For Monica Tilley and Theresa May,
who told me to get the man out of the house

If you're in combat and your troops are lost
Beg God come to your rescue if the enemy is Navajo

Epa nava, ene yo saca Navajo, heyo,
yayo jene ya heyo yayo heyo heieieieio

If you go to Navajo land beware of the danger
Because Death over there is firm and unyielding

—from a traditional New Mexico *coplas,*
a verse song of the Southwest

SHADOW
PLAY

skinwalker

Children told the first of the skinwalker stories at night, but it took several weeks before the number of these stories accumulated and spread around the Navajo families at Monument Valley.

Most stories began in the same way.

"There was a family," some kid would say. "Sleeping in their hogan, but this girl, she heard something on the roof, uh, some scratching sound up there, and she woke up the family and they all heard the scratching too. So the dad built up the fire, real hot, smokey-hot inside the hogan, and the scratching stopped, so this boy, he went outside and climbed on top of a flat rock and watched the roof of the hogan and pretty soon he saw somebody walking up there, something hairy, hair all over the body and on the feet and hands, and in the hogan, they let the fire down, they thought nobody was bothering them no more, and stuff came down the smokehole. Pollen, but not sacred corn pollen, it was like gray ashes, the dad said it was the ground-up bones of little babies."

This story spread, who knows, probably one story led to another, it was a very hot summer and the People just wanted to sleep after a long day in the sun, watching their sheep, because it was time for shearing of the lambs.

So when the Navajo Tribal Policeman heard about the stories, they were everywhere, every family had another story, and so it spread that a *yenaldlooshi* was taking babies and cutting off children's heads. And so he made his rounds at twilight instead of dawn, stopping at hogans through the evening, where one night he visited Martin Yellowhorse and his family of five, and young John, aged eleven, was eager.

"Okay," John said. "There was this family."

The policeman wanted to hear the family's name, but being Navajo, couldn't and wouldn't interrupt the story, it had to come out from the teller.

"The two boys, they got together with some other boys and their dogs and they went out to camp one night, up at Thunderbird Mesa. Okay. So one of the dogs got to howling, something was out there, the dog ran away from the boys, ran away chasing something into the dark and next thing, okay, the boys heard a different kind of howling, not dog howling or coyote, some animal they'd never heard before."

The policeman waited, but that was the whole story.

"*Yenaldlooshi*," the dad said. Everybody nodded, but nobody said anything more because the mom took the mutton off the stove just then and the policeman had to eat with them, to leave would have been discourteous.

Over the next few weeks, he heard many skinwalker stories and he made a map, pushing little colored pins into spots where skinwalker incidents occurred, or where the stories seemed to indicate. Gradually, he found a pattern that centered on Right Mitten, one of the most photographed places in Monument Valley, and also the one-time home of the Begay family.

The policeman made careful inquiries about the Begay family, since he knew one of the brothers, had served in Vietnam with this brother. The father had been murdered decades before. The one brother was in the army Rangers, the other brother was a movie star, so nobody wanted the old man's belongings and according to custom they were smashed to pieces, a hole was knocked in the roof of the hogan, and it was a *chindi*, a ghost house. Over the years, part of the roof fell in, and pieces of the eastern wall, but the People left this hogan alone.

The skinwalker stories grew and the People around Monument Valley were afraid and watched over each other and their children and their kinship children. Even in those places where skinwalkers weren't reported, the People watched because ghosts can travel, they get into the body through curly hair and fingerprint spirals and through the mouth and nose and ears.

Then one night Charlie Sand Castle thought he heard something outside his hogan and his dog took off, howling and yowling. He loaded his 1894 Winchester pump shotgun, a sixteen-gauge old-timer, some of the bluing rubbed clean off and the stock cracked when a horse stomped on it, but Charlie glued it together. Some of the People said that only certain guns could kill a skinwalker, so Charlie passed up his .30-30 lever Winchester for the old shotgun, put several double-ought buck shells inside, ran out of his hogan and saw somebody running and running and Charlie ran after him, he was seventy-nine years old but could still run all day, the running man stumbled in a dry watch and Charlie stood on the rim of the wash and blew the man's head off, Charlie saying at first he looked down at the head bouncing in the moonlight and the eyes rolling around, as the head rolled the eyes kept turning so they focused on Charlie and he blasted the head just in that instant when he recognized he'd just shot his best friend Nathaniel Yazzie, who was always scared of dogs and ran away from them. Nathaniel had some fry bread his wife Yolanda had made up, he was bringing it to Charlie, but the dog howled and made him run away.

A manilla envelope arrived at the Tribal Police substation the next morning. Postmarked in Green Valley, Arizona, addressed to Vincent Begay, return address of the Pima County Sheriff Substation. The policeman happened by the mail delivery and so he opened the envelope and read the short note inside, asking that the surviving family of the enclosed named deceased be informed. The policeman knew from the devastating pictures inside that he must now make a choice between the natural harmony of not interfering, not disturbing *hozho*, the harmony, and the policeman's way, which was the outsider way no matter how much any policeman wanted to be one with the People, he worked according to different laws and rules of action.

Since he now had nearly two dozen colored pins on his map, clustered around the old abandoned Begay hogan. He went out one night on his horse, a five-gallon can of coal oil hanging off the saddle. Stopping along the way, resting for minutes at each stop, wary that he might be seen, working over the bad thing he was going to do, but he couldn't see any other way out of it.

He studied the stars and those constellations recognized by the People, thirty-seven in all. As always, since he was a child, he marveled at how Black God kept the stars inside a folded blanket, but Coyote came along one night and snapped the blanket open to the night air, scattering the stars.

Enough of the old ways for tonight, the policeman thought.

He touched the gasoline can.

I'm an outsider, he thought. *I can't forget Black God and Changing Woman and Monster Killer and Spider Woman and all the legends, but I'm an outsider*.

With these thoughts, he knew that the flavor, the meaning, the harmony of the legends had died within him. Reaching the old Begay hogan, he wasted no time emptying the gasoline can, dousing first the roof and then the cedar walls, the cedar so dry that the fire sprang full-blown from the single match he threw down, and for some time the brilliance of the flames forced the stars to hide. The hogan burned quickly, within half an hour reduced to just embers.

Nobody saw him, but he'd crossed a line, his only justification that one man had killed another. The stars came out of hiding, the policeman rode to his trailer, got in his '97 Dodge RAM pickup, and thought that was the end of things.

Some time during that night, Yolanda Kaye's youngest baby, a nine-month-old boy named Slimmer Pete, disappeared and at noon the next day a sheepherder found Slimmer Pete's headless body on the desert. Firing the Begay hogan touched the community, the clans, the families, the children. In six days, the People discovered six more headless bodies of Begay clan re-

lations of all ages. One a day. Until the only clan rela-
tion alive was Frank Everwool, who'd driven over to
Gallup for a funeral and hadn't yet returned.

This was no *yenaldlooshi* story about shadows on
the roof, this was what skinwalkers did to babies and
teenagers and good mothers and aunts and uncles.
Good Fellow requested a week's personal leave from
his captain, got back into his pickup and didn't stop
driving until he reached Tuba City for gas and put
through a collect call to his old friend Nathan Brittles.

suicide

At sunrise the breeze shivered between the mesquite and palo verde trees, gusting in puffs and snorts strong enough to shake my lantana bushes. From the south-southwest, the top edge of another monsoon working up from Mexico. It was the middle of an unusually fierce August monsoon season, so much rain driving north into Tucson that at times the foothills shimmered with green, trees, bushes, even grasses once dead but revived by the water.

I'd wanted a long run in Sabino Canyon that morning, at least fifteen miles up and down the roads for a serious muscle-burner workout, but when the breeze became a wind with twenty-mile-an-hour spurts, I stayed close to home, running a quiet loop through the Randolph Park section of Tucson around the two golf courses and along the wide sidewalks. Skateboarders wove between and around joggers, runners, and women pushing baby carriages, roller-bladers swooping in and out with their own internal rhythms or whatever popped on their CD player headsets. Nobody really working up a sweat, the breeze cooled us off.

Dust devils rising on the baseball field and dirt playground.

Nearing home, the vibrator of my cell whanged against my right hip. Close enough to slow down and read the LCD panel, caller ID showed me it was Nathan.

"You free later this afternoon?"

"Free for what?" Playful.

"I need you," he said.

"What did you have in mind?" Both playful and needy, wanting to see him. Instead of spending last night at his place up in Casa Grande, I stayed home because my daughter Spider said we'd catch a movie, but her boyfriend's lowrider snarled into our driveway before dinner. A black-pearl '78 Caddy convertible, rigged with all conceivable hydraulics, huge sub-woofer audio system, chromed spinner hubcaps, whatever there was to buy, Carlos had it. Spider vaulted the closed passenger door into the leather seat, waved at me while Carlos backed into the street, she five months pregnant and not bothering with the seatbelt.

"It's work. Can't explain now, are you free?"

"I have a Reiki session, lunch with Spider, a doctor's appointment." I didn't tell him about what kind of doctor. "Maybe, I guess. Later. Why?"

"You're a registered PI," Nathan said. "Also certified to do photographic forensics at crime scenes. Meet me down south, past Green Valley."

"This a fresh scene?" I've done both murder scene and autopsy photographs, but hated fresh scenes, hated the blood and body parts.

"No." He gave me directions.

"How old?"

"Week ago. It's been closed as a murder-suicide.

Shotgun. Look, I just don't have time to tell you much."

"Why are we going there?"

"Two old friends," he said. "You'll be there at four?"

That was a question I'd ask myself many times in the next week. Well, not quite that question. *Will I always be there for you?* That question, the answer so far a big *yes, but*. I'll tell you about that later.

Two *dead* friends? I wanted to ask. One murder the other, turned the gun on himself? *Her*self? "Four o'-clock," I said instead. "Yes, of course I'll be there."

He'd already disconnected.

"Alex," I said. My seventeen-year-old partner, computer hacker Alex Emerine. "Stand by this afternoon, okay?"

"What's up?" she said.

"Stress call from Nathan, I have no idea what, but stay at your keyboard, just in case. What are you working on?"

"The ATM scams. Six-figure pledge to a nonprofit, funds no go."

"Is this a new client?"

"Tohono Chul park. Some guy pledged two hundred and fifty large, gave them a cashier's draft, guy committed suicide, draft no good."

"Work that as priority," I said. "That's a good place. Good people. I'll call you later if I need you."

Nathan Brittles is my partner and my lover. These are not the same two things. Our hearts are one with each other, our spirits intensely overlapping and intensely different. To relieve this intensity, we live in separate houses at this time.

Also, Nathan now struggles to learn more of the traditional *Dineh* ways. *Dinetah* people are Navajos to the rest of the world. I can't connect to my Hopi past. Like, I've gone through some desired ethnic change despite the realities of my birth.

2

Georgia Roan held both her palms an inch away from my right shoulder.

"Wait for the heat," she said. I'm just too impatient, some days I can't let myself relax into Reiki sessions. "Laura. Unlock your knees." I'd crossed my ankles, legs straight out on the massage table. "If you don't bend your knees, the energy just doesn't circulate, it bounces back up. Locks up the energy."

"I know, I know," I said. "Just for today, be grateful. Let go the stress."

Removing her hands slowly, she extended a thumb and jabbed right into my lower neck muscles.

"Ow!" I said.

"You're way too tense today, Laura. I don't know, I can give you some shiatsu massage, but Reiki isn't going to work for you. Just for today, let go the stress. Let go your anger."

"I'm not angry," hearing the barking words, sighing, "well, I might be angry but I don't know why." I knew why. "Give me the massage then."

"It's your daughter, isn't it." Squirting massage oil on her hands, she slapped my naked thigh so I'd roll on my stomach. "Or the guy. Or both."

I buried my forehead on the brace, didn't say another word as she worked my neck and upper back
muscles. Usually I fall asleep when she does this. Not
today.

Later, while I was dressing, Georgia watched me
clip my Beretta inside my belt, snuggled hard in that
small hollow down there just above my butt.

Shaking her head, disapproving the gun. "Why do
you carry that around?"

"I have a permit."

"No, I mean, why have a gun at all?"

"Protection," I said, snarking a smile sideways, "for
snakes and sich." Clint Eastwood, *Unforgiven*.

"We're going to start all over again," she said.
"Reiki, guns, I can't reconcile the two in one."

"Because I'm a woman?"

"No. Because it's a gun. Don't bring that in here
anymore."

On time at the railroad car diner, on Valencia near the
Air National Guard buildings, I waited for Spider to
show up for lunch. By two o'clock, I knew she'd
blown me off again.

Spooning mouthfuls from a bowl of intensely delicious chili, medium-hot jalapeno peppers on the side, I
read three more articles from *FitPregnancy* magazine.
BREASTFEEDING PROBLEMS SOLVED. PRENATAL FOOD
RULES: WHAT TO EAT, WHAT TO AVOID. You'd think I
was having the baby, not Spider. SEX. KEEP IT FUN THE
WHOLE 9 MONTHS. I fumbled at the first pages of a
large section on the best new baby products, spilled
chili on the magazine, and asked the waitress for another napkin. She looked fondly at the magazine, then

at my face, figuring I was either a bit old to be having a baby or a bit young to be a grandmother. I raised my eyes to her, but she just smiled and went to pour coffee for two men at the far end of the counter.

I left her a big tip and went to my doctor.

A close friend I'd met through Reiki claimed she could astral travel. Get out of her body, her consciousness free to roam the planet. I'd like to do that, I'd like right now to project myself at the murder house, but I haven't reached any stage yet where I'm logically able to believe in stuff like astral traveling.

Surprisingly, Nathan accepted Reiki without question. To him, to a Navajo, things floated in and out of the body, good things, evil things. But he'd renounced guns, I don't quite know why, I'm not sure. More on that later.

Reiki helps the arthritis pain in my right shoulder.

Reiki channels universal life energy. In Kanji, Rei is the Japanese ideogram for a universal, transcendent essence, spirit, and power. Ki, like the Chinese Chi, is the energy of the vital life force. I revel in my life force these days.

3

"Lab results are back," Dr. Wallace announced.

"Good?" I said.

"Inconclusive. Chromosomal issues."

"You sound like a therapist. Issues."

"A useful word, nowadays. Whenever the lab results are . . . inconclusive."

"So?"

"Let's see, how long has it been?" She pillaged my patient's folder, yanked out a stapled report and tossed it in the wastebasket. "Duplicate," she said. "So much paperwork, nobody checks for duplicates."

"Except you."

"Mmm. Here. Six weeks. Have you had your period since?"

"Yes."

"Good."

Something chirped underneath her jacket. She retrieved a pager, glanced at it. "This can't wait, Laura. I apologize. Mmm, I'll be a few minutes. Do you mind waiting in here?"

I was already pulling out my laptop as she left without waiting for an answer. Billie Wallace paid a heavy price for being one of Tucson's best OBGYN doctors.

She took few new patients, never refused a direct request from a friend or fellow doctor, worked fourteen hour days for weeks at a time.

Nathan left a cryptic message, just two names. I called Alex on my cell, asked her if she'd run data checks on Leon Begay and Jodhi Patroon.

"Nothing on the woman," Alex said. "Driver's license has to be a fake. The address doesn't exist. Social security number was never issued."

"Try running the name through INS databases. See if she's in the country illegally, maybe you'll get lucky."

"The guy, though. Begay. Tons of data, I've got his whole life in front of me. Bet you didn't know his brother was a big Western movie star?"

"Begay?" I'd seen almost every Western made in the past fifty years.

"No. His brother is Vincent Basaraba. Big, in the sixties and seventies."

"*Billy,*" I said.

"Yeah. I see that, a movie about Billy the Kid. Says here, the brothers grew up in Monument Valley. Their father worked for John Ford. An extra, in all those movies Ford shot with John Wayne."

"*Fort Apache,*" I said. "That trilogy around nineteen fifty. I know about that. What else?"

"Basaraba is the executive manager of that casino in west Tucson. The new one, looks like a huge pueblo, with fountains."

"Tucson?" The brothers lived twenty miles apart, did they know about each other? "My ex was a Begay," I said. "But on the rez, that name's like Jones or Smith. Anything else?"

"Nyet."

"Nyet?" I said.

"Don't ask, I mean, like, ask me later."

Dr. Wallace came back, tapping my files, wanting me off the phone.

"Gotta go," I said to Alex. "Get some general background on Basaraba. I'll meet you for lunch tomorrow."

"Sorry," Dr. Wallace said. "Six weeks after the miscarriage, one normal menstrual cycle since. Okay. The labs."

Six weeks.

I'd not told Nathan anything. Away in Atlanta for a training conference when I had the miscarriage. Worse than that, he'd never known I was pregnant, since *I'd* barely known. The miscarriage happened somewhere around ten weeks. The first trimester. The pregnancy an accident, a blessing, a wild hope to be a mother.

"How are you doing with this, Laura?"

"Sorry. Guess I was drifting off into . . . whatever."

"Have you talked to Nathan about this?"

"No."

"Why not?"

"He doesn't want children."

"Anybody else?"

"You're somebody."

"Do you want me to put you in touch with a support group?"

· "Miscarriage? A twelve-step program?"

"It's not a joke."

"No," I said. "It's *def*initely not a joke. An accident, but not so funny."

"You feeling guilty?"

"Say what?"

"Guilt. As in, Why me?"

"No."

"Embarrassment?"

"You mean, like, Is there something *wrong* with me? No."

"Talked this over with Nathan?"

"Yes," I lied. She studied me closely.

"Laura, you're lying through your gorgeous Julia Roberts lips."

She wrote something on a lavender Post-it, peeled it off, stuck it on the right sleeve of her coat. "Let's go through the obvious," she said, peeling two reports out of my patient's folder.

"First trimester pregnancies. One-quarter of all miscarriages happen during the first trimester. Lots of reasons. Irregular menses or ovulation, no ovulation, uterine fibroids . . . dah dah dah . . . Okay." Noticing that I was looking at my hands, she put her palm under my chin until I met her eyes. "Laura. When the maternal age is thirty-five or greater, things get kinda dicey. Law of averages, law of statistics, whatever. In your case, I've ruled all of those conditions out as the problem with having another baby."

"So why?"

"I'd say, my sweet Laura, mostly, you're just a tad too old."

"God*damm*it," I sobbed.

She dropped the patient's folder, knelt in front of

me, grabbed my hands, put my hands around her neck, moved into me, hugged me, held me, I just couldn't stop weeping, all those days, those weeks when I wanted to tell Nathan and didn't.

"Thank you," I said finally.

"Mmm." Her emotional objectivity slid back into place. "It's not *just* your age. The lab reports. From that D&C we did, after the miscarriage. I requested a detailed chromosome assessment. Because of your age, I'd asked for that. I'd asked for a lot of things, but most of it came back negative. In the uterine macroenvironment, no indication of polyps, adhesions, fibroids . . . dah dah dah . . . yada yada yada . . . just stop me if you don't like all this jargon. No horned bicornuate uterus, no T-shaped uterus, nothing suggesting the need for a laparotomy."

"Whoa," I said. She could make me laugh when she talked technical. "Get back to my chromosomes."

"In a word? Two words?"

"Yeah."

"Genetically unlucky."

"Plus I'm too old."

"Laura, why?"

"Why do I want to have a baby?" She nodded. "It's simple. I had a child, but I never really got to be a mother."

I'd already gone through everything about my daughter Spider, how I'd been sixteen when I had her, how my former husband Jonathan took her from me when she was barely two years old.

"There's always adoption," she said.

Oh yeah, I thought. *Nathan and I will go to China*

*or Cambodia or Vietnam or Rumania and bring back
a little baby boy and call him Nathan Junior.*

"I'll call around. Just to know about adoption.
Okay?" Her pager chirped again. She read it, started
to turn from me, stopped. Put hands under my elbows
and urged me to stand close. "You can keep trying to
get pregnant, Laura. But the odds are really bad. We
haven't even talked about the likelihood of Down syndrome with older mothers. Imagine that you're pregnant again, you survive without a miscarriage and go
into the second trimester, you do a test and the fetus
has Down syndrome. I don't like those odds. You
shouldn't gamble on them, either. Let me show you
something."

Opened my patient folder, removed a picture and
laid it in front of me.

"Your last sonogram."

I couldn't recognize anything, the images fuzzy, a
picture from some primitive technology, like airport
controller radar, a funnel-shaped cone rising from the
bottom, inside, a small shadowy object like an approaching UFO.

"Can you tell the sex from this?"

"Wouldn't even try to guess. Does it matter?"

"I want a girl."

"Laura, you *have* a girl, you have a daughter. This is
a tiny fetus. Mostly a shadow. You can't see much, but
I can. The head is wrong, the body . . . even at that
primitive stage, it wasn't normal."

"Shadows aren't dead," I said. "I photograph the
real thing. I know *dead* when I see it in my lens."

"This is *my* lens, Laura." She stood up, patted my

hand, suddenly matronly. "See you in a month." And then she was gone.

I never kept pictures of my baby daughter. Baby Spider.

Like all mothers, I have my memories, my . . . mental images. But no pictures. And nobody remembers exact details of a baby, when it's twenty years later.

4

Green Valley is a seniors residential community, twenty miles south of Tucson. The closest I'd ever come to it was driving by, back and forth from Nogales. Housing developments sprawled on both sides of I-19, grouped around the three major cross-streets: Duval Mine Road, Esperanza, and Continental.

The Green Valley Mall lay off Esperanza.

That means *hope* or *wish* in Spanish, but most of the seniors living in Green Valley spoke little Spanish. I saw Nathan's dark-rust-red Nissan pickup in the parking lot. I pulled up beside him, facing the other way with our driver's windows close together. Like when you see two highway patrol cops taking a break, parked side by side so they can shoot the shit or drink coffee together or more probably discuss who's going to have the radar gun and who's going to be the chase car.

"Say hey," I said. Reaching across to touch his nose through his open window. "What's the haps, good buddy?"

But he was already cranking up his windows. Locked his pickup, got into the passenger seat of my

Grand Cherokee. I turned sideways, ready to kiss him, but he was all business and no play.

"Get out on Camino del Sol," he said. Pointing until I shifted in Drive.

We took the frontage road, looking for an address he didn't tell me about. I hadn't been this far south since two years ago, when Meg Arizana was kidnapped in a shootout at the Nogales border crossing. Since then, new housing developments sprouted everywhere.

Whatever was in his head, it lay unopened between us.

I got ready for anything. We exited at Continental, passed another shopping center, losing our sense of direction after weaving for ten minutes through several subdivisions with one- and two-bedroom row houses.

Ahead of us, huge cumulonimbus clouds anviled their way up thousands of feet. Awesome thunderheads, deflecting air travel for miles around. Beyond, to the southeast, sullen, sodden gray clouds streaked with downshafts of rain, completely blotting out the Santa Rita mountains.

"Monsoon looks like it'll pass right over us," I said.

Nathan flicked his eyes around the horizon. "Not for half an hour," he said, driving on. "Let's find this place."

But when we did, nobody seemed to be home. After ringing the bell and pounding on the door, Nathan came back to the Cherokee.

"Let me drive. Shoot a few pictures of the house," he said. "Get the street sign."

"Is this the crime scene?" I asked.

"No. Just want to remember where this place is,

we've got to come back later." Consulting a map. "Go back to the frontage road. South, to the Canoa exit."

"So," I said. Three miles later. Trying to brute-force a conversation, I had *no* idea what we were doing down here or why. "Who's the person living back there?"

"Don't know."

"Um, why are we here?"

"An old friend."

"How come if you know him," I said, all right, I'm thinking, let's *pull* this tooth, "you don't seem to know just where he lives?"

"Laura, there's no logic in any of this. Yet. Don't go looking to pry something logical from me."

"Oh-kay."

"When this guy moved up to Monument Valley, up in the rez, I lost touch. I thought he was still there."

"You didn't keep in touch? An old war buddy, you didn't keep in touch?"

"Canoa. There's the golf course," he said. "You ready?"

"Nathan," I said. Laying a hand on his right thigh while he drove. "I've got to talk with Spider, before she disappears for another night. Got to be home by six."

"This is more important." Moving his right foot to the brake, not really needing to brake, but it moved his thigh and my hand fell off, I've learned these signals, *now's not the time,* so I just let my hand fall, thinking that we'd crossed further into the dimension where one thing is important to one partner but irrelevant to the other. Like a problem in theoretical logic.

Momentarily lost on a side street, I finally pointed at a strand of yellow crime-scene tape hung fifteen feet up in a mesquite tree.

"Fourteen twenty-two . . . sixteen . . . over there. Fourteen oh four."

Nosing the Cherokee at the carport, I parked twenty feet away and turned off the engine. I started to get out, but Nathan just sat still, looking at the front door. Screen set in heavy wrought iron, with a small and larger saguaro design.

"What's wrong, sweetie?"

But he didn't even hear me.

"Nathan. Look at me." Ducked his head, cocked it sideways. "Look at me." I held his head, held his eyes on mine. "I need *some*thing, I need . . . your friend, was he . . . you said it was a murder-suicide? Sweetie? Help me here."

"Leon Begay," he said finally.

"Your friend?"

"Yes. But he'd *never* kill himself." His head twisting gently from my hands. "And what I haven't told you . . . Leon's clan family? On the rez? Six people have died in the past week or so."

"More suicides?"

"Worse. Uh, I'll tell you later. One thing first, then another." Pushing away.

There's a logic tool called a Venn diagram. A simple thing, two overlapping circles. There's a common, shared area where they overlap, plus each circle has its own special identity. Sometimes, if you've got a wonderful partner, the circles almost entirely overlap. Or sometimes they don't. Reiki celebrates the shared area.

Some years ago, I hiked with thirty other people on a butterfly watch in the Baboquivaries, the sacred To-

hono O'odham mountains. The butterfly guide, a lep-
todopto . . . something, she explained that when you
see two butterflies in a circling pattern. Sometimes,
she said, as we watched two zebra longwings courting,
neither recognize the sex of the other, they get closer,
the male patrols above or behind the female, flutters
his wings, rapidly, rapidly, until insemination.

Other people think that the courtship spirals really sig-
nify antagonism, one trying to escape the other.

5

These days, I often question myself.

Who am I? We all do this, I tell you, we unexpectedly find ourselves in transition zones with no comprehension of how or why we got there, but we enter those sentimental, melodramatic places of the heart that no longer thrive.

I am in my early forties. Married at fifteen, had a daughter within two years, my husband Jonathan abandoned me when my baby, Spider, was two years old. She lives with me again, having no other place and pregnant with an unnamed father.

As a younger woman, I was active in Indian resistance movements, but drifted from this to live in one place or another, with a succession of unsatisfactory men. While Nathan Brittles has been my steady partner and lover for almost a whole year, we live in separate houses since both of us retain a private mystery of our past that leaves us not yet willing to commit to and share the same space.

See? I told you this was melodrama, but I don't understand why. Yet.

I've broken a variety of laws within the past ten years, mostly because of illegal computer hacking.

Even though I now own a legitimate business, I struggle to become a better person, not wanting to depend on something else or someone else to make me whole.

My daughter is the exception to this. I want to share her pregnancy, I yearn to bear a child myself, or at least, I *think* so, I'm confused about this.

Years ago, I called myself an information midwife.

I found people who believe they'll never be found.

I never met them. I just sold their secrets.

I didn't ever *want* to meet them.

Using computers, I cracked (hackers = good guys, crackers = black hats) into networked databanks, gleaning unlisted phone numbers, bank accounts, credit card histories, airline travel itineraries, telephone and medical histories, records of birth and death and marriage and divorce and supermarket shopping purchases, anything to compile in electronic dossiers and hawk to those willing to pay my fee. I could find almost anybody who thought they'd skip out and remain untraceable. I never advertised, never solicited work, rarely had an unsatisfied customer.

*Every*body leaves traces.

You just have to know where to look.

I'm confused about my current role as a private investigator, how I've gone from the privacy about living alone to meeting clients and suspected identity thieves, I'm concerned about carrying a gun, about photographing crime scenes and dead people. I don't much understand why I do this. To counter this acceptance of violence, I work to heal myself holistically, I exercise with long runs and working out with weights.

I fall into these sentimental moments too many times these days, sentimentality and melodrama are so seductive.

Questions too often lead to betrayal of worth.

6

I sat sideways, legs outside the Cherokee while I fitted a wide-angle lens to my Fuji S2 digital camera and attached the flash package.

Dirt over all cars nearby, sidewalks, windows, patches of pavement underneath the carport where rain couldn't wash the dirt. Sand, actually, brought up by another monsoon a few days before. Wind bursts to eighty miles an hour. Rotation of the monsoon winds, snatching Sonoran desert sand, caliche, dirt of all manner and color, cradling the dirt two hundred miles north from deep inside Mexico.

"What do you want me to shoot?"

"Everything."

"Everything in the house?"

"Inside, outside. Set a procedure, don't miss a thing."

"Nathan," I said, "sweetie," I said, "don't miss a thing? Why?"

"Because it won't be here tomorrow."

Okay. A riddle. Answers only when ready.

First rule of forensic photography. Get your perspective, look, and shoot.

Don't even go to the door until you've drawn all the exterior visuals into your gut, your head. You start the analysis right away by not taking anything for granted.

A whole lot different than seeing everything on a computer monitor.

Nathan didn't want to get out of the Cherokee.

Not saying anything, I checked my equipment.

Flash memory card loaded in a FinePix S2 Pro digital SLR camera with a 6.17 megapixel proprietary Fuji advanced ccd, octagonal pixels for higher image quality than the standard ccd with square pixels. Built by Fuji on a modified Nikon N80 chassis, using all Nikon lenses and accessories.

"Let's get this done," I said. "Before the monsoon hits."

He didn't move except to finger a manila envelope.

"Why are you sitting there? It's gonna rain like hell, let's do this."

Opening my aluminum carry case for lenses, taking out the 12mm to 24mm f4 Nikon G series zoom lens for interiors because it's an ultra-wide-angle optic at the 12mm end, equivalent to 18mm on a 35mm film format.

"*Chindi,*" he said finally. "It's a Death house. Hard for me to go in there."

"It's a modern, stand-alone, lower Arizona housing development. This isn't the rez, Nathan. I'm ready," I said. "If you're not, just give me the keys, I'll shoot whatever I see inside." I took out the Nikon 28mm to 100mm f3.5 to f5.6 G series cheapie zoom lens for whatever general shots I'd need and snapped the hinges shut on the lens case. "Give me the keys. I'll shoot the outside later."

Nathan pulled a key ring from the envelope and we walked to the front door. He tried a few keys until one slotted into the single lock. Inside the door I jumped, startled at seeing my reflection in a floor-to-ceiling mirror creating the illusion of a tiny entryway. Directly ahead, what looked like two bedrooms, two baths, a kitchen area with a counter and two high wooden chairs, a dining nook with a four-foot round fake oak table and two chairs.

The whole place sized about eleven hundred, maybe twelve or thirteen hundred square feet, I guessed. Small. I'd lived in smaller, but this place had few windows, making it seem smaller than it was. Well lighted. At least two skylights, one in the hallway and another in the first bathroom. The master bedroom also bright, so there was either a window or skylight or both.

In the living room, a too-long entertainment center crowded one wall opposite a sofa and matching chair, both heavy and inexpensively plush, dried blackish bloodstains mingling into the sofa's fabric design, patterned in light and dark browns with reddish stripes and vaguely Indian-looking rock art shapes. Blood spatters up the wall, smaller ones like inverted apostrophes, with upper points as the splatter spread to the ceiling. Heavier spots with points top and bottom, splatter and drip.

An intensely close atmosphere, a closed-up house smell. Mostly that dry, musty, hot-temperature smell of a single-level desert home that gets a lot of sun with closed windows. Underneath the sun smell, a heavy metallic dried-blood odor, coppery-smelling to some, but for me it smelled of zinc, mostly because when I bled, I used my fingers to rub blood off, then sometimes licked my fingers, it tasted of the zinc supplements I took every day.

I swished the front door back and forth, trying to get some fresh air inside.

"Back door?" I said.

Nathan pulled photos from the envelope, held them up one at a time as he matched them to the living room. He pointed down the hall, jerked his chin at me.

"End, to the right, should be a sliding door out onto a patio."

"All right to open it? I can't hardly breathe in here."

He grunted, located the aircon control and turned it on. Passing the kitchen, my eyes to the right as I went down the hall under the skylight, I almost walked into the louvered doors at the end, next to a bathroom. Behind the louvers I could see a washer and a dryer. To the left, a king-sized bed and two dressers filled a room. To the right, drapes. I found a pull cord at the end, drew them back, unlocked and slid open a six-foot glass door. Went out on the small bricked patio to a small, intensely packed garden. Beyond, the ground sloped down into a ravine, mesquites partially blocking the view east of a golf course on the other lip of the ravine. A threesome putting on a green, a single player waiting behind them.

Shafts of rain fanned out from the clouds, maybe five minutes away. Thunder rumbled somewhere to the southeast. Lightning flashed and veined in all directions, at times two or more strikes joining together.

Switching to my zoom lens, I carefully bracketed the entire backyard, one hundred and eighty degrees of desert and mountains views. Across a thick row of pink-flowered oleander bushes, down thirty feet or so on this side of a ravine and up the other, lower side reaching to the golf course. Lots of bushes, branches, leaves, natural debris in the ravine, I wouldn't walk down in there, I have a terrible fear of rattlesnakes. Finished, I went back inside and pushed open the door of the second bedroom.

"Anything out back?" Nathan said.

"Golfers. What next?"

"Check those computers."

I looked inside the study. Nathan heard my gasp of amazement.

"Your friend really into computers?" I said.

"Wouldn't know. Everybody's got a computer these days. Play those games, surf those webs."

"Not you," I said. "C'mere. Take a look."

We huddled together in the doorway.

"That's a lot of gear," he said finally. "Looks like your office."

"Who was this guy? What did he do?"

"Leon. He's got a name, Laura. Use it."

Dead people, I don't *want* to use their names. One way to keep yourself separated away from emotional attachment, shoot autopsy photos of somebody anonymous. It bothered me somewhat that Nathan knew this man.

"So what this, what did . . . Leon . . . do?"

"Coordinated other customs agents out walking the desert, looking for carpet walkers. Drug smugglers."

"Would he have used computers for his job?"

"Unlikely. That stuff is coordinated by the Nogales and Tucson offices. This must have been just casual stuff. Hobby, game-playing, whatever."

"No way," I said. "There's at least ten thousand dollars worth of equipment in here. Computer, hub, router . . . he had a whole network in here. Two brand new Apple G5 PowerMacs. That looks like a thirty-two-inch flat display screen, that alone must cost five thousand dollars. Wait a minute."

I went outside, walked down the road backward, a few drops of rain splattering loud on the galvanized rooftops of the carports. I kept looking for something on the flat roof.

"What?" Nathan opened the screen door.

"You see a ladder anywhere?"

The wind kicked up, nine veins of lightning zapped off the main plume dancing to the ground.

"Come back in here," Nathan said.

"Got to see what's on the roof."

"Get underneath something."

Nathan ran back through the house. I stayed where I was, waiting. The first rain hit the galvanized tin carport roof, one *tink* and another *tinktink* and suddenly fat raindrops plunked on and around me. I didn't move, almost impossible to keep dry when the monsoon wind slapped the rain sideways, under the carport. Nathan suddenly appeared at the front of the roof, waving at me to go inside. A hard rain now, pushed almost horizontal by increasingly heavy winds. I ran to the door, stood under the front eaves, half soaked, but loving the clean ozone-fresh air. Thunder crashed every twenty seconds as the monsoon blew almost directly over the housing development. Two houses away, a huge multiveined lightning stroke smashed a big mesquite, knocking off a main branch twenty feet long, a *huge* chunk of wood flying across the road to partially crunch a parked Buick, thunder crashing right on top of us as the wind gusted well over fifty miles per hour and finally uprooted the mesquite, top branches just missing some windows, crushing the galvanized tin carport roof.

"Get *in* here!" Nathan shouted.

"What's on the roof?"

"Metal pizza-size dish," he said. "Antenna?"

"High-speed data uplink."

A heavy smash in the back bedroom, splattering tinkle of glass. Down the hallway, we looked cautiously into the room. A huge branch had blown off one of the mesquites down in the ravine, near the golf course, other smaller branches still flying around. Rain blew like shotgun pellets into the room, shredding part of the drapes and pushing the sliding-door metal frame out of alignment.

Nathan nodded to himself, almost a tight smile on his lips for a moment.

"Come on," he said. "Shoot everything you see."

I went to Leon's office, sat in Leon's chair, started to inventory the room. I booted up one of the G5s, waiting to open the File Finder, waiting to check files, to see what applications were installed, especially what email program so I could look for traces of what he'd been doing.

"This is a little weird," I said. Calling Nathan back into the room, waiting for the G5 to boot up. "Equipment's brand new, seems right out of the box. That's pretty high-tech stuff."

"What does it mean?"

"I don't know. I'm waiting to look at his personal files and email."

A brilliant lightning stroke flashed nearby. The air vibrated and a second later, my body throbbing as intense as standing near the transformers of a major power substation, except with lightning, *every*thing throbs.

The electricity went off a second later. We went to the back window of the bedroom, watched the lightning moving across the golf course toward us, wind whipping the mesquites to slant toward the ground. Down below, the lone golfer whacked a ball, got in his electric golf cart, and headed to the green.

"One crazy bastard," Nathan said. "Okay. Power's off. Shoot pictures everywhere. Let's do this, let's finish this."

"What are we finishing?"

He waved the manila envelope, pulled several large photos halfway out. Hesitant. *He doesn't want to do this,* I thought.

"What's in those pictures?"

"Computer room first," he said. "Then we'll go back to when it happened."

"You said these deaths happened a week ago?"

"Eight days. Why?"

"Look at the dirt. From that monsoon two days ago."

Dirt coated everything in the house, walls, floors, furniture, the coating thicker as we went into the back room. "Somebody's been inside," I said. "Just recently. And come look at in here." Steering him to the computer room. "Look at that wall. Sideways, at a slant toward the light. See it?" A two-by-three-foot spot almost completely free of dirt, centered roughly at eye level. "Map? Chart?"

"And look here," Nathan said. Pointing at shelving underneath the window.

"Picture frames," I said, ducking as I focused the Nikon lens. "Four by six, five by seven. These had to be taken yesterday, or last night."

"Or this morning. How many shots can you take with that thing?"

"A thousand or so. Plus I've got another high-speed minidrive out in the car. How many pictures do you want?"

"Everything at least twice. And from different angles."

"The whole place?"

"Here."

"If the windows stay closed, the dirt won't blow away."

Paying no attention to me, he counted off marks on the shelving. "I figure, six or seven pictures are missing. Make sure you cover the pictures that are left."

"Ocotillos, saguaros, Mexican gold poppies. Flowers, landscapes," shooting while I talked, "so what kind of pictures are missing?"

"When you're done," he said, "come to the living room."

7

But first, the master bedroom. Nathan removed three crime scene photos from the envelope. Polaroid digital photos, I couldn't believe a crime scene tech didn't shoot in digital, had to be a reason. Nathan laid the photos in a row, against the headboard.

A dead teenager, no more than seventeen. If that.

"What's her name again?"

"Jodhi Patroon. Arizona driver's license in her handbag, also an INS card given only to Mexican nationals. Same name."

"Probably both fake IDs," I said. "Patroon? What kind of Mexican name is that?" Got Alex Emerine on my cell, gave her everything else on the driver's license so Alex could run it through all of our identity databases, not bothering with a description, we'd handle that with more complex software. "Young and poor," I said to Nathan.

Short cropped brown hair, blond highlights in two bunches sprouting from behind on either side, a strange haircut but nothing that teenagers did surprised me anymore. Streaks fading from a cheap cut and dye job, probably done by a friend. Wal-Mart stonewashed jeans pulled down to her knees, white panties with a lollipop pattern at midthigh, a TULANE GREEN WAVE tee hiked up past a red bra with the right side totally shattered by a shotgun round. Lower torso down to her thighs ripped by shotgun pellets, panties and bra so drenched in blood that the patterned and faintly red hibiscus flowers sewn into the bra barely registered because of the blood.

Blood spatters up against her face, drops against the headboard and streaking the wall. In the photo, I saw the sliding glass door at rear wall, not smashed by the wind but locked with a foot-pedal bar and a one-inch-thick wooden rod lying in the slider track. Eyes open wide as double eagles in extreme surprise at what was about to happen to her.

While looking at the pictures, another fierce gust of wind drove against the remains of the slider door, the drapes dropping occasionally when the wind slowed, only to shiver from the impact of rain slamming horizontally against them. Down on the golf course, his profile blurred through wet shards of glass, another lone golfer swung a club, got in his cart, and drove out of sight. Room closed, musty, thick blood and urine smells from the saturated mattress.

I shot the entire room.

"What next?"

"In here," Nathan said.

Three crime scene photos laid on the blood-drenched leather sofa.

Most of Leon's head blown away by the shotgun round. His lower jaw was in two or three pieces, nothing north of his upper jaw. One eyeball rested on the back of the sofa, mired in a sea of blood and brain, and the remains of Leon's head spread out like a flower, like a very, very large hibiscus, very dark red in color, hypnotic, the color Polaroids so vivid they drew you into the bloody face as though it was a flower, like Georgia O'Keeffe's bright red poppies.

I shot thirty-five pictures of the room, but nothing matched the bluntness of the crime scene photos, these in more vivid color as though the tech had switched cameras or run out of Polaroid film. Leon's skin peeled away from the skull, head the same as a hanging side of beef. Red marbled meat, orange-yellow spongy, fatty tissue, white cartilage and tendons and ligaments and bits of bone.

I was surprised, as always.

We never think of what our bodies will look like when we're dead.

Dressed only in jeans, nothing on top, his body extremely fit and muscular, six-pack abs, a big Navajo torso, but also that of a man in extraordinary physical condition. A muscles triangle up his waist. As somebody who worked out regularly with free weights, I could see the results of years of curls and crunches.

"You got everything?" Nathan asked.

"From this room, and the bedroom. Anything else?"

"Medicine chests in the bathrooms."

I nodded. All kinds of things revealed by what's in those bathrooms. But when I opened the mirrored doors, it was all ordinary. I shot both medicine chests, meticulously went through the kitchen and shot each cupboard. Shot the inside of the refrigerator, various juices, milk, cheeses, nothing extraordinary.

The crime scene full-face photos. Like actors' head

shots, not a pun, I said to myself, really, they really *are* head shots. Something bothered me, dug at me, scratched the unconscious, semiconscious, enough of metaphors.

Nobody ever bothers to clean up a death scene, unless the property is immediately resold or put up for rent. Even then, takes a lot of dedicated scrubbing to get rid of that coppery blood scent.

Stared at the living room crime scene photos. Leon on the sofa, damaged head against the wall. I turned Leon's picture over, in the bedroom I then laid out every shot of the teenager, working through her mind as Leon, or somebody, brings the shotgun into the room, he's probably already pumped a shell into the chamber. What does the teenager see? Does she even see the shotgun?

On her side of the bed. Several books stacked together, one open facedown. *The Prophet,* Gibran. Pages dog-eared, pencil and pen marks, notes, underlinings. A Michael Connelly mystery, half read and discarded. Headphones, a small portable CD player. I popped it open, read the CD. Ambient sounds of relaxation. Nothing eccentric. Surf, rain, wind, bubbling brook. Another CD of Yanni.

Getting a sense here, a woman who mellowed out. Why? A teenager? On her side of the wide oak dresser, old pictures of a woman, probably Leon's wife, Leon, and five somewhat younger people, obviously their children, two women and three men, three of them with spouses or partners, and nine, counting them, what had to be nine grandchildren.

I stood directly opposite her body, represented by the photographs. I knelt, put my arms out, crawled closer to the photos, sat back, rump on my heels. The teenager's last moments. Leon suddenly in the room, shotgun to her body. I stared at the bloodstains on the carpeting, pulled back my imagination, thought of the angle of the shotgun wound to her chest. The number-four buckshot angling down, thirteen pellets in her chest, removed during the autopsy, the rest of the twenty-seven pellets through and through, embedded in the mattress and the wall.

Back to Leon. Trying to be in his head, what the hell *was* in his head, did he do this, loading an old shotgun with only two shells, walking into the living room, leveling the barrel at the teenager, pulling the trigger without hesitation. Trying to imagine the teenager seeing him and the shotgun, what was she thinking, he's got the gun on her, she's probably been around his guns all her life, she knows he means to pull the trigger on her, she can't believe it, doesn't know why. Fright, panic.

No.

I picked up the crime scene photo showing her face. Rictus of astonishment, horror, disbelief. What's wrong with this picture? With the New-Age books, CDs, if it was Leon, the man she loved, trusted, would not her face be composed? *What are you doing? I'd like you to take that weapon away. No, Leon, please.*

But if it was a stranger, somebody else with the gun, unsuspected, that's the look of horror. And what if *she* was also a stranger?

"Nathan," I said, calling him into the bedroom. "What's wrong in here?" He looked around carefully, he'd already looked three times, finally shaking his head. "Look at those things on this teenager's side of the bed. Are they Leon's? If not, are they hers? With all this stuff, she looks like she's come to stay, or has been staying. But why is she sleeping in the same bed as Leon, if they're not sleeping together?"

"I don't know. Got pictures of everything?"

"Yeah. But taking pictures isn't the same as getting answers."

"We're done here," he said finally.

The monsoon thundered westward, wind whistling through mesquite and yucca trees, the rain finally stopping enough for us to go back to the Cherokee and drive to the Green Valley Mall. Raindrops scudding across all the Cherokee's windows.

He opened the passenger-side door, waited until I sat, stood holding the door half open, palms across the window ledge, both index fingers pointed at me.

"Let's set some ground rules," he said. "First rule. Computers, your thing. Everything else? Mine."

"Everything else?"

"You got a problem?"

"What does that mean, *everything*? What are you saying?" I cocked my head, trying to look up into his eyes, but the sun sparkled indirectly behind him, prismed through raindrops. East, toward the Santa Ritas, I could see a double rainbow and on the edge, the faint color bars of yet a third rainbow. I'd never seen a triple rainbow in my life. "Why are you telling me this? What did you notice, that you're saying this to me? Like we've never worked a case together, like we've never been partners?"

"Division of responsibilities," he said. "You check out all that computer gear. You check out their financials. Leon and the Patroon woman, you look at their digital records. I check out the real people involved. I interview witnesses, suspects. Whoever. Whatever."

"You don't trust me around people?"

"Laura." He bent down, his face level with mine. "I trust you 100 percent. I trust you with my life."

"But?"

"You got a history of getting near killed."

Irritated, I pushed the door against him, trying to swivel my legs out. He held the door firm, the physical control setting off a flood of anger.

"Two people dead here, Laura. A murder-suicide, maybe, maybe not."

I pushed hard on the door, quickly pulled it to me and just as quickly pushed it out hard before he could adjust to the back-and-forth pressure. The door banged his right kneecap.

"Okay. All right." He grimaced, smiled, stood away while I struggled out of the car. "Let's try this another way. It's my thing, okay?" Rubbed his knee. "I saw your eyes light up, all that computer gear. You're thinking, hey, you could be a real part of this. Here's the deal," Nathan said. "One. You don't talk to anybody involved in this unless I say so. Two, you don't come along when *I* talk to people, unless I say so. Don't answer the phone until you run caller ID."

"I understand. You chief. Me just working Indian."

"Works for me." Not missing my sarcasm. "Okay, tell you what. You want people? I give you that."

"Gee. Thanks, chief."

"So now we cool?"

"Oh, dude," I said. Smiling, laying my hand below

his belt buckle, on top of the zipper. "Now you *know* that I'm cool."

"Not now," he said, turning away from my hand.

"What?" I said.

"You see any TV sets here? Books? CD player?"

"No."

"Lives by himself, doesn't watch TV, read books, or listen to music. Look at the carpeting in that computer room, the wheel marks from his chair, back and forth. He spent a lot of time in this room, which means a lot of time at the computer."

"I'll run the hard drives up to Tucson," I said. "Leave them with Alex after I talk with my daughter. C'mon. Let's go, gotta be there."

"I want you to do something else first. That place we stopped? The house, nobody home? Go back there, see if the woman's returned."

"Woman," I said. "Aha. You'll let me talk to 'people' long's it's a woman. Okay. Who is she?"

"I don't know. All I have is the name and address. Antoinette Claw."

"Navajo? Where you get her name? Her address?"

"A friend," he said shortly.

"Will I get to meet this friend?" Nathan considered, nodded. "What's his name?"

"Bob Good Fellow. He's a Tribal Policeman. Staying at my place. Can you meet us tomorrow morning, at Casa Grande?"

"Afternoon," I said. "Alex and I will work on these computers. Two o'clock all right? I miss being with you, Nathan."

Another heavy blast of wind. Glass tinkled, probably from the sliding back door. He got that tight smile, nodding to himself as we went to check that the room was secure enough from more damage. Across the ravine, the golfer ducked his head at us, bent sideways for some shelter against the rain, then he swung again.

"That's odd," I said. "Who hits golf balls into heavy wind and rain?"

Nathan stared and stared, abruptly ran into the living room and returned with a pair of binoculars, focusing them on the golfer.

"No ball," Nathan said. "He's not swinging at a ball. He's looking at us, he's got binoculars." Nathan slipped between shards of glass, hurdled the row of oleander bushes, and sprinted down the ravine. The golfer backed up quickly to his cart, turned on the small engine, and swung through a wide U-turn toward the far end of the fairway. Nathan slipped on some wet leaves, climbed to the lip of the ravine just as the golf cart disappeared in a flurry of rain.

"Who could that be?" I said ten minutes later, Nathan dripping all over the carpet. "Why was he watching us?"

"Not us. Watching the house. Listen. I'm going to stay here. You go see if Antoinette is home. Take the computers. I'll finish up."

"Finish up what?" He grabbed the G5 computer carrying handles, one computer gripped in each fist, carrying them out to the Cherokee.

"Keep your cell on," he said, disappearing back into the house.

Back at the Green Valley Mall, a woman from the bookshop pushing the outside sale-book racks inside, closing up the store. I walked around his pickup, the far side window open several inches. Using my extra key, I opened the door and switched on the power long enough to roll the window completely closed. A catalog lay on the seat, addressed to me at Nathan's address, the catalog creased open somewhere in the middle. Shoes by Jimmy Choo.

This sounds so frivolous, wanting a pair of expensive shoes. Part of my new, social self was the realization that I had few good clothes. Absolutely no frivolous underthings, sports bras and Jockey panties, nothing frilly or suggestive, I usually slept with nothing on. My shoes? Nearly three dozen pairs of running shoes, some sandals and flipflops, a single pair of heels, low heels, practical heels. While Tucson isn't a high-fashion shopping center, I could find nearly anything I needed, never thought of shopping in Phoenix for something expensive or seductive or even colorful. Figuring I'd start where I had the least, I began looking at shoe catalogs and after three months decided I wanted a pair of Jimmy Choo four-inch heels. Totally impractical, almost totally unobtainable, just a fancy, something out of reach.

People skills. A running joke between Nathan and me. In the past few months, more truth than humor, Nathan an old-fashioned cop, me one of the first of an entirely new breed of private investigators. The Internet barely ten years old, I'd been checking people's identities for most of that, including the early years when databases were so new that getting into them was pretty much illegal.

Now, my small business, created by Donald Ralph and managed by him until his Cessna 172 crashed and burned in a Kansas cornfield, we'd increased from nine people to nearly two dozen. Most of them young kids, a few with college degrees, two still in high school, all of them huddled over their laptops and wide display screens for long days, often curled fully clothed into sleeping bags under their desktops, crashing for an hour of sleep while computers crunched through powerful databases both online and owned by my company.

I never cared if they had college or even high school degrees. With these kids, the personal interview pretty much started at a keyboard. I only wanted to find people with curiosity at solving puzzles, or even if they showed facility at such diverse things as computer games, crossword puzzles, nontraditional IQ tests, anything that made them eager to solve something, to provide an answer.

Corporations now routinely ran background checks on some employees. First-time daters checked out financial, medical, or criminal pasts of their new companions. In addition to these jobs, we recovered data from suspect computers, rebuilding supposedly deleted email messages and personal files and address books. Thirteen of every hundred people had done something negative in their past. If criminal charges were filed, we almost always discovered what happened.

Unlike the old-time PIs, like the Jake Gittes character played by Jack Nicholson in *Chinatown* and *The Two Jakes,* I refused what used to be the meat-and-potatoes jobs, uncovering sexual infidelities of husbands or wives. There's just too much money to be made at a computer to bother with hours of fruitless surveillance. For a short time, I considered offering electronic surveillance, like those software programs where you can track keystrokes on a remote computer, or read your husband's email from his office computer, to me that was too much like ambulance chasing, like sneaking long-lens pictures through a hotel window.

Some of the kids working for me probably'd never had sex, anyway. What seventeen-year-old had time for cruising and telephoning when I paid nearly fifty thousand dollars a year for them to pry into databases and networks.

Network hacking remained the toughest job. Any computer hooked to another computer is capable of being hacked. Any network, no matter how strong the security firewalls, can be probed for access, either from outside the physical premises or, occasionally, by paying an employee to provide information, something completely illegal that we didn't encourage except in cases that involved whistle-blowing of some corporate misdeeds.

Nine years ago, operating from my single-wide trailer in Tuba City, I'd dial up through an old-fashioned modem, taking hours to penetrate another computer miles away, once I'd solved the log-in identities and passwords, I spent hours on a single job. Now we had thirteen high-speed Internet connections, including access to satellite time if a client paid the expenses.

So. People skills. Nathan insisted that any private investigator had to deal with people, it couldn't be computers all the time. He got me to stop cursing like a sailor, I'd startled too many corporate suits with my potty mouth. And Nathan encouraged me to carry a gun in case my people skills didn't keep somebody from trying to hurt me. I've got your back, he'd always say, unless I'm not there.

I had all kinds of toys, sneaky cameras and recorders and microphones and wireless gadgets, usually I had time to pick and choose.

This afternoon, none of them were available.

I found the right neighborhood in a roundabout way, I followed a zone-tailed hawk circling a small ravine south of Green Valley. Looks like a turkey vulture, except this bird dove low over the roadway, almost filling my windshield with a blur of raptor-feathered wings and I saw the grayish-white band across the middle tail feathers.

In the 1870s, so it's told, Major Charles Bendire of the U.S. Army, climbed an old cottonwood tree to investigate a zone-tailed hawk's nest. At the exact moment that he spotted an egg in the nest, from his high perch he saw a small band of Apaches, all of them surprised to see each other. Or so Major Charles's writings seem to indicate. Yikes, he must have said, what comes first? Hawk or savages? Stuffing the egg carefully inside his mouth, he got out of the tree and on his horse, riding five miles back to Fort Lowell in Tucson.

Which gives a whole new ending to an old question. Which came first, the Apache or the egg?

Looking back from the hawk to the road, recognizing the street, I went looking for the right house.

9

Somebody was home. Front door half open, an almost new Ford XLT SuperCrew pickup in the driveway, facing out to the street. I slowed beside the high curbing, then inched forward until I blocked the truck.

Four full-size doors, split-bench seats in the front with a transmission console shifter, backseat bench loaded with boxes, more boxes in the stepside cargo bed.

"What do you want?" she said.

Short, squat, flat-nosed but a beautiful face. Greenish velveteen blouse hanging over extrawide jeans that almost hid her boots.

"Nice truck," I said. Moving behind it, the hinged tailgate hanging down over the license plate. Lifting the gate, I saw it was a Budget rental.

"Move your car," she said, laying another box in the cargo bed.

"Are you Antoinette Claw?"

"No," the lie flickering across her eyes, "she left town."

"I thought this was her house."

"It's not."

She went back to the house, closed the door care-

fully. Walking to the street, slowly, trailing my fingertips along the silvery sides, fingering the F-150 emblem and then moving quickly around the front to the
passenger door. Keys in the ignition. I opened the
door, yanked out the keys, shut the door with a solid
click and waited.

Five minutes. I went to the front door, pushed the
bell button, knocked. Another few minutes. I rang the
bell again, raised my hand to knock just as the door
opened and she stood there with an old lever-action
.30-30.

"Give me the keys."

I held out the keys in my left hand, slid the right behind my back for the Beretta, but had enough sense to
stay away from it. People skills, time to try them out.

"Look," I said. "I really need to find Antoinette."

"Don't know her. Now go move your car."

"I've got a message for her." She hesitated. "You *do*
know her?"

"Maybe."

"Let me write down the message."

"Don't care *what* it says. Who's it *from?*"

"I'm, my name is Laura Winslow." Staring into eyes
like coal-black buttons. "My partner's name is
Nathan Brittles?"

"Umh. What's his clan name?"

"I don't know."

"Mother's name?"

"I don't know, I don't know."

The .30-30's barrel drooped a few inches. "His
middle name?"

"Nathan? Oh. Nathan Cutting Brittles. Cutting."

"Cutting Tongue," she said. Uncocked the .30-30,

lowered the barrel until it pointed somewhere at my right running shoe. "Don't know him."

"But you know his middle names."

"Don't know him, never said I'd didn't know about him. What's the message?"

"Um," I said, "well," I said, trying to create some message, "look, he just wants to see you. Talk to you."

"About what?"

"Leon Begay." She staggered, brought the .30-30 up again. "Nathan, he's an old friend of Leon Begay. And another old friend just came down from Monument Valley. A Navajo tribal cop. Bob Good . . . Good something, I can't remember."

"Good Fellow. Umh." She went slowly to the pickup, opened the passenger-side rear drawer to fumble inside one of the cardboard boxes for a very worn silver picture frame holding an old black-and-white photo. Three young men, hardly more than teenagers, standing slightly apart but all pointing at the camera. In the background, what looked like Right Mitten, one of the most photographed rock structures in Monument Valley. "Who are they?"

She held out the picture.

Two of them I'd never seen before. On the left, Nathan, a fierce grin underneath a battered straw cowboy hat.

"That one's Nathan," I said, pointing. "Never seen the other two."

"Leon and Robert, that some call Bob. Come on in. Have some coffee."

Her house was small, but neat except for a half-dozen or so empty cardboard boxes in the living room. She packed nothing in the kitchen, I didn't want to look elsewhere.

"Where'd you get that picture?" I said, coughing at the coffee, incredibly strong and black, she had no milk or sugar. Sipping from her pink mug, no handle, staring over the rim at me, only halfway to trust. "Wait, wait a minute."

I ran to my Cherokee, got my camera and turned it on, cycling thru the pictures until I found the one I wanted to show her. "It's kinda small. Do you need glasses, can you see it?" A picture of the shelving in Leon's computer room, showing the spots not marked by monsoon dirt. "You've been there," I said. "Yesterday?"

"This morning." Put down her cup. "I was afraid he'd come back for them."

"Who?"

"Sheriff's had a volunteer watching the house until early this morning. When she left, I went inside, got some things. I was afraid, I didn't want him coming back."

"Who?"

"The *yenaldlooshi*."

"Who? I don't speak Navajo."

"The thing what killed Leon."

"What thing?"

"Skinwalker," she said, standing up. "Got to go, got a long drive."

"No, wait, Antoinette, you *are* Antoinette Claw?"

"Umn." Carrying the picture to the pickup, holding out her hand for the key.

"Where are you going? Back to *Dinetah*?"

"*Dinetah*. Yup."

"Where?" Like pulling a yard of weeds, never getting to the root of what she could tell me. "Where on the rez?"

"You talk to Robert Good Fellow, he knows my family."

"If I tell you where Good Fellow is, will you go see him?" She twisted the key in the ignition, the V-8 rumbled quietly and she pulled the center-shift lever into Drive. "Casa Grande," I said. "Whoever you're afraid of, he's never been to this place, he doesn't know about this place. Please." Grabbing a restaurant receipt and a ballpoint pen from my handbag, I wrote down Nathan's address and drew a rough map, adding the phone number at the bottom.

"Good Fellow is here. I'll call him. I'll tell him you're coming there. Here's *my* phone number. Call me if you have," starting to say trouble, biting my upper lip, "if you have any problems."

"Maybe," she said finally. "Move your car."

"Wait. Just, wait, one more question. Why did you say that Leon was killed by a skinwalker." For the first time, I saw a wave of fear ripple down her cheeks and neck. "The girl, too? Were they both killed by a skinwalker?"

"Are you *Dineh?*"

"No. My father was Hopi."

"Hopi." Spat the word out. "From up there?"

"Hotevilla. Until I was fifteen."

"Hotevilla. Umn, umh. You grow up with witches?"

"No. Except television. *Bewitched.*"

"What's that?"

"TV show. Once in a while, my dad would hook a TV to his truck battery."

She abruptly shifted into Park, reached through the seats behind to pull another picture from a box. "Take this," she said. "I get near Casa Grande, I'll call Robert." Two youngsters, maybe twelve or thirteen, and an older man, probably their father, sitting outside a single-wide trailer. "You and your friends, you tell me who these people are, you call Robert at Casa Grande and tell him, then I'll call Robert when I'm near there, if he gives me the names . . . maybe, I'll stop for gas."

"I don't believe in witches," I said. Brought up my Nikon and ripped off three pictures of her face.

Livid, she jumped out of the pickup. "Give me that film," shouting, half-running toward me as I backpedaled. "You can't keep my face."

"It's digital," I said. "There is no film. But here. Look." Holding up the back of the Nikon, working the buttons to show her picture. "I'm sorry. Watch." She stuck her face a foot from the camera, tried to grab it but I'd called up her picture. "Okay, I'm deleting it." I backspaced to a picture of Leon's house. "See?

"That picture is gone?" Unbelieving.

"Yes." The truth, that one picture was gone. Two more images left on the flash card, she didn't seem to know what I was showing her. "How many pictures did you take from Leon's house? Was there also a map, two by three feet?"

"Ah!" she snorted, waddling back to her pickup, cramping the steering wheel to the right, jumping on the gas pedal to drive across the caliche front yard, the pickup bouncing slightly as it rocketed off the curb, the heavy sixteen-inch tires spewing a rooster tail of dirt and small stones that rang like hail against my car. I ran to my Cherokee but had to fumble for my keys, finally starting the engine before I looked up to see her pickup at the five corner, but I lost sight of it when she lurched around the corner since I had to stare through five starry cracks in my windshield.

In all my life, I've only heard one real ghost story. Here it is.

10

A *giant Kachina stood just inside Patrick Valasnu-youoma's rusted screen door.*

My own witch story, from five years ago. Up on the rez, Tuba City, story of a vision, told to me by a Hopi elder. Adam, Anthony . . . no, Abbot, no, that was Abbott Pavatea, wanting me to find his missing daughter. Judy.

I hadn't thought of Judy Pavatea in a long time.

And a Hopi elder, a *kikmongwi*, he'd told me the ghost story, yes, that's who it was, I remember now. Johnson . . . Johnson . . . something.

Pongyayanoma.

And in remembering his name, I remembered the ghost story with absolute certainty of Johnson's exact words, they rushed into my head, each word crystal clear, like seeing all the drops in a monsoon rain. Each grain of sand in a dune.

Blue prayer feathers stuck in thick, flowing black hair.
  Come, Patrick, he said.
  Why?
  Travelers, the Kachina said.

Seeking the Home of the Dead. We must protect them from Powakas.

Two Hearts? Patrick said. Witches? he said.

Come.

The Kachina beckoned with his right hand. He backed outside, rusted hinges squeaking like mice in the winter corn. They left the ancient stone house and they flew over cornfields and peach trees, above and beyond ancient stone villages on the three Hopi mesas until the Kachina pointed down at hordes of travelers, gaunt, haggard with fatigue, begging for food and water. Staggering under gigantic bales of firewood, serpents braceleted and struck their arms, scorpions thrust into their thighs, hundreds of cholla thorns pricked the soles of their feet, their armpits, their genitals. All these punishments for bad things done to others, or maybe just for speaking up against rain.

They flew until they landed upon a high desert plain.

Someone sat motionless behind the wheel of a derelict, completely stripped pickup truck. No tires or rims, no hood, no doors or tailgate, the engine throbbing at full speed, a throaty pulsation, the enormous power of a diesel semi double trailer, shifted down into crawler gear, muffler blatting as it climbs full out up a three-mile hill and the longbox pickup bed overflowing with girls and women of many ages, all bearing enormous scars or bruises or wounds or holes through their bodies, some carrying their hearts, livers, a hand, fingers, their heads.

The Kachina pointed toward the south.

Many creatures moved toward them at tremendous speed. As they drew near, Patrick saw they were young maidens with butterfly swirls of black hair braided behind both ears. Some of them ridden and spurred by five winged creatures with sharp beaks and enormous erections. As the women passed, Patrick saw their faces clearly and he was astonished that he knew many of them.

Four of the creatures drifted by, but the fifth circled above him, above the pickup. A woman came out of the pickup cab, her fisted right arm extending, stretching upward, striking the creature and then plucking him from the woman he rode and the arm swinging like a lasso and throwing the creature beyond the horizon.

Astonished, mute, Patrick saw the woman settle into the now empty pickup bed and the pickup drove away. The other creatures returned in a long ellipse, the dust of their travel rose, filled the air, swirled around until they passed and then things changed again.

One thing more, now my mind could not stop picturing Leon's destroyed head. In the Kachina ghost story, how he looked entering Patrick's stone house.

Head cradled in his left hand, shoulders thrust against the beamed ceiling.

Enough of these old memories, my old life. Most people think the trick to dealing with the past is to push it out of conscious memory. Nope. The *real* trick is to deal with your life and recognize you've moved beyond it. Why else would Dr. Phil and Oprah be so popular, if not to tell us to get a new life?

* * *

I tried calling Spider but she wasn't home. About to
flick the cell shut, I had an idea. If I was going to im-
prove my people-person skills, I needed to meet somebody new.

11

"Anasazi Flamingo Casino."

"Vincent Basaraba, please," I said.

"Who is calling?"

"Laura Winslow."

"Does he know you?"

"No."

"What company or concerns do you represent?"

"Computer Forensics," I said.

"Um . . ."

"Data integrity. Computer security, that kind of thing."

"Security. I'll ring you right through."

On hold. Then a number rang, immediately rolled over to another number, probably a cell phone, and somebody answered immediately.

"This is Wes."

"Actually, I'm trying to reach Mr. Basaraba."

"The operator said you worked in computer security."

"Yes, but this is a personal call."

"I screen all of Mr. Basaraba's personal calls."

"Screen them for what?"

"Who am I talking to?" Voice harder-edged. "Winslett, is that your name?"

"Laura Winslow."

"Computer security, right?"

"Yes, but . . ."

"We handle our own computer security, thank you." His voice faded after the first word, sounding like he was either hanging up or switching off a cell.

"It's about his brother," I said.

A long silence, but no click of disconnection.

"Who *are* you?"

"Who are *you?*" I said.

"Wes McCartney. Director of casino security. Uh, to my knowledge, Mr. Basaraba doesn't have a brother."

"You're right. He's dead."

"He's what?"

"Enough of this jackshit," I said. I've got this voice, I can lower my pitch almost an octave, I get even quieter, but it gets results sometimes. "Just let me talk to Vincent Basaraba. What's the problem here?"

"You're not a reporter? Trying to get some inside story?"

"Story about what?"

"We had a suicide here today."

"Not . . . Mr. Basaraba?"

"Gambler. Owed lots of money. Jumped from the roof."

"No," I said. "I'm *not* a reporter."

"All right," he said finally. "But I'm gonna brief him first."

"Okay. I'll take what I can get."

I waited three minutes, then the line clicked live again.

"Miss Laura Winslow?"

"Yes."

"This is . . . I'm Vincent Basaraba." Baritone, very modulated, carefully exact with pronunciation, but also a current of concern. "About my brother? You're calling to tell me my brother is dead?"

"Last week."

"We're talking about my brother Leon?"

"Yes."

"Leon Begay?"

"Yes."

"I'm only asking because . . . I haven't used that last name in years. But Leon, I knew he was in Vietnam, I heard he moved back to the rez. Did he die up there? In Monument Valley?"

"In *Green* Valley," I said.

Sharp intake of breath, hand covering the phone but not entirely, I could hear another voice in the background, a woman's voice and then that of another man.

"Who *are* you?" he said. "I mean, I've never heard of you, I've not heard any news about Leon, nothing in the papers. How do I know you're not just somebody trying to get an edge at the casino?"

"He died last week," I said. "The medical examiner's office held off with his name because a young woman died with him."

"A car accident?"

"No." How could I explain this. "Can I make an appointment to see you, Mr. Basaraba? Tomorrow? Any time tomorrow?"

"Yes . . . I suppose so, but . . . how did they die?"

In for a penny, in for it all.

"It's been ruled a murder-suicide," I said.

"Jesus Christ." He gasped, didn't bother covering the phone, I heard him say *murder and suicide* to the other people. "Who was the woman? Why did she kill Leon?"

"I don't really know how to tell you this, Mr. Basaraba. Leon killed the woman. Then he turned the shotgun on himself."

The phone clattered onto a desk or table, something wooden, I could hear it bounce a few times.

"This is McCartney. How soon can you be here?"

"You told me he didn't have a brother."

"Tonight?"

"No."

"Tonight," McCartney said. "Any time, all night. Any time is okay."

"I'm on my way to Green Valley right now," I said. "Then I just want to go home, and I live in . . ." I stopped, right there, sometimes, I tell you, I get this instinct not to reveal personal things, like where I live. ". . . a long drive from here. I'll be at the casino at nine tomorrow morning."

"How do you know this?" McCartney said. "About Leon, and the woman?"

"Somebody contacted me."

"Contacted you? In what capacity? Does this have anything to do with computer security? What *somebody*?"

"Tomorrow morning at nine," I said. This guy asked *way* too many questions.

"Don't misunderstand me, Miss Winslow. A lot of

people, they know Vincent from the movies, a lot of other people want an edge at the casino. I have to be really, *really* careful about who I trust.

"Let me ask you a question," he said. "There's a horrible plane crash *exact*ly on the border between Arizona and Mexico. Bodies everywhere, wreckage across a dozen acres, plane seats, teddy bears, shoes, so tell me, if it's exactly on the border, where do they bury the survivors?"

"Survivors live on."

"Not the right answer. Tomorrow."

"Tell Vincent I'm a big fan," I said.

I heard the three people talking, Basaraba's voice clearly audible at one point. *A fan? What the hell is this?* I disconnected and started to power down the cell so they wouldn't star sixty-nine the call, but it rang.

"Where are you now?" Nathan said.

"Outside her house. Antoinette Claw, I met her." I started to tell him about Vincent Basaraba, but he interrupted.

"Come back to Leon's place," he said.

"Nathan. I told you, I have to talk with my daughter. I can't meet you."

"I need your help," he said, his voice over the edge of control.

12

"I don't know what's going on there," the old man said. White shorts, calf-high white socks, white golf shoes, and a cream-colored guayabera. Standing next to an elaborate electric golf cart, lime green and the roof curved up from the front. Holding his titanium Big Bertha driver in one hand and an open cell phone in the other. In the middle of the street, looking into the open doorway of Leon Begay's house.

"What do you mean?" I said. Parking the Cherokee in Leon's carport.

"Smashing up the place," the man said. "I just came back from thirty-six holes, I see Leon's door open so I stop my cart, he shot himself, you see, and I knew nobody lived there, I wanted to find out who's in there, see if I should call the sheriff's office. Or what."

"It's all right," I said.

"Up my ass it's all right," the man said. "Somebody's in there smashing up the place. Listen, what are *you* doing here?"

"I don't hear any noise." Getting out of the Cherokee. "What kind of noise?"

We both listened, but heard nothing.

"Chopping wood. Breaking up wood, I don't know. I'm calling the sheriff."

"It's all right." I started up the walkway. "When we were here earlier, the man in the house, he's my partner, we're here investigating Leon's death."

"Badge me," the man said. I shook my head, not understanding. "Your badge, what kind of cops are you? You don't badge me, I'm calling the sheriff."

"You want ID," I said. Opening my purse, I handed him one of a half-dozen different business cards I kept for any occasion like this. "Security," I said, not explaining what kind of security.

"Homeowner's security?"

"Related, yes. But I can probably tell you about the noise. When we were here, two hours ago during the monsoon, a mesquite branch flew into the back sliding door. Smashed the glass door, did a lot of damage. My partner in there is probably chopping up the wood, so it can be removed."

"I'm going out back to look."

"It's all covered up, drapes, not much you'll be able to see." Having no idea what Nathan was doing inside, but not wanting anybody seeing it before me.

"There's a community walkway in back. Development property. I'll just walk around there, have a look."

At the front door, I paused. "During the monsoon," I said. "Were you playing golf?"

"Yeah," the man said. Matter of fact. Still gripping the Big Bertha, at least he closed his cell. I left him there, went inside, closed the front door.

Total disaster area.

"Nathan?"

Front mirror smashed. Just inside the door, a Mexican painted giraffe statue crunched into fragments. Every single bit of living room furniture crumpled into pieces, no real design to the destruction, just smashed beyond use. Bits of the entertainment center surrounded smashed TV and electronics.

"Nathan!"

"Back here."

I stopped just outside the computer room, distracted by the broken bed frame and dressers, more destruction in the back bedroom, the drapes now hanging across the broken glass slider. I looked inside the computer room and saw Nathan, both hands clenched on the hickory handle of a sixteen-pound sledgehammer raised over his head in front of the large LCD display monitor, huge veins popping out on both temples and another zigzagging down his forehead, arm muscles rigid, every muscle etched under his skin, so close to the edge of destruction.

"Nathan, *Nathan! What are you doing?*"

"Breaking up his possessions."

"Nathan." Quickly went to raise my hands across his. "You can't . . . this is a crime scene, this is . . ."

"This is a *chindi* house," he said.

"Put the sledgehammer down."

"I'm not done," he said. Hesitant, almost as though for the very first time he was aware of what he'd been doing. "Just this room, then I'm done."

"Put. The. Sledge. Down."

"I . . . I . . ."

Gently, carefully, I pulled against the hickory handle, pulled it downward. Reflexively he resisted, but I thrust my face two inches from his, nodding, smiling.

"It's all right," I said. More pressure on the handle. "You're frightening me, Nathan. I don't know what you're doing. I need you to put this sledgehammer down, I need you to do that first and then tell me what you're doing."

"*Chindi,*" he said finally. Alert to the smashed computer desk and chair, relaxing his grip on the hickory. "Break up his possessions. He's dead."

He let me grip the handle, take the sledge hammer and lower it to the floor. I wrapped an arm around his torso and led him into the hallway, the only place without smashed objects. I pressed both hands on his shoulders, pushing him down, both of us finally sitting on the floor, facing each other across the narrow hallway.

"Okay," I said. "*Chindi.* I know you're really working at your Navajo roots, or traditions, or . . . hell, Nathan, I don't really know *what* you're working on. But start by explaining what *chindi* means."

"Ghosts."

"Skinwalkers?"

"Where have you heard that? I haven't told you that."

"Antoinette Claw. I found her, she said something about skinwalkers."

"I need to talk to her."

"She's gone," I said, "she's driving back to the rez, but she's going to call Robert Good Fellow."

"She's going to see Bob?"

"Forget Bob. Forget her. What's happening in here, what's *real,* Nathan. I need to know what's real in all of this."

"You really want to know?"

I kept myself from sighing, from showing any irritation or displeasure or negative reaction to him, so I kept my smile, I worked at keeping the smile in my eyes and I held his hands until he slumped, nodding his head, gathering thoughts.

"When somebody is born, they receive the breath of life. When the person dies, that breath, that wind, goes out of the body. And becomes a *chindi*, a ghost."

"A ghost," I said. Encouragingly, trying to get him to talk, but my never having believed in ghosts. "And?"

"Well, it's not like all of that person is a ghost. Some of the People believe that the better nature of the person goes to *ciditah*. The afterworld, the underworld, no, like inside the Hopi kiva, you know the hole? The place of emergence? Into the next worlds, that's where the better side goes. The *chindi*, they wander here, in this world. Skinwalkers, some people call them. Ghosts."

"Skinwalkers, like coyotes, like wolves?"

"Owls are bad, bad things to see. But it could be something as small as a mouse. Or a dust devil on a calm day. Strange fires at night. Or one of the dark spots at night, so dark and black it's like a hole into . . ."

"You're really spooking me, Nathan. I mean, you're freaking me out. Do you really believe in this ghost stuff?"

Wrong question. He pulled his hands out of mine, stood up, went into the living room. I followed quickly, I didn't want him picking up the sledgehammer again and I especially wanted us to get out of there before the old golfer called the sheriff.

"Can we just go?" I said.

"Right," he said.

I led him out the door, shutting the door firmly, led him to the Cherokee, opened the passenger door. Didn't want him driving. The electric lime-green golf cart was still parked in the middle of the road, the old golfer apparently in his house. I got into the driver's seat, started the engine, and slowly drove out of the development.

"You think I'm over the edge. Don't you?"

"No. It's just ... well, Nathan, why did you smash things up, back there?"

"Destroying his possessions. That mesquite branch, smashing out the window, it was to the east, making a hole for spirits to leave the death house. I had to complete the destruction so nobody would be harmed, if they went in there."

"Harmed?"

"At night, skinwalkers return to the *chindi* house. Anybody there, skinwalkers could ... could ..."

"I really want to hear more about skinwalkers, Nathan. I really, *really* want to understand all of this. But right now, it's not the time. I saw an old man, outside. You know that golf cart? That old man heard you smashing furniture. I tried to tell him it was just you chopping up the mesquite branch, but I don't think he believed me and I bet he's already called the sheriff's office. So that's where we're going. Right now. I know exactly where it is, and we're going in there."

"Why?"

"First of all, if that old man called, they're going to want to know what we were doing. It's probably a good thing," I said, "if we go to the sheriff's office right now. Can you handle that? Can you? . . ."

"Pull myself together? I'm not over the edge," he said. "I had permission."

"For what?"

"Leon's family, Leon's aunt. She gave permission to destroy Leon's belongings. I've got a letter, I've got . . . you're right, I need to see the sheriff." He reached over to touch my nose. "I know I've been hard on you, I know . . ." Starting to smile, some darker thought crossed his mind and he pulled his finger away from my nose and stared straight ahead.

"Who are these people?" I showed him the picture Antoinette gave me, the three men side by side. He swept over it quickly, stared out the window, did a double take and took the picture into his hands. "Is one of them Leon?" He pointed at the youngest boy, rubbing the old grainy black-and-white photograph, trying to make it sharper. "Older man must be Leon's father?"

"And this guy is Vincent. Always handsome, see, his shirt's tucked in, jean bottoms turned up two inches."

"Just like John Wayne," I said. "He always did that."

"So she took this picture from Leon's house?"

"Yes. She showed me one other. You, Leon, and Good Fellow. Whatever else she took, she didn't show me. Just told me, if you knew who these three guys are, I should call Good Fellow and describe each one, from this picture."

"Bob's an honest man. Let's hope she trusts him. Let's go see the law. I want to set this right, I want no trouble with the sheriff."

13

Navajo men. Hadn't thought much about Navajo men, even knowing Nathan a year and eleven days, he remained first and last my man, and until recently when he started building the sweat lodge, almost never a Navajo.

My first husband, Jonathan Begay. Born to *Dibé izhiní*, the Black Sheep Clan, and born for *Hasht 'ishnii*, the Mud Clan. *How long ago was that?* I wondered. *How long ago did I believe so much in Jonathan I thought he'd hung the moon?*

But in the last years with Jonathan, we rarely talked. Both of us said *Listen* because neither of us did. To communicate anything, we had to force our angry words sideways into the gaps between what the other said.

"Laura," Nathan said.

"What?" Shaking my head.

"You've been silent for nearly ten minutes."

I'd actually been thinking about my husband.

"My husband's name was Jonathan Begay," I said. "And your dead friend is Leon Begay."

"On the rez, Begay is a common name. Like Jones. Like Smith."

"Still," I said. "I wonder if they were related. If they knew each other."

"I don't have time for this, what are you thinking?"

"I've always wanted to tell you about him. You've heard so much about what my father did, but you've never really heard about Jonathan. And whatever violence I suffered from men, it was more from Jonathan than my father."

"All right. Tell me."

"In the beginning, nothing but happy times."

"When you say, in the beginning, how many years was that?"

"Five, seven. We got married after eight years, and the troubles all started then. But in those first years, we thrived as lovers, soul mates, and guerrillas for Red Power, ready at a moment to load our half-ton Jimmy and travel to any Indian nation needing help. We'd had some fantastic times in that old Jimmy. We'd bought it nearly brand-new from a Bittersweet Clan woman who couldn't make the payments. Jonathan drove and I learned how to do tune-ups, reline brakes, adjust the carburetor, usually because we had to clear out of some place with no money for mechanics and wouldn't have chanced a regular garage anyway because we skipped out on the bank payments and usually changed license plates depending on what state we were driving through.

"Did you love him?"

"In the beginning, I loved the way Jonathan handed me commitment. Straight out, with no fancy dinner plates underneath. We lived with the constant hope of change, of making things better. Our taps wide open, love flowing for all things Indian, always primed to square off against the entire Bahana world. Brights flicked on all the time, no turn signals needed. Roaring arrow straight toward trouble. Hold back the dawn against the whites. Off the BIA, the BLM, the FBI.

"I once hoped I could freeze dry the best of those moments, storing their essence away for later nourishment. But then we got married, came back here, and the barbed wire went up on Black Mesa, separating Hopi and Dine families by fenced boundaries, forcing some of Jonathan's clan to give up centuries-old family land and move outside of the fence. Our troubles marinated like spoiling summer meat. Never once believing that troubles on the rez could possibly touch *our* partnership, we suddenly found ourselves at war because I wouldn't support armed resistance of the Dine Second Big Walk.

"Just like the land dispute partitioned off families, Jonathan increasingly partitioned his life into different political activities, shutting me out of most of them. Our only passion was sex, which somehow got more and more violent. Wow. Did you hear that, about how I used those words in the same sentence?"

"You mean sex and violence? Are those the words you mean?"

"It was a terrible life. We couldn't talk to each other because neither of us wanted to listen. Jonathan took to supplying guns all over the country, talking up armed struggle from Montreal to Pyramid Lake, while I took to speaking out in public. Show me a bullet, I'd tell people, that'll kill drunkenness and unemployment and such on the rez. People got tired of listening to me, I got so preachy and shrill. So I asked him to move out. He did, but only because he had to go to Wyoming, or some place, I never knew where.

"Two months after we'd separated, Jonathan came back to the house and even when I told him to leave he'd come whenever he pleased. One day I came home to find that he'd sold my pickup, a beautifully reconditioned old Chevy stepside, nineteen years old, only thirty-eight-thousand miles after the engine rebuild. Even though we showed joint ownership on the title, he'd forged my name for the sale and used the money to buy a Blazer four-wheel drive plus a twenty-four-foot power cruiser, fully trailered and now parked defiantly in my driveway.

"I spent hours with a hacksaw sawing through everything metal I could find on the power cruiser. He threatened me so bad that night I knew that I couldn't stay in the house any longer. When he went out for some beer and groceries, I packed a bag and left for Flagstaff. Jonathan became so enraged that he put on his second-hand police flak vest and cammie clothing, loaded the shotgun, grabbed two boxes of shotgun shells, his Fairbairn-Sykes commando knife, his .357 with the six-inch barrel and four autoloaders, and the .30-06 10X scoped hunting rifle with the 180 grain handloads, crammed everything into his pickup, and started cruising the streets in Flagstaff looking for me. I was walking from the bus stop and so he saw me before he'd been out not more than a few minutes. I often wondered what would have happened if I'd walked faster, or turned down another street.

"But he found me. He took me home and did whatever pleased him for hours and hours. The next morning he dared me to complain to the police, boasting that nobody'd much care about what a husband and wife did in their own home. To my astonishment and despair when I went to the police station, he was right.

"Everything ended abruptly one night when he got sloppy drunk in a Flagstaff bar and savagely beat up a Havasupai who kept pulling me to the dance floor. After serving ten days in jail, furious because this time I wouldn't go him bail, he walked out of the cell, came home to pick up our daughter, and they both disappeared from my life. I kept hearing about Jonathan getting in worse and worse trouble, about how there were both state and federal warrants out for him, how some of those warrants named me, too. Finally, I just drove off into Mexico."

He'd stopped driving. We were in the sheriff's office parking lot. "I'd like to hear more about him," Nathan said. "Some other time. Let's go inside."

14

The monsoon had completely blown over by the time we drove up to the Green Valley substation, Pima County sheriff's department, a small complex of buildings just off La Canada. Sunset beyond the Pima Mine, its striated color lines completely dark now, rim barely lit by the last rays of the sun.

We parked outside the substation, both of us hesitant to start this ball rolling. A pileated woodpecker worked deep inside the crevices of a huge mesquite, retrieved a grasshopper and carried it away. Mesquite pods lay all over the caliche, some old and blackened, others still green, the seed balls hard against the skin of the pods.

"Ready?" I said.

"If I have to stay here," he said, "if they keep me here, call Bob at my house. Tell him I'm here, ask if Antoinette checked with him."

"Why would you have to stay here?"

"That letter. Authorizing me to destroy Leon's belongings."

"You have it, right? Oh, please, tell me you have it with you."

"There's no letter," he said.

"So let's not go in here."

"Call Bob. He'll arrange a letter, he'll get it faxed down here."

"You don't have to do this."

"Laura," he said. "If this was *Dinetah*, we'd be in a different world. The tribal police, they'd understand. Down here, we're in the system. I have to be true to this."

"Then let me handle some of it." Digging in my handbag for my PI license.

The desk sergeant took my business card, flicked it with his thumbnail, checked my PI license, made notes on a rust-colored Post-it pad, peeled off the Post-it and stuck it to his left thumb.

"Is there a problem?" I said.

"And just tell me again, you're here because . . . ?"

"Leon Begay. We've been asked by his family to look again."

"Murder and suicide," he said. "It's closed, the whole business, it's been signed off up the line."

"Just a few questions," I said. "And Mr. Brittles here also has something to tell you. About Leon Begay."

He checked Nathan's name on the Post-it, frowned.

"Is there a problem?"

"Nope. Just trying to remember who all caught that mess, I wasn't here that night. Think it was a volunteer patrol, let's go ask Billy."

Lieutenant William Mangin. Small and round, halo of white hair, half-moon reading glasses on a silver chain. Ducked his head to look at us over the glasses.

"Billy," the sergeant said, "this is"—reading from my card—"Laura Winslow. And Nathan Brittles."

"Brittles," Mangin said. "Winslow." A guy thing, putting the man first. "Don't know the names. And you'd be here for?"

"I'd like to ask some questions about Leon Begay."

"Ugh," Mangin said. "Nasty, nasty. I've seen a lot of suicides, I just hate it when they take others down with them. What interest have you got in a murder-suicide?"

"He was an old friend."

"I've got lots of friends, too. So?"

"Also friends of Bob Good Fellow."

"Who'd be what?"

"And you've got a lot of attitude," Nathan said.

"Jim," Mangin said to the sergeant. "You know anybody named Good Fellow?"

"Nope."

"Navajo Tribal Police," I said.

Instead of going outside to his desk, Mangin picked up his phone, ran his hand down a speed-dial list, punched numbers, and then put it on speakerphone.

"Navajo Tribal Police, Window Rock."

"Who's this?"

"Sergeant Healthier."

"Hey, sergeant. Bill Mangin here. Pima County sheriff's office. How you?"

"You're on one of those tin-can speaker thingies. You got somebody there?"

"Nathan Brittles. You know him?"

"Nope. Heard the name, that's all."

"Who is he?"

"Last I heard, a U. S. Marshal."

"And how about a Bob Good Fellow?"

"Tribal Police at Monument Valley. What're you asking for?"

"Just checking on some names."

"There are channels for this kind of thing, Lieutenant."

Mangin blinked, stared at his desk blotter, ran a bandaged thumb across myriad notes until he found what he was looking for.

"I sent an envelope to the Tribal Police station in Monument Valley. Addressed to Vincent Begay."

"Yes. There are lots of Begays up here. What was in the envelope?"

"Autopsy photos."

"Then call up to Monument Valley. Ask them."

"I'll do that," Mangin said. "Thanks for your time."

Mangin hung up his phone. "What's this all about?" he said.

"Leon Begay and Bob Good Fellow are very old friends of mine," Nathan said. "We go back to Vietnam."

"Hey," the sergeant said. "Semper Fi."

Mangin waved off the sergeant who'd rolled up a sleeve to show Nathan a tattoo. "And who is Vincent Begay?"

"Leon's brother," I said. "Vincent moved to Hollywood. Changed his name to Vincent Basaraba. And now he runs the new casino in Tucson."

"He ask you to come down here? Look into this ugly business?"

"No."

"Murder and suicide. Begay committing the murder."

"He swore he'd never fire another weapon," Nathan said.

Mangin stretched his arms over his head, linked his

hands behind his neck, stretching his head back and forth, arthritic cartilage popping in some of the vertebrae on his neck.

"Okay," he said finally. "Jim, call the volunteer's office. If Arletta Vezo is working this shift, have her come on over. If she's not there, not at home, probably having her afternoon burger over to the Mercado del Sol. Ask her to come here, please?"

Mangin got out of his chair and he suddenly wasn't so short anymore. One of those people with extra long legs. Wide leather Resistol belt holding up his uniform pants, flat stomach, and torso. Woven leather equipment belt creaking as he unbuckled it and set it with a thunk on his desk.

"Twenty pounds. You wouldn't believe, just sitting down, how much those twenty pounds pull on your back." He watched Jim put on his straw cowboy hat and go outside to a patrol car. "You're wondering, I know you're wondering, why's a substation sheriff not readily extending courtesies to a fellow lawman.

"You a law lady?" He read my business card closely, looked at the back. "Computer forensics, I don't much know what that means."

"Data security," I said. "Who is Arletta Vezo?"

Instead of answering, he abruptly yanked open his middle desk drawer, took out a business card, placed it carefully in front of Nathan. "This guy, he came just yesterday. Also asking about Leon Begay."

Nathan read the card, handed it to me.

WES MCCARTNEY
MANAGER OF SECURITY
FLAMINGO CASINO

"You know him?" Nathan shook his head and I clamped my mouth shut. "Me neither. But that's who he is. Security manager, at that same new Tucson casino. Something, I don't know, odd about him, I didn't tell him anything. Coincidence, about them both at the casino? What do you want to know? About Leon?"

"You've already decided," I said. Both men looked at me. You sent the sergeant to find Arletta Vezo. My guess, Vezo was first person at the crime scene."

"Two thirty-five A.M.," Mangin said. "Neighbor heard the shots. At first, thought maybe somebody devastated a rattlesnake near their patio. But the neighbor calls us, anyway. We've got sheriff's office volunteers down here in Green Valley. You know, a high-profile neighborhood-watch kind of deal. Ex-cops, usually, retired, bored, we give them a uniform, train them, give them everything they need except a gun, and they catch all the usual nuisance stuff."

The patrol car returned with the sergeant and a woman in shorts and a tank top, eating French fries off a paper plate. I thought she'd leave the plate outside, wash her hands, but she set it on Mangin's desk. Short torso and long legs, large breasts tightly wrapped under the tank top, hair gathered behind her head with a scrunchy. At least sixty years old but leathered and muscled, the three officers looking like they could be from the same family tree.

"Arletta, this is Nathan Brittles. And Laura Winslow." Arletta pulled off her scrunchy, shook loose her white-and-gray hair. "I'm not really sure who they are, but this guy says he was a very good friend of Leon Begay. Just tell 'em about last Tuesday night, Arletta."

"Jesus *God*," she said, repositioning the scrunchy. Pulled a small spiral notebook from her hip pocket, flipped the pages nervously. "I never expected to walk into a slaughterhouse. Desk gets a call, oh two thirty-five. I'm cruising Camino del Sol, get the address down in Canoa. Not our regular circuit, but nothing's happening all night except the gas station fiasco, so I respond at oh two thirty-eight. Guy's standing at the end of the street, there's a wash right there, still water in it from the monsoon. I light him up with my flash, it's Karl Inklemann. He's smoking a cigar. 'Begay's house,' he says, 'sounds like somebody there shot a diamondback, except, usually, people don't usually shoot 'em middle of the night. And two shots. I heard two. Sounded like a choked twelve-gauge, except I don't know anybody what uses a choke, I've seen some weapons down here. But hearing the gun, I'm not gonna go over to there, check it out. Called you people. You get paid for it.' "

Flipping through her notebook.

"Pretty much what he said. I ask which unit is Begay's, Inklemann points. I respond to the front door. No lights on inside. Ring the bell, knock, ring the bell. Nothing. That subdivision, it's five homes in a row, you can walk the common property all around. So I go out back, I go to the patio slider. Locked, drapes closed. I bang on the slider with my flashlight. Nothing. I go back around to the front door. At this point, Inklemann says, 'You want a key?' He's right behind me, cigar in his mouth, neither of us is sorry the other one's there. He holds out a key ring. 'Neighbors,' he says. 'We look after each other.' I ring the bell, knock again, unlock the door, go inside. Inklemann is right behind me, he knows where the light switches are. 'Begay,' he hollers, and then he lights up this Jesus God slaughterhouse."

Arletta sat down, fast, started eating the French fries. We waited.

"Woman's lying in the bedroom, blood everywhere, I can tell she took a round directly in the heart. Man's slumped on the couch, head back, back of his head everywhere. Shotgun's laying half on and half off a mirror-top coffee table, cracked the mirror. Twenty-three years, Chicago PD, I've seen a lot of gunshot fatalities. I back out of there, literally, I walk backwards, trying to match where my boots might have been. Inklemann's still got his cigar in his mouth, but nearly bit in two. I respond to the office here. Didn't touch a thing. Office gets Billy here out of bed, he took over the scene."

"And you'll be wanting to see this, too."

Mangin unlocked a wall cabinet, took out a shotgun, laid it across his desk.

"Must be damn near a hundred years old," Mangin said

"Double-ought shells?" I said.

"No," Mangin said. "Number four buck load. Twenty-seven pellets a shell. Why there was so much damage to Leon's head."

"Who was the ME?" Nathan asked. I stirred, flexed my hands in surprise. "Who did CSI work?"

"Pima County sheriff's CSI. Team came down from

Tucson, three guys were there in less than an hour. We taped off the place, they took photos while I was getting the local coroner over. With all the senior citizens down here, we had to elect a coroner. Heart attacks, mainly. Ambulance from Green Valley fire station takes them up to a Tucson hospital, if they're still alive. Or morgue. That's about it, far as this office goes. You want to know more, contact Tucson."

"No lights on in Leon's house?" I said.

"Nope."

"Anything else we can do for you?" Mangin asked.

"No. Wait. Yes," I said, tapping the security man's card. "What'd this guy say, what was he doing down here?"

"No idea." Mangin said, studying Nathan. "Look. I'm sorry about your friend. Didn't know him. Was he Law of some kind? Like you, maybe?"

"Uh, Billy?" the sergeant said. I hadn't noticed he'd left the room, the door now open, sergeant standing there with a surprised look on his face. "We got Karl Inklemann out here. Drove his damn golf cart all the way up from Canoa, says he's got information about the Begay house."

"Not now," Mangin said.

"You oughta see him, I think. He's saying that the Jeep Cherokee in the parking lot, belongs to these two people, Karl is saying it was at the house."

"I can explain," I said quickly.

Mangin frowned, a scrunchy disbelieving frown. "You two, wait in here." He went to the outer office, closed the door.

"I did it alone," Nathan said to me. "Make that old

man remember, you drove up while he was in the street. I did everything by myself. I'm going to tell them everything, tell them why I did it."

The door opened. Inklemann thrust an arm through the doorway, pointing at Nathan. "Yeah, *yeah*," he said, "that's the man that came out of the house. I went around back, the glass sliding door was smashed, I went inside, I tell you . . ."

"Jim," Mangin said to the desk officer. "Take Karl's statement." He shut the door. "Mr. Brittles," he said. "I thought that gas station shootout was enough, we don't get much real police work down here. A few break-ins, somebody smashed a rock through the front door of the Old Chicago Deli, that's our usual style. But I'm gonna have to lock you while I sort all this out."

Nathan put his hands on Mangin's desk, next to the equipment belt and the holstered 9mm automatic. Mangin tensed, half crouched, but Nathan went to him and held out his hands. Mangin started for his handcuffs, stopped.

"Am I gonna have to hook you up?"

"Call Bob," Nathan said to me. "Tell him what's happened. Get that letter."

"And that letter would be what?"

"We have permission," I said. "From Begay's family. We have a letter giving Nathan Brittles total permission to take possession of Leon Begay's belongings."

"I'm hoping to see that letter right now."

"At my house," Nathan said. "In Casa Grande. Can I ask, where's Leon now? His body, I mean, where is it now?"

"PCSO handled the investigation and the scene," Mangin said. "Homicide and Forensics come down from Tucson because of the mess at the gas station. At Leon's house? To my knowledge, after the processing of the scene by PCSO is complete the bodies were turned over to the transport guys from the medical examiner's office, or maybe to the contract body-recovery firm. I don't know if one was used, we had so many bodies that night."

"What Nathan is asking," I said, patient, slowing down my words, lowering my tone, wanting to be the only person in the room not so hyped. "Where is Leon's body right now?"

"The bodies were driven to the medical examiner's office next to Kino hospital in Tucson, that's where the autopsies were to be done. Since our substation was the primary at the scene, I got copies of the autopsy photos. The ones you have there, the ones I sent up to the rez. As required by Arizona statute. Autopsies required when death is by violent means. Typically within three days, depending on how busy the ME was. They might have been done that same day."

"Where is Leon's body?" I said again.

"Well. That's why I sent the material up to the rez. Trying to locate next of kin, the autopsied body could only be released to the next of kin. If none, the state or the county would bury the bodies in a public cemetery. Call the ME's office. That's all I can tell you. Now, I think we're done here. You want to ask me any more questions, Miss Winslow, I'll lock you in the same holding cell, you can talk things over with your partner. Maybe you'll even change your story?"

"No," I said. "That's the story." Nathan opened his mouth, I could see his lips moving, nobody else looking at him, mouthing the words *Call Bob Good Fellow*.

"I'm missing something here," Mangin looking from Nathan to me to Nathan, "aren't I?"

"Two things," Nathan said.

"I handled this business perfect," Mangin said.

"Nothing you missed. Somebody went into the house, probably early this morning. Took a few things from Leon's study."

"We had a volunteer on that place," Mangin said. "Until this morning. What's missing?"

"Don't know. Picture frames, most likely. We saw spots in the dirt, maybe six frames missing. And a map, something two by three feet. Tacked on a wall."

"And what else?"

"A week ago, the night Leon died, did anybody report a stolen golf cart?"

"Yes," Mangin said, puzzled, "indeed they did. Found the next day. Kids do that down here once in a while. Not much here for kids to do."

"Suppose somebody else shot Leon. No unfamiliar cars out front, the neighbor would've seen them. Just suppose, somebody came at the house from behind. Stole a golf cart, rode it to the ravine behind the house, left the same way."

"Coincidence," Mangin said finally. "Case is closed. Murder and suicide. Anything more to tell me?"

"No," I said.

"I'm wondering, why do you want to see Leon's body?"

"He's Navajo," Nathan said finally. "The body

needs to be prepared for burial. Shoes on the wrong feet, corn pollen . . . buried up on the rez."

"I sympathize," Mangin said. "Nothing I can do. Contact the medical examiner's office, they'll tell you where they've stored the body. Anything else?"

Nathan said nothing about the mysterious golfer, or about Antoinette Claw. In the parking lot, Inklemann saw me and quickly started his electric cart and scooted off. I began the long drive back to Casa Grande, dialing Nathan's home phone every ten minutes, finally leaving messages for Bob, five messages, Nathan's answering machine cut off messages after thirty seconds, in*fur*iating, I kept punching redial, forgetting some of what I'd already said, repeating until I got it all and left my cell number and the number of the sheriff's office.

Once I got home, Spider still wasn't there, but not quitting on her yet, I settled for waiting all night. I took a shower, got a huge aluminum pot of water on simmer, ready to throw in the rigatoni when she walked in the door, chopping tomatoes and onions, fresh from Mexico, lettuce not so fresh from Safeway, and three different kinds of lo-cal salad dressing in the fridge.

I sorted through some CDs, tried some Mad Squirrel rap, I just couldn't listen to rap these days, I couldn't write my own raps, couldn't enjoy music. Waiting for Spider, I ran through half a dozen small tasks at my computer.

A year before, Spider came abruptly into my life after an absence of almost twenty years. Never expect-

ing to see her again, astonished at her appearance in
the Tucson city jail back then and the wild ride we'd
had through a series of murders, she'd not left my
mind a single day since. She'd flown off from the Tucson airport, half promising to see me again only to disappear for six months and reappear one night with
two duffel bags of clothing and a backpack of computer gear. She rarely explained anything to me about
those years, about any other years, even about her days
and nights while living with me.

Some nights she'd be home, other times she'd be
away for two or three days with a crew of Mexican
men and women. One night I found her sobbing in her
bedroom and I lay beside her, stroking her arm, trying
to cradle her body into mine. *I need your help,* she'd
said finally. *I'm two months pregnant and I don't
know what to do.* She wouldn't say anything about the
father, wouldn't even say if she wanted the baby. It was
a particularly bad time for me. Nathan and I wanted
to live together again, I struggled with which of the
two people was more important and to his great credit
and love, Nathan finally decided for us, telling me that
my daughter needed me.

Weeks stretched to months, Spider now in her second term, triggering my own instinctual desire to have
a baby of my own. I grew more and more anxious and
started carrying my Beretta everywhere I went.

Some time after nine I realized Spider wouldn't be
home. I ate some sharp cheddar and slices of fresh pro-
sciutto and called my anxiety counselor.

Never wanting to deal again with panic anxiety attacks, I'd been working with a counselor from the

Tucson Center for Anxiety and Related Disorders, run by a former meth addict and heroin smuggler named Choochee Madona.

Choochee's method was as peculiar as his name. Instead of doing traditional relaxation exercises, meditation, waterfall imagery, and other soothing practices, Choochee made people confront anxiety by deliberately concentrating on whatever people dreaded the most. One woman so dreaded claustrophobia she rarely left her house, keeping all the doors and windows open. Choochee had the woman crawl into the trunk of her Buick, curl up inside with the trunk door open, until one day Choochee shut the door on her and quickly opened it and from there she went to staying inside for an hour and her claustrophobia gradually disappeared.

Since I'd participated in so many gun-related deaths, Choochee instructed me to carry a gun and take target practice once a week. *Blow up the cardboard targets,* he said, *until the sensation of terror at the destructive power of a bullet is reduced to something immaterial.*

A gun is just a tool, I joked. Alan Ladd, *Shane.*

So is Prozac, he said. *So which tool do you want to use?*

gun

15

I did something I'd promised Nathan I'd never do again.

Home alone, restless beyond control, I left for a ten-mile run.

While I ran almost every day, Nathan made me pledge that I'd never do it at night. In the dark. Even during my early-morning runs he demanded I carry Mace, a fold-out metal crunch baton, and my cell phone set on Vibrate so even when I cranked volume through my headphones I could get a call. Never really understanding technology, Nathan didn't think about me needing to make an emergency call in a hurry, but I had a mike-and-earplug cord attached to the phone, clipped to the top of my sports bra along with the pulse-monitor sensor.

This night, after two hours making unanswered phone calls, I inserted a freshly charged battery in my cell and got suited up with my usual running gear. Running ten miles over the same route is so repetitive that I'd miss my MP3 player and headphones, but I wanted to keep making calls until I at least reached Bob Good Fellow and Antoinette Claw. After one call to the Green Valley sheriff's office, with a new deputy on duty and Mangin not there, I gave up, concentrated on finding Good Fellow and having him fax whatever kind of authorizing letter would get Nathan released.

Extra strips of orange light-reflecting tape on my running shoes and shorts. A ten-ounce Bauer .25 automatic in a mesh holster, clipped uncomfortably in the small of my back, canister of Mace, totally overprepared but after the first mile the weight of the .25 steadied into a spot that didn't chafe and reminded me it was there with every step, reminded me this wasn't an ordinary run.

"Bob Good Fellow?" I said, finally connecting.

"What . . . here . . . what?"

At the bottom of a dip in the roadway, I knew signal strength was fading, dashed to the top of the hill beside the road.

"Can you hear me now?"

"I've seen that commercial," he said. "I've got some news."

"Listen, just listen to me, Bob. The connection's not great, you've got to hear what's happened."

"You all right?"

"No, I'm not."

"You running away from something? You seem, a bit out of breath."

"I'm out running, just something I do. Nathan's in jail. We went to Leon's house, first, the power went off, I couldn't check Nathan's computers but I took out the hard drives, they're being looked at. But I left to talk with Antoinette Claw."

"She's here now. Why's Nathan in jail?"

"He destroyed almost everything in Leon's house."

"*Chindi* house," Bob said shortly. "Doesn't surprise me, him doing that."

"Surprised the hell out of me, Bob. Why did he do that?"

"Hard to explain to somebody not Navajo."

"Bob, Bob, don't give me more ghost stories, no more skinwalker stuff. This is real trouble, somebody heard Nathan breaking up furniture, reported him to the sheriff just when Nathan and I were there asking about Leon."

"Okay, don't worry. Yesterday I found one of Leon's uncles. Frank Everwool. One of the elders in the Begay family. By rights, Leon's property belongs to him. I've got a sworn statement that Nathan did the right thing, the traditional way of dealing with a *chindi* house. I can bring the statement with me, that oughta get Nathan out of jail."

"Fax it," I said, giving him the sheriff's fax number.

"About *chindi*," he said. "You don't understand much of what Nathan's dealing with." Not a question, saying it to himself. "You contact the brother?"

"Tomorrow morning. At his casino. He wanted to see me tonight, but I refused. He didn't say much about Leon. Sounded, I don't know, strange, something's not right about his response."

"Frank wants to tell me more about the family. Hard to get him talking, I've gotta go through all these rituals, can't push him. Laura, this will work much better if I don't come down until tomorrow afternoon. I can rest up, I really need it, I can get official leave for the next few days, however long it takes. And I can get the statement from Frank, can find out what else he wants to tell me."

"Any clues what he wants to say? Does it have anything to do with Leon?"

"He's worked up about skinwalkers."

"Bob, I don't want to hear that kind of talk. I don't even believe that Leon was murdered, there's nothing at his place makes me believe it's not murder and suicide."

"And Nathan?"

"Nathan," I snorted. "He works a sixteen-pound sledgehammer, but he doesn't really seem to care about explaining why he smashed furniture."

"I can help, Laura. Give it time. Talk to the brother. Tomorrow's another day."

"Tomorrow's almost here," I said.

"Does running help you deal with things, get you settled down? Just go on running for a while, then get some sleep." In the background, a voice on a radio. "Tomorrow, okay?" He hung up.

Tomorrow.

I started running again, almost at the return road on the ten-mile loop, decided to take a shortcut through a patch of leveled caliche and something leapt at me from behind a creosote bush, not really *at* me, something hiding there until I went past, but exploding only two feet from my legs and then *between* my legs, high enough to brush my thighs as it plunged on behind me, a long hairy tail wrapping my thighs and my heart rate cycled between panic and fear, blood pounding my temples. I yanked the Bauer .25 from the mesh holster, fumbling with it in the dark, trying to find the safety and clumsy with the weapon, it squirted out of my hands and disappeared. I dropped to my hands and knees, not even looking for the .25, just wanting to huddle into a protective ball if the beast returned, but I could see it running toward the full moon and momentarily cresting a small rise at high speed.

A coyote.

I'd startled a coyote. I'd seen several hundred coyotes, I knew what to do when they came close, they scared off easily but this one had waited behind the creosote bush. *Waiting for me*, I thought, gripped by the irrational fear that it was a skinwalker, that the coyote lay waiting for me. I quickly fanned my hands over the caliche, trying to find the .25 and there it was behind the creosote bush, right next to a half-eaten jackrabbit that the coyote hadn't wanted to give up.

Finished the return loop in seven-minute miles, anxious to return home, take stock, make sense of . . . *nothing* made sense.

But I never believed in ghosts. Inside my mind, sure. Outside, in the world, no ghosts or child-eating skinwalkers or *chindi* spirits with hairy bodies.

I usually peeled my soggy running clothes off and took an immediate shower, but now, sweat running off my face, stringy-wet hair tickling my bare shoulders, runnels of sweat between my breasts and on my legs.

Equipment, that's my mind-set. Got my gun and cell phone. Poured French Chablis, looked at the gear, thinking how much they reflected my real world. That, and my computers. Ejected the small clip from the Bauer .25, racked the slide to pop the chambered shell, laid the weapon on the table for a moment and went to the gun cabinet in our bedroom, my fingers moving automatically on the digital touchpad, I'd done it a hundred times in the dark so I'd know how to open it quick.

Ignoring Nathan's unused and dusty weapons, I took out my shotgun and a box of double-ought buck shells, remembering the first time Nathan showed me what to do if I was ever awakened at night by a stranger inside the house.

"You really want to use that thing?" he asked when I bought the shotgun.

"I might need it."

"For rattlesnakes?"

"Whatever."

"Where you going to keep it?" he asked.

"I figured, under the bed?"

"On your side."

"If you're that worked up about it," I said, "I'll keep it in my study."

"Not worked up. It's just, if you want it, in a hurry, you want to roll over, stick your hand under the bed and find it."

"I won't need it that quick."

"You won't?"

Two weeks later, he burst into the bedroom at two in the morning. Shaking me awake, he had that look in his eye. The *I-want-something-from-you* look.

"What?" I said. I'd been waiting for some kind of a look, we hadn't had sex for a long time. "*What?*"

"It could hurt," he said.

"Oh."

"I think your shoulder would be sore."

"Kinky. And just how are you going to hurt me?"

"Not me," he said. "C'mon."

A long box lay on the kitchen counter. In the dark, I

thought it was maybe some long-stemmed roses, except the box was too big. He took the lid off the box, turned on the lights.

"A Benelli," he said. "Super 90 autoloader. It's got two shells in it."

Outside, he turned on the workshop lights, led me to the lower lip of a small wash and pointed.

"Chamber up the first shell," he said.

"I know how to shoot one of these," I said. "But lemme go back inside, get something to pad my shoulder. These things kick like hell."

"No padding. In fact, take off your nightie."

"Say what? Nathan, I don't even have panties on. I'm not getting naked just to fire off a shotgun."

"Please," he said. "I'd do it myself, but I want to see how you handle this. If anybody breaks into the house while you're sleeping, what would you do."

"You bastard," I said, laughing. Pulled the pink-elephants nightie over my head, dropped it on the ground. "You're gonna pay for this. Stand back. More."

Once he got five feet behind, I pumped the Benelli, chambered the shell, hesitated, but knew I'd better get it over with fast. Put it firmly against my shoulder and *wham wham* got both rounds off.

"Jesus! That really hurt, Nathan."

He took the Benelli while I pulled my nightie back on, rubbing my right shoulder. It hurt bad, my ears were ringing.

"Sorry about the noise," he said. Led me into the bathroom, turned both the regular light and the heat lamp on. "Let me see."

I looked at my shoulder. A rapidly spreading red mark, I'd probably be purple and green by morning.

"Yeah," Nathan said. "That's what I thought."

"Never mind what you thought," I said, putting his hand on the red mark, moving it down to cup my breast. "You can tell me later."

Usually, when I did that, especially when I'd come back from running, sweaty, I'd pull off the sopping clothes and pull him into the shower.

Months ago, we'd shower together.

"Now you know," he said.

"Know what?"

"You wanted a shotgun, but you never worked out how to get at it when you needed it the most. Which is always gonna be when you least expect to use it."

"Point taken," I said, rubbing my shoulder.

"Here," he said. "Let me rub you up a little bit."

16

Just a coyote, I kept reminding myself. Just an animal. At one of my computers, I Googled skinwalker.

Between man and animal, one website said. Skinwalkers exist between the gap of order and chaos, between being alive or dead, but contrasting a symbolic metaphor of this dialectic with the inescapable reality that man *is* animal.

No books really exist about skinwalkers, another website said. There are only stories and conjecture, usually by white academics and avoided by Navajos. Nothing to read, anywhere, to give understanding to a skinwalker's behavior or personality. One discovered a skinwalker by oneself only. One watched, experienced, observed, and learned. Through patience and respect for both tradition and nature, one learned.

Tony Hillerman's name everywhere, his wonderful novel, a movie with Wes Studi as Joe Leaphorn, I could see that. Out of habit, I went to my browser menu and clicked on Reveal Source to look at all the hidden search terms for the web page, hoping I'd find some better reference to skinwalkers. Instead, I found politics.

The Forbes web page search terms included Conservative, Reagan, Homeschool, Republican, *National Review,* Worldnewsdaily.com, Christian, Regnery, Conservative Leadership Series, Ann Coulter, Rush Limbaugh, William F. Buckley, and Matt Drudge. I'd never thought Hillerman's wonderful books could be used by a political group. I wondered if he knew about it.

Damn! I'd forgotten to tell Bob about Antoinette.

After three calls, nobody picking up, I left the same message twice. The Begay father and sons. Left to right, Leon, father, Vincent. Get Antoinette to stay the night, call me when she arrived.

I checked all the door and window locks before I took my shower, then lay awake for an hour on our bed, the shotgun beside me, wondering what we'd become. And in the morning, a slender strand of drool running down my cheek, a very small sensory feeling on my cheek, I awoke to find myself hunched up on my side in a ball and staring at the shotgun. I threw the sheet and duvet over the gun and got dressed to meet Vincent Basaraba.

17

Fighting the morning Tucson traffic on Speedway, Tucson no longer a funky little city but stretching toward a population over a million with main streets meant to handle a third of the cars.

Nearing Fourth Avenue, police flares ignited all over an intersection two blocks ahead, traffic diverted onto the side streets, impossible to move more than a car length every few minutes. Like everybody else, I cut people off, tried to take shortcuts, even drove half on the sidewalk to get around two Mexicans with locked bumpers and drawn pistols.

Stalled, not yet late, fuming, for no logical reason I remembered my first gun.

It was a Spanish .22-caliber pocket pistol. A Bersa with a ten-round magazine. I bought it in Flagstaff, five years before. I remembered the salesman. Freddy. Had a bumper sticker behind the cash register.

TEDDY KENNEDY'S CAR KILLED
MORE PEOPLE THAN MY GUN

"First one out takes just a little more trigger pull," Freddy'd said. " 'Cause it's double action. But once the

slide racks back, the pull is easy and smooth. You want
to shoot off a magazine?"

"No."

"No offense, but have you ever fired a handgun?"

"No."

"Again, no offense, but guns kill. You don't look
like you much know what to do with this piece. I sug-
gest, no offense intended, that we just take just five,
ten minutes of your time, so you learn how to load it
and fire it."

"This is a shooting range," he said in the back of his
store, handing me some yellow foam earplugs. "Stick
these in your ears before we go in."

He pushed another set of plugs into his own ears.
After I inserted mine, we went through double doors
into the shooting range divided into four sections by
upright partitions. We stood at a waist-high Formica
counter inside the first section. Empty cartridge brass
was scattered everywhere on both sides of the counter.
Freddy laid the Bersa on the counter and opened a box
of shells. Showing me a small lever on the side, he
flicked the lever and the magazine dropped into his
other hand. He gave me the magazine and positioned
it open-end up and handed me a shell.

"You've got to slide it in. Go on. Go on. Try it."

I pushed the shell into the magazine. It took more
force than I'd have thought. One at a time I inserted
six more, each time getting easier as I learned to push
down with my thumb on the rim of the casing and
then slide the shell backward. Without thinking I
swiveled toward him and he ducked as the barrel
aligned with his chest.

"Jesus, Jesus, don't *ever* point that at somebody unless you mean it."

"I'm sorry."

"Okay. You got six in the pipe. Six is enough. Six is plenty. Now. This is a semiautomatic. A lotta people think that all you gotta do is pull the trigger, but that's just TV, that's just the movies. First, you gotta get the first bullet into the gun so it will shoot. Grab the barrel with your left hand and pull it back until it clicks."

It clicked.

"Now, let the slide go back to normal."

I did. And felt a strange satisfaction at the precise mechanical movement of cocking the hammer, then a metallic *snick* as the slide racked forward.

"Feels good, doesn't it?"

"It's very strange," I said, "to be holding a gun and learning how to fire it."

"Well, it's ready to shoot. Just remember, don't point it if you don't want to shoot it. See this little button? See here? See here? That's the safety. Push it to the left, it won't fire. Push it the other way, you're all set."

He punched a button on the wall. A motor hummed somewhere and a line above my head started moving, bringing a paper bull's-eye target toward me.

"Okay. That's ten feet away. Aim right at the middle."

I held the gun out in front of me, turning my face slightly away.

"Wait. Use both hands. Take your left hand, put the palm underneath the gun butt. Good. Wrap the fingers of your left hand around the right hand. Good. Look right down over the barrel. Take up the slack on the trigger. When you're ready, like they say in the movies, just squeeze slowly."

The barrel wobbled and I tightened both hands and pulled the trigger fast, the sound incredibly loud in the small room. My ears started ringing.

"Don't I have to cock it again, or slide that thing back?"

"No. It'll just keep shooting until you run out of slugs."

I lined up on the bull's-eye and squeezed until the gun fired. Without waiting for him to say anything, I carefully aimed and fired twice more.

"There's two left. This time, as soon as you've fired, do it again. Bang bang. It's called a double tap. Most cops shoot twice. Go on."

Tap tap. The slide stayed back and I looked at Freddy. All six holes were grouped within the second smallest ring, and two were directly within the black bull's-eye. He held the doors open for me and as we went back into the shop I dug the plugs out of my ears, which were still ringing.

"Lady, you're a *natural*. Look at this. Group of six, two in the bull."

The *bull*. My father, the rodeo bull rider. George Loma. We remember our parents as *Mommy* and *Daddy*, *Mama* and *Father*, we're they're children, we don't call their names, I'd not remembered for a long time his name. George Loma.

I've got only two pictures of my youth. No baby picture, no picture of the mother I never knew. In one picture, my father's face etched against the sky, left arm bent at the elbow, holding the reins of a bareback bronc, right arm extended in a long graceful arc, hand flat like a knife ready to slice off a large chunk of life. The picture always reminded me of one I'd seen in a magazine of an Indonesian guerrilla, his hand clutching a machete-like knife, his smile revealing an eagerness to pose. At the guerrilla's feet lay a corpse, its hands tied and its severed head lying several feet away.

The other picture showed myself and my father, both smiling. I remembered the day specifically because it was my seventh birthday. I was having fun playing with a girlfriend while my father read a circular about a Sears sale in Flagstaff. Mingled with sales notices for clothing and energy-saving air conditioners, he found one of those special picture deals, one 8 × 10, two 5 × 7s, and four wallet-size, all for four ninety-five. I didn't want to go, but he carried me to the pickup. When we got to Sears and it got to be our turn in the lights I wouldn't stop crying, twisting my face away from the camera while the photographer fidgeted and frowned, a long line of other reluctant children waiting with their beaming parents. But I stopped crying immediately and smiled for the camera when my father put his hand around behind me, like he was holding his wonderful daughter. Missy, he said, if you don't smile quick I'll heat things up for you when we get home.

I don't remember being *heated up* by my father, I'm not sure these days what he meant. But then I don't remember much love, either. *Wish I'd known my mother.* And then traffic cleared and ten minutes later I pulled into the casino lots.

18

Tastefully lit signs, no blinking neon, no outrageous
colors, little on the huge electronic signboards except
advertisements for performing stars or boxing matches.
Colors somewhat like Santa Fe sand and pale greens
and sky-washed turquoise blues, but with highlights to
make them unique.

ANASAZI FLAMINGO CASINO

Built like a massive pueblo, not a solid wall anywhere from ground to top, the eight floors staggered,
adobe-like facings, suggestive of legendary pueblo villages. Keet Seel. Chimney rock. The White Palace, at
Canyon de Chelly.

Under a drive-entrance with valet parking, the entrance topped with real wooden beams, and giant
wooden ladders extending four stories up to the main
restaurant floor.

Outside the front door, I started to hand my car keys
to a valet, but a uniformed security officer came over
quickly, checking a clipboard. His pastel blue name tag
said CHAVEZ SLIDING. Underneath in smaller letters,

VERA CRUZ, MEXICO. Mexican Indian of some nation I couldn't even identify, although his thin face and hatchet nose reminded me of an Apache I'd once dated.

"Are you Miss Laura Winslow? Photo identification, if you would, please."

"Do I have to take my shoes off?" I said. Handing over my driver's license.

"Pardon?"

"Sorry. Nothing. Are you Apache?"

"Jicarillo Mountain," he said. Smiled. "My grandmother was brought back from a raid into Sonora, seventy years ago. And you are Hopi."

"How do you know that?"

He flexed the clipboard. "Mr. McCartney, he does good background security checks on everybody who comes to visit Mr. Basaraba." He waved at the valet, who took my keys. "Follow me, please."

Inside the massive glass doors, whooshing open like Star Trek when we got near them, I could hear the dominant tones of the slot machines. When you first go into a big casino, you think it's cacophony, all the different slots and their flashing lights, each machine seems to have a different noise and it becomes unbearable until you either start gambling or leave. But I knew that many casinos carefully orchestrated the electronic notes, allowing individuality while blending them all together by having enough machines playing the notes of a perfect major triad. Usually in the key of C, sometimes E.

The Anasazi Flamingo emphasized the first, third, and fifth tones of a triad, a key I hadn't the ear to identify, but some machines also featured music that rose and fell in water-fountain arpeggios, so the total sound invited you onto the slot floor.

Unlike many of the smaller casinos, this one must
have had powerful air filters, sucking up the cigarette
smoke so that as Chavez Sliding led me through the
machine maze I only smelled cigarettes when I passed
nearby a smoker.

"How many slot machines?" I said.

"Almost two thousand."

Young men and women, all of them with some kind
of Indian blood, circulated in carefully arranged uniforms, offering free drinks, change for the slots, smiling at anybody who approached them. Men in
vaquero pants, flared at the bottom, braided-pattern
jackets with high collars and golden buttons in the
front, halfway up so the top of the jackets lay open.
They wore no shirts underneath. All had woven black
leather belts with buckles large enough for small
rodeo trophy buckles, except these all had an inter-
twined AF. The women, most of whom couldn't be
much older than early twenties, wore short skirts and
spaghetti-strap, brightly colored tops, some of them
clearly bra-less, but the tops tight against their bodies
so if they leaned over no cleavage showed. Women
with that slimmer-than-slender look, and raised horizontal waves rising under the skin from their rib structure, plus above their uniforms, collarbones in all
manner, some straight out to the shoulders, others vee-
ing upward, most with well-defined muscles and good
skin tone. Same body shapes for the men. Nobody
overweight or over twenty-five, nobody underfed, all
with genuine glowing skin and wide smiles and thank-
you nods for gamblers who stuck chips into whatever
part of the clothing was accessible.

I'd dressed for the meeting. The few expensive pieces of clothing I owned.

An off-white cotton shirt, tailored with no collar but material rising an inch around my neck, unbuttoned a third of the way down, long sleeves, every inch thoroughly starched and ironed by my laundry, with the sleeves unbuttoned at the wrist, the starch holding the fabric steady.

High lightweight wool slacks, black, sewn by a Mexican seamstress after a Calvin Klein design I ripped out of a *Vogue* at my dentist's office, when he was so overbooked he kept me waiting an extra hour. Zelma, the seamstress, extended the waist up, like a stovepipe to emphasize my narrow waist and hips, making my legs seem longer than reality. Model legs, in those slacks.

My taste only went as far as the shirt and slacks. I wore a lady's black Resistol belt, a string of white beads sized somewhere between a golf ball and mothballs. Only one pair of decent-enough shoes in my collection from Payless, black suede slip-on pumps with a two-inch heel, slightly flared at the bottom.

I usually wore this outfit when I visited a new client, never thinking I looked anything but above-adequate. Today I wanted some Jimmy Choo shoes.

Chavez Sliding led me past several poker rooms crammed with all kinds of games. No Limit Texas Hold 'Em, Omaha, seven-card stud. At least thirty blackjack tables, very few low-limit tables. He stopped in front of an elevator, inserted a special key card, and pushed the single button. The doors opened immediately. I thought he was going to follow me inside, but he swept his hand, turned his back, and the door closed.

No floor buttons, just two pale purple triangles, one pointing up, the other down. The cage rose swiftly, stopped, the doors opened before I had wits enough to think about what to say, trying out a smile, a movie star fan's smile, deciding nothing much interested me in smiling this morning, frowning with indecision as the door slid open and I stepped forward, arm raising to shake Vincent Basaraba's hand, but it wasn't him at all.

"Come with me," the man said.

Well over six feet tall, skinny as a fencepost, pock-marked cheeks and a rash of marks down the right side of his neck, but handsome, face narrowing toward the chin like the actor Wes Studi. Long denim *vaquero* pants, flared on the outside with inset gores highlighted by brass buttons, a wide black Resistol belt with a rodeo buckle that I couldn't read it was so faded, but silver, not pot metal. His faded, black tee-shirt bore the legend IF YOU CAN'T LIMP, YOU AIN'T SHIT and as he turned without a word for me to follow him, the back of the shirt had a Harley-Davidson emblem. He didn't limp.

Leading me to a small, windowless office. Almost a cubicle, no desk, just two wooden chairs, looked like a police station interview room. He kicked the door shut behind him with a worn kangaroo-skin boot with a two-inch digger heel.

"Wes McCartney," he said. "Security. What are you doing here?"

"You look like an actor," I said, struggling to gain some composure. "Wes Studi. You know that actor?"

"Cut the pleasant shit. What are you doing here?"

I stood up, tried the door handle. Locked. "Please," I said, looking around for hidden cameras or microphones. "Take me to Mr. Basaraba," I said, resisting the anxiety of being locked in, resisting another test of the door handle.

"Why?"

"We have an appointment."

"Yeah. Well. Vincent's the actor in this place. I'm head of security, I check out *every*body who makes appointments with Vincent. What are you doing here?"

"Your CD is slipping, you keep saying the same thing." I sat down in the other chair, locked my knees together. "Zero," I said. He cocked his head. "The plane crash was so horrible there weren't any survivors."

"What are you doing here?"

"Leon Begay," I said. His persistence outlasted my patience. "Vincent's brother. Leon and Vincent Begay are brothers, I know this, you know this. Leon was shot last week."

"Shot himself," McCartney said, laying a pack of unfiltered Camels on his right knee, "murdered a woman, then shot himself." Shook a Camel loose, took out a worn silver-plated lighter, got the smoke going, and tucked both lighter and cigarette pack back into his pants.

"It's just about the body," I lied. "Somebody needs to claim the body, Vincent is the only surviving family member. If he doesn't claim Leon's body, nobody will."

"The body," blowing smoke sideways, "that's why you're here?"

"Yes," I lied. Now more curious than ever why he was interrogating me.

"How'd you know they were brothers?"

"A friend told me."

"Friend name of who?"

What is this? I thought. McCartney's questions made no sense.

"Navajo Tribal Policeman," I said finally. "The Green Valley sheriff sent autopsy photos to Monument Valley, asking if the Tribal Police up there knew of any surviving family member that could claim Leon's body."

"Name of who? The policeman."

"Good Fellow."

"Monument Valley Tribal Police. Good Fellow." Said to himself, repeating the name twice as he rolled it around in his head. "Okay. Two standard questions for everybody with an appointment to see Vincent. You looking for employment in this casino?"

"No."

"You're some kind of computer security pro, right?"

"Right."

"No need for anybody doing that here."

"I said, I didn't want a job. What's your other question?"

"Somebody gives you two coins totaling fifty-five cents. One of them is *not* a fifty-cent piece. What are the two coins?"

"One of them's not a half dollar. But the other one is. Plus a nickel."

"After hiking all day in the wilderness, you reach your cabin at dark. Inside, there's a wood stove all stuffed with fresh oak kindling and some newspaper, there's a kerosene lantern, and there's a propane stove. But you only have one match. So what do you light first?"

"The match. Do you study history?" That brought a smile to his lips, not too much of a smile, his lips stayed shut. "How many *an*imals," I said, "of *each* species," I said, "did Moses take aboard the ark?"

"Two," he said, quickly, too quickly, realizing his mistake when I kept silent. "Very good. Misdirection. You emphasized those early syllables, got me in the rhythm. Well, this is a casino. We have magicians from time to time. Illusionists. No tigers, no vanishing elephants, nothing in Vegas style. We also have all kinds of cheaters. Dice shavers, card counters, chip stealers . . ."

"Are we done here?"

"Not by half. But, that doesn't really matter," he said finally. "Come with me." Took a small remote device from his pocket, like what you use to lock and unlock car doors and alarms. Pressed a button, the door latch clicked. He opened the door and didn't bother holding it for me, walking away before I got up from the chair, hurrying to the door to grab it before it closed, afraid it would lock me inside.

McCartney took me to another elevator, inserted a key card in the slot.

"A word of advice," he said. "Most people, when they see Vincent, they see the movie star, they think Vincent is just a movie star and they work real hard to get to know the real man underneath." The elevator door opened. "There is no real man underneath."

"What do you mean?"

He reached around the open door, pressed a red button, pulled his arm out as the door slid shut but I stuck a foot against the door, it reopened, the elevator clicked and whirred.

"What do you mean?" I said again.

"What you see in the movies, you think you see everything, but nobody really sees anything. Never. You watched the people on the screen, but you don't really understand them." The door started to close again, hit my foot, reopened. "You're not what I expected. Woman of computer mystery. Hacker, cracker, invisible, calculating but never seen. But in person? What do I see? Sensuality. He's waiting."

I pulled my foot back, the door closed, but the elevator didn't move.

What's happening? I thought. *Where the hell am I?*

19

"One moment," the digital female voice said.

A panel slid aside in the rear wall of the elevator, a small oval seat levering out of the panel until locking.

"Please. Be seated. Your anticipated wait is . . . two minutes."

"Then open the door," I said. Pounded a few times on it. Took off my right shoe, banged on the door.

Like being in a vortex.

My good friend Monica had two vortexes on her property in Arivaca.

One is incredibly powerful and good, she says. When I need to feel energized, when yoga isn't enough, or I'm tired from working all day, or there's a monsoon and the roadway floods into Arivaca, and I have to get in line at mile nineteen marker to get across the wash, I finally get to my trailer and I take off my clothes and put on a swimsuit, sometimes I don't put on anything, and I move into the power vortex and it lifts my spirit.

"Waiting time is now three minutes," the digital voice said.

I mean, I ask you, have you ever been kept in an elevator that won't go anywhere? Telephone menus, sure, no corporation wants you talking to a real live person, they want you to hunt around the menus until you give up.

Willy Wonka. His elevator went sideways.

What is a vortex, anyway?

I've been to the power spots in Sedona, Arizona. Four magnificent-colored red-rock formations, one on the steep hill to the airport, then there was Cathedral Rock and Butterfly Woman, I forget the fourth spot. I visited there a long, long time ago, when I lived in my trailer in Tuba City and wound up tracing stolen artifacts in Sedona.

The elevator didn't move, I heard something clicking in the control panel. I punched the triangular pale purple button pointing up. Nothing happened.

So many theories about vortexes, are they vortexes or vortices? One guy claimed that because the planet Pluto was first discovered from a telescope at Lowell Observatory in Flagstaff, about twenty-five miles to the north, Sedona remained under the influence of Pluto, except now astronomers claim that Pluto really isn't a planet, just a cloud of space rocks that rotate somewhat in unison around the sun.

Monica also had a negative vortex. Don't go near there, she says, it's a downer, a bummer, you feel energy sapped out of your body. But I always wonder how she knew it was there, if it was negative, did she ever go through it on purpose? What if one of the free-range cattle got into a vortex? A javelina or coyote or jackrabbit, did they feel worse or better?

My head running around my body in circles, this is totally weird, I'm thinking, but who ever gets stuck in an elevator with a digital voice menu? Maybe it's just that I only had two or three hours of sleep last night, but my head was foggy, so many planets swirling around in there. Leon Begay. Bob Good Fellow. Nathan, Nathan, crushing furniture because he believed in ghosts. Maybe it was because I hadn't eaten any breakfast, had too much wine last night, too much adrenaline, too tired because I went on a late-night run, threw off my body rhythms.

Some astrologers believe that Pluto in your personal chart of the heavens brings about major transition and rebirth.

Weak-headed, you must be kinda weak yourself, reading this, hearing me babble without meaning, except all I had for meaning were two things. One Navajo supposedly shot a young woman and then turned the gun on himself. Another Navajo believed in *chindi* power.

I rubbed fingers across the oval seat. Some kind of metal, anodized a metallic almost platinum color. I sat down, slumped against the back wall of the elevator, incredibly fatigued. My eyelids wavered, you've seen that in the movies, the star falls into a sleepy trance, they're trying to stay awake, they can't.

Scientists never agree on much, they certainly don't agree on the scientific reality of vortexes. Vortices. Electromagnetic powers or mental confusion, that's pretty much the two poles of the argument.

Have you ever been to one of those Mystery Spots? You see the signs for a hundred miles on the interstates. MYSTERY SPOT! WHAT IS IT! FIFTY MILES. TWENTY MILES. MYSTERY SPOT, NEXT EXIT. Don't believe until you've seen it yourself. Or they're called Spook Village or Gravity Hill and Anti-Gravity Hill and Mysterious

Tomb. And around the world, psychics and mystics and hundreds of thousands of tourists and wanna-believers claim their bodies go through astonishing changes in these Mystery Spots. Weird houses where short people are taller than their six-foot high boyfriends. Strong stomachs suddenly queasy, unexplainably.

The Oregon Vortex supposed to be the kinkiest Mystery Spot of them all. Even featured on an *X-Files* episode.

Total bunkum, right out of P. T. Barnum, some scientists claim. People believe what their senses tell them, right or wrong, sensual perception controls mental and intellectual faculties.

Look at our survey maps, other scientists say. Electromagnetic forces pulling in a dozen different directions. Compasses go mad, people get happy.

The elevator abruptly started moving upward, jolting me awake. I barely had time to stand up, think where I was and why I was there, when the doors slid back and a huge black mastiff sat directly opposite me, a paw extended and his nubby tail whopping back and forth, four inches of tongue lolling out the left side of mouth.

And behind him, coming toward me, there was Vincent Basaraba.

20

Vincent Basaraba.

I inhaled everything about him.

Five-ten, incredibly fit under his suit. I work out and I know good bodies when I see them. Profile, chiseled, there's nothing but clichés that fit his wonderful, chiseled profile. He turned sideways to let me through the door, turning back to smile at me with capped teeth like perfectly formed white slabs of sugar. Black hair cropped to about an inch and a half, carefully layered, random flecks of gray close to matching his light gray silk suit, with a white linen shirt open at the collar.

"Hi," I said. Feeling like an idiot, there for such a serious thing, and I was ready to go on about his movie roles, except there were three other people in the room. Wes McCartney, another man, and a woman.

"Vincent Basaraba," he said. As if there was any doubt in my head. He reached out, took both of my hands in his. "Glad to meet you, Miss Winslow."

"Laura. Call me Laura." *Yikes,* I thought, *like a teenager here, Call me Laura. I'm probably even blushing.*

"So Laura," looking at my left hand, at my ring finger, "married?"

"Yes." *Was* married, not a dishonest answer.

"Widow," McCartney said. "One daughter, age approximately twenty-three, served a few months in federal prison for theft of credit card numbers, pardoned last year. Laura Winslow, aka Laura Marana, possible other aliases. Federal warrants served, then voided when she helped the U. S. of A. solve some crimes."

"That's not necessary, Wes."

"I'm an old fan of yours, Mister Basaraba. From the movies, I mean . . . that elevator," I said, trying to recover, "it's like, this will really sound weird, the longer I waited, the more I felt like I was in a vortex."

His eyes and smile, controlled until that moment, crinkled with delight.

"Do you believe?" he said.

"In vortexes?"

"Their magnetic power?"

"I can't say I *don't* believe."

"Ah." He turned to the three other people in the room.

"Wes McCartney. Security manager. Wes, this is Laura Winslow, the computer security person."

"We've met." I said.

"Of course. My apologies for the elevator problem. Wes realized it wasn't working, called the security room to check the electronics. Hope it didn't scare you. Who'd have thought, elevator as vortex. And this is Mya Nguyen. Manages all the hostesses, floor and bar girls."

"Miss Winslow," she said, a slow, ready, and practiced smile that moved only because she'd opened her mouth. *And aren't you two a pair?* I thought. Wes and Mya, professionals to the bone.

"And Clive Davis. My gambling floor manager."

Another tuxedo, but an honest face, cherubic, glowing cheeks, earnest smile. He stood two feet apart from the others, a delineation of power.

"Clive took second place once in the poker world series."

"Second place at the fifth table," Davis said.

"Clive and I should work on one of the cameras over pit six," Wes said.

"And I've got to check on next shift replacements," Clive said. "Two dealers called in sick, one pit boss."

"First time with a movie star?" Wes asked.

"Almost," I said. Not totally goo-goo.

Davis smiled. "Had a crush on Audrey Hepburn," he said. "Been in love with her for years. Well, Now, I'm thinking of transferring my love to Cate Blanchett."

"Anything else you want?" McCartney said.

"Nope, no problems here," Vincent said. "I just wanted you all to meet Miss Winslow. In case she needs to talk to you later."

"Laura," I said. "No, I'm only here to talk with you." And maybe it was the elevator, maybe I was having a vortex moment, but something occurred to me and I usually give my instincts a shot.

"I knew one of your dealers," I said to Mya. "Or maybe she was wait staff." She smiled, paused. "Young Latina. Jodhi Patroon."

Not a flicker from Mya or Wes. She shook her head at the door. "I know all my staff from the day we opened. I don't believe that woman ever worked here."

Wes whispered something in Vincent's ear. The mastiff lurched against my legs, pressing hard before it sat down and offered a paw. I reached down to shake the paw and the mastiff immediately went to a far corner of the room and curled up on a large sheep-skin pad.

I scanned the rest of the huge office suite.

Just me and the movie star.

I'd better get over this I-had-a-teenage-crush-on-you attitude.

"I saw all your movies," I said, bulling ahead what-the-hell-am-I-*say*ing right into it, like a teenager on Hollywood Boulevard, you're standing on one of those sidewalk stars and look up to see the actor in front of you.

"I think I was in movies before you were born."

"Well. Not really, I mean, I did see them, though. Most of them in a movie theatre, the rest on TV, you know, VHS tapes."

"Let's sit down over here."

Led me to white-leathered chairs in front of the window, Vincent waiting until I was comfortable before he sat down.

"My father was an extra in *Fort Apache*," Vincent said. "One of the Navajo actors, except they played Apaches in those movies. *She Wore a Yellow Ribbon*, um, I've forgotten what the third was called."

"*Rio Grande*," I said. "Another of those Ford things where you believe you're right on the Rio Grande, the river, except the scenery is Monument Valley."

"New Mexico, Arizona, and Apaches. All in Monument Valley."

"Your father, what was his name? Was he an actor?"

"Franklin," he said. "Franklin Begay. No, he was

just an extra among all those Navajo extras Ford hired. He needed the money. Food, sheep, whatever. He got jobs for me and my brother Leon. I was a kid, a child extra. Leon didn't want his face on camera, he tinkered with things, they had him working with the grips."

I started to ask about Leon, hesitated because I didn't want to spoil the moment, *my* moment with a movie star. If you've ever been around a movie star, you know what I mean. It's their presence, it's *being* in their presence, you see them on a big screen, in magazines, and on TV, then you meet them and they're just people, except, somehow, special. I couldn't ever remember feeling so giddy in my life.

Vincent Basaraba.

After the shootout at Pine Ridge, on the run with my husband Jonathan, just a teenager dodging from one low-down motel to another, I'd duck out to the movies every chance I'd get.

For the first time, I looked around the office. Movie posters and memorabilia hung from every inch of wall space, artifacts piled on shelves and cabinets.

"Would you like the tour?"

"You look just like you did in *Hangman*," I said, admiring one of the posters.

"I was only sixteen then. Maybe seventeen."

"You played James Coburn's young brother. Turned out bad, sheriff killed you early in the movie and Coburn swore revenge, killed the sheriff."

"Oh, yeah. The bad brother. I played that part a little too good. They always cast me as a bad guy after that."

"Like that gambler in *Back to Tombstone*. And the

lead role in *Billy*, well, not the lead, that was what's-his-name, from the Clint Eastwood spaghetti Westerns. The Mexican who played Billy the Kid. And you were sheriff."

"You really saw all those movies?"

"I even bought some of them the last few years. On DVD."

Somebody knocked on the door, opened it.

"Security's back up for pit six," McCartney said. "And Deborah, in the cage, asked if you'd okay ten large for a Mrs. Brenda Mayfair. From Nashville."

"Nope," Vincent said. "She already owes us seventy." McCartney left without comment. "I need the money, I need action from people like Brenda Mayfair. But I don't like to see them get into the barrel without I show them I might put the top back on and nail it down. What were you doing in Pine Ridge?"

"When Joe Stuntz was killed. The siege."

"Most people remember that two FBI men were killed. Not an Indian."

"I loaded rifles for some AIM people. My husband, except he wasn't my husband yet." On the far wall, over his desk, two fabulous posters, one of his best movie. *Billy*. "Julie London was in *Billy*. Owned the saloon, wanted your body, you thought she was too old."

"Julie." I saw him do the flashback, his eyes glazing for a moment. "God, she was beautiful, I'd've loved to spend a night with that woman, but Jack Webb might've arrested me." He laughed, shook his head at the words as he came out of his memories. "Said that too blunt, I guess, but I sure loved every woman I could get my hands on, back in those days, they all wanted me."

"She played a whore. They should have written a scene between you two."

"Thirty years ago, they didn't call 'em whores. Bar girls. They let the audiences imagine the whoring. Dressed the actresses in tight dresses, bunched their breasts up out of the lacy front, let 'em lean over to the camera and swish their petticoats. I don't remember they ever cast me with a *good* woman character."

And the other poster. I had to walk over there, reached out, realized I shouldn't touch it before I saw it was under glass.

"*Man of the West.*"

"It's one of the few remaining original posters."

Gary Cooper upright, almost the entire right side of the poster, knees flexed, six-guns in each hand. Wide-brimmed hat, red bandanna flowing out, as though blown by winds ahead of the reddish cloud banks across near the bottom of the poster.

GARY COOPER
AS THE
MAN OF THE WEST

"The role that fits him like a gun fits a holster," Vincent read.

On the left side, the dark outline of another six-gun, a still from the movie inset showing Jack Lord holding a knife to Cooper's throat as Julie London looks on.

"Take those clothes off, girl," I said, not even bothering to read the print, it was one of the best-known lines from the movie. "Real slow like. Great movie."

"You really liked it?"

"One of my favorite Westerns."

"So. Why are you here?"

I couldn't make the shift that fast and he saw it in my eyes.

"I haven't made a film in over twenty years, Miss Winslow."

"Laura."

"Laura. I hardly even think about those days, except for the money I made and my agent was good enough to bank for me. That's how I set up the syndicate that owns this casino, with movie money. I'm raising funds to make another movie."

"What was your last?" I said.

"No idea. Look it up online. I'm told it's really easy to get movie data that way." He looked at his wristwatch, a Rolex of some kind. "So. I was having dinner with some people from the state gaming board. But, why don't I cancel them out? You'll have dinner with me?"

"Well," I said. "About your brother."

"Leon?" His head shivered, just for an instant. "My brother Leon?"

"Yes."

"Leon left my village a long time ago."

"Uh," I said, thinking *What is this?*

"Mr. Basaraba," I said. "Your brother died just last week."

"Yes. I suppose you think I'm . . . uncaring? Not sad enough?"

"I wasn't implying anything."

"Green Valley." Astonished, unbelieving. "Just south of here. Three nights ago. My own brother commits suicide and I didn't even know he lived so close."

He looked all around the room, eyes picking into

every corner, for two or three minutes he seemed to forget I was even there. "I'll, uh, do you have a phone number? I'll call Michaela."

"Well. I don't know how to say this. His wife Michaela died several years ago. Last week, your brother, before he committed suicide, well, first he killed a young woman, and then he killed himself."

Vincent rose, steady, walked to a side table, began leafing quickly through a stack of newspapers. *The Tucson Arizona Star, Tucson Weekly,* and the *Republic* from Phoenix.

"Last week?" he said. "There's nothing in here. Leon Begay? You're sure about this?"

"Yes. The sheriff's office didn't release their names."

"Why?"

Because something wasn't right, I thought. But I wasn't going to tell him that, since I didn't know yet what was right or wrong here.

"Nobody's claimed his body yet. For burial. So his name's been kept out of the newspapers."

"Um." He picked up his telephone, finger poised over the speed-dial buttons, realizing finally that his brother's number wasn't there. "Haven't seen him in thirty years. We weren't close, not after my father committed suicide. And now Leon."

"*Man of the West,*" I said. Unable to take my eyes off the poster. "One of my all-time favorite Westerns. Julie London was great in that movie, right?"

"Would you like to see my fantasy?"

He took me through a locked door, a small room, nothing in there except a landscape model, easily the size of a Ping-Pong table, four feet of space on all sides. Most of the model showing a large valley, cradled by several mountain ranges, three entrances to the valley across saddles in the ridgelines. Small white flags on silver hairpins, stuck at various places on the model.

"May I?" I said, pointing at but not touching one of the flags. He nodded, smiling his perfect white smile, but not at me, I seemed to have no effect on him. I pulled out the hatpin. The label said KINO'S GOLD.

"You don't recognize the valley?"

"No. What is this? Some real estate development? Another casino?"

"Up here," removing a billiard cue from under the table and pointing to one edge of the model, "Sedona. Tucson, here. Arivaca, Nogales. How long have you lived in southern Arizona, Miss Winslow?"

"Six, seven years."

"And you don't recognize this valley, you don't know it's name?"

"I've heard something," I said. "From my Reiki master."

"Reiki." Always reassessing me, whatever else grasped his attention, he shifted back to me, the desire to communicate higher with each transition.

"When you first came in, I asked, do you believe?"

"The last time somebody asked me that," I said, "I was in a broken-down old car, no muffler, brakes failing, and a cop stopped me, wrote me a ticket, and asked if I believed. I'd just bought that junker for a hat, that's how bad the car was, and I never noticed the fish symbol on the trunk."

"Do you believe?"

"In Christianity?"

"In anything."

"I believe in myself," I said finally, the only true answer I could give.

"Me, too. Well. I must insist on your company at dinner. Agreed?"

How do you turn down an invitation from a movie star. Judging my hesitation, he clasped both of my hands again. "Agreed," he said. "Where can I send my car?"

"Here. At the casino."

"Eight?"

"So what is this model?" I said, not sure of my answer yet.

"Eight," he said.

"All right." Already thinking of what to wear. "Oh. And this model, this three-dimensional landscape. What is this?"

"Where I'm going to make my next movie."

"What's the movie about?"

"A remake of *Man of the West*. I play the Gary Cooper part."

"And this landscape model?"

"Where I'm building my sets, where we'll shoot the entire movie."

"And where is that?"

"Here. Right here." He swirled his hands over the valleys of the landscape. "In the Palm of God."

"I've never heard that expression," I said.

"Shamans use it for this area. Healers, mystics, psychics. I'll tell you later. Now, I apologize, I've got some unpleasant business to take care of. One of our guests at the casino, unfortunate accident."

"The jumper?" I said. "The suicide?"

"I'll pick you up here tonight." He clicked his tongue and the mastiff leapt off the sheepskin and followed Vincent into a closed room.

21

"Georgia?"

"Yes. Laura."

"Glad I caught you," I said. "Can you talk?"

"I've got a few minutes before my next session."

"What is the Palm of God?"

A sniff, an intake of breath through the mouth, a pause. "Why are you asking about that?"

"Somebody mentioned it. You know about it?"

"The Palm of God."

"Yes. Is it, what, the palm of a hand?"

"A palm, yes."

"Palm reading?"

"No," Georgia said. "What's the context, whoever mentioned it?"

"I saw a, I guess, a model. A three-dimensional landscape."

"Of a valley?"

"Yes. And mountains."

"Several different mountain ranges?"

"Yes," I said. "Around the valley."

"That's the Palm of God."

"A valley."

"Several. And more mountain ranges."

"Where?"

"Not on any map," Georgia said.

"In a book?" I said. "A movie, what?"

"We've talked about vortexes."

"So this valley, it's a vortex?"

"Laura. It's many vortexes. You've been to Sedona?"

"Yes. The power spots, yes."

"Some people believe that the Palm of God runs from Sedona south almost to Mexico. If there was only one valley, I'd say, it would be near Arivaca."

"Arivaca? That weird community, near the drug corridor to Mexico?"

"To outsiders, weird, maybe, I would never say that. I did my training down there with a Reiki master. Why are you asking this? Are you on a case?"

"A case?"

"As an investigator, as a private investigator. Is this a case?"

"Georgia," I said. "It's *not* a case. It's actually about a movie."

"Have I seen it?"

"A movie that's not been made."

"Oh. Yes, just a minute," she said, a woman's voice in low register asking a question. "Tell me more at our next session. But, Laura. Are you going down there?"

"Where?"

"To Arivaca."

"No . . . I just heard the term, heard about the Palm of God. I just wondered what it meant, where it was if it really existed."

"Don't go down there alone. I'll see you next Tuesday."

"Why shouldn't I go down there?" I said.

"Lots of drug smuggling. Border Patrol is all over the place, plus, somebody strange shows up in Arivaca, it's a small community, a tight community, but with so many cops a stranger sticks out. Do you know anybody there?"

"Can you take me?"

"I could, if I had time. Why?"

"I want to find a movie set," I said.

"Okay. I know a stunt man down there. We could talk to him, if any movie's being made, he'll know about it."

"So when can you go?" I said.

"Day after tomorrow? Can you wait?"

"Sure," I said.

But I'm not the waiting kind and started to make my own plans.

22

"*Hola,*" she said, hands fluttering welcome. "*Sí, sí,* this is the place."

She squeezed into a tiny nook, an old-fashioned cash register with plastic pearl keys of her combination grocery and *taqueria.* Three aisles crammed floor to ceiling with cans, boxes, and jars of Mexican foodstuffs, pink and green prickly pear cactus paddles, stacks of fresh tortillas in several sizes. Six-inch corn, fifteen-inch flour, packaged by one or two dozen. A wire rack of vividly erotic comic books.

"In the back," she said. "Your daughter, *no?*"

"My daughter, no," I said. "*Mi compadre y mi amiga.*"

"Ah." Her smile never wavered. "*Por favor,* please, in the back. Eat some *antojitos.* Enjoy."

"Laura?" Alex Emerine called. "That you?"

Slender as I am, I almost had to turn sideways to get down the center aisle and into the lunchroom. Three tiny tables, plastic hibiscus flowers layered in cereal bowls on each table, chairs scattered around to be pulled up anywhere, all of it old-style cheap kitchen furniture. Salsa blared from a boom box, TV tuned to a Mexican soap opera, the volume down.

Alex half rose from a chair, turned off her iPod and parked the headphones carelessly atop her rave-shaved-sides haircut, the wild curly top dyed incredibly pink. Except for earrings, no other noticeable body piercings, I was glad to see that. Alex rarely paid attention to her model-slim looks other than dyeing her hair and meticulously selected sandals, some of them I knew worth several hundred dollars. She saw me looking at her feet and raised one leg to display a lime-greenish flip-flop.

"Rubber," she said. "Really hot in Singapore."

"How much?"

She shrugged, which usually meant over a hundred bucks. "Juanita," she said. An incredibly tiny woman straightened up to smile at me over a handmade countertop. "Laura, Juanita." She waved in both our directions, Juanita's smile growing impossibly wider. "Juanita's got some corn steamed, a fresh tub of *masa* to make our *taquitos*. You want *barbaco* or *carnitas*?"

"Goat," I said. "Only if it's got that toughness stewed out."

"*Mas carnitas,* Juanita. *Y dos cecina flautas.* What do you want to drink?"

"What's that?"

"*Agua fresca,* flavored, um." Sipped from the brown plastic glass, ran her tongue over her upper lip. "Mango, I think. Here. Try it."

"I'll have one," I said to Juanita, who'd already poured it and was pattypatting the corn tortillas.

"Great place," I said. "Never heard of it. I thought the best *taquitos,* food like that, came off those neighborhood trucks."

"On the weekends, she makes this fantastic *pozole*. *Tacos* with salsa smothered on *cecina* or *tengue*."

"Tongue, no way."

"So what's the haps?" Alex rarely bothered with small talk, or at least she didn't with me, especially when I disagreed with her about something. "The fake ATM scam thing? Monster job, I've got five computers cranking on it. Nothing yet, though."

Juanita set paper plates in front of us, we dug into the delicious stewed goat *taquitos*. "I can't work on that for a while. You able to handle it by yourself?"

"Stefan's helping me. We'll make out for now, until the databases are set up and we need some qualifiers to start sorting all the people. Nineteen months, I had *no* idea how many people don't bother to see if the ATM they're using is really an ATM. I mean, we've found a couple that were pretty much cardboard crates put in place over the existing machines, with a fake digital plate and a very real slot that took your ATM card for keeps. Rough guess, we're tracking on twelve hundred people, past and present. Okay. Must be those two computers from last night."

"Any files on them?"

"No. That's the mystery. Ah, look at these."

More paper plates. *Cecina,* the salted beef wrapped in three *flautas* for each of us. Juanita set another place between us.

"Try," she said. "No pay, this time."

"No pay, yeah, right," Alex said, poking at the cornhusks of the tamale. "For sure, once I get addicted. Oh, looky. Sprinkled with cheese and cream. So what's this new job?"

"I don't know yet."

"Oooo, this is de*licious*." The *tamale* disappeared in three bites. "Sorry, hadda eat it all. You want, I order some more?"

"I'm already full."

"*Dos, por favor*," she said to Juanita. "Probably already got them dished up."

"What's the mystery?" I said. "What's on the hard drives?"

"Nothing."

"I don't understand."

"Somebody ran a simple reformat of both hard drives."

"Somebody thought they were erasing data," I said. "But they didn't use a high-security program, they left tracks."

"Exciting tracks. I can retrieve most of the data, but not all. Then I'll run a few software goodies of my own, see what I find. First new G5s I've seen, me being a Windows person at heart. Anything you want to tell me?"

"Power went off before I could even boot up the machines."

"I mean, where'd you get them?" She saw my frown, studied the hard drives and my face, eyes flicking back and forth and settling on me. "You and Nathan? You and your daughter? Still problems?"

I told her everything about Leon Begay and Green Valley.

"Yuck. Lotsa old farts down there." Alex seldom bothered with tact, but she saw my frown. "Sorry. Did you know him? Leon Begay?"

"No."

"Jail time for Nathan. What's up with you two,

anyway? Don't tell me. Okay. I'll get on the hard drives, do some data crunching. I'll get help from Stefan. You have any, I mean, *any* idea what I'm looking for?" Stuffing her mouth, she talked around the *tamale*. "Leon Begay." The last forkful of *tamale* paused halfway to her mouth, thinking. "Might be just a coincidence, but the casino manager? Vincent Basaraba? I think he's related to somebody named Leon Begay."

"Yes," I said. "I met Vincent this morning. He's invited me for dinner."

"Oooo. When?"

"Tonight. About the data?"

"Okay, okay. Let's check something." Pulled her cell from the shoulder bag, punched up a number. "Steffi. Yeah, don't tell me I'm hot, not right now. Pull up any data you can find on a Vincent Basaraba. Check also on a Leon Begay. No. I'm *not* into that right now, Steffi. Pull up the file. I'll hold."

"Steffi?" I said. "He plays tennis?"

"Stefan's bedroom name. What's that?" Face twisted at a puzzle. "Thanks." She held the cell in midair, studied my face. "Leon Begay *is* Vincent Basaraba's brother. Did you know that Vincent used to be in movies?" Turning her head to murmur something to Stefan, probably what he should *not* say to me about their relationship. Handed me the cell.

"Ya, Laura, okay?" Stefan sounded Russian. "Reading from the screen. Vincent Basaraba. Born Vincent Begay, Tuba City, Arizona, tenth day of March, nineteen hundred fifty-three. Nine years old, hired by John Ford as extra for a Western movie in Monument Valley . . . ya*da* ya*da* ya*da* . . . moved to Hollywood at age of sixteen, took stage name Basarada, was in thirteen movies, starring roles in three. For sure, Laura, okay? How much detail you want?"

"Everything you can find about the entire Begay family. They live near Monument Valley, probably don't have telephones, good chance they don't even have electronic records. Try Indian Health Service, the Navajo Nation records at Window Rock. Just upload it when you're done. Alex will tell you where."

Alex watched me disconnect.

"What aren't you telling me?" she said. "You twist your lips around while you work on what you want to say or not say."

"Something's happening to that family. Lots of death the past weeks."

"Meaning . . . what?"

"Meaning I don't have anything in focus. Nathan pulled me into this."

"You *should* go meet the guy for dinner. Vincent. He sounds kinda neat. Who was that, oh, Al Pacino is a Vincent somebody in *Heat*. People are saying Vincent, they push on that first syllable." Juanita dropped a handwritten check on the table. "I got it." Fumbling in her bag. "Gotta run." Already standing up, she hesitated. "What's this about, Laura? Murder-suicide? Nathan destroying furniture, ghosts?"

"I don't know."

"Maybe just a coincidence. Oh. Got you some presents." Dropping two packages on the table. "One of them's a toy. En*joy*." She blew a kiss, disappeared.

I opened both packages inside my Cherokee. One a miniature Zen sand garden, five tiny rocks, a miniature rake. *Chill out with some sand waves,* Alex's card read. The other with no card. Fifty yarrow stalks. A complete guide to the *I Ching.*

Which was the toy?

I drove the fifty miles to Casa Grande National Monument. Avoiding the back road where Spider and I almost wound up in a monster leaf-and-brush compactor. Stopped at a roadside table, alone, and threw the *I Ching.*

23

The bottom trigram emerged

$$\equiv\!\equiv$$

Kan. Water.

An old method, using fifty yarrow stalks. I can't remember when I first threw them, I was young, maybe early twenties, somebody knew the easy way, flipping three coins to get it over fast. I think I read the Wilhelm book, that's where I got the yarrow stalks. Manipulate the yarrow three times to get one line, three lines form a trigram, six lines the complete ideogram, but separated into two parts, the upper trigram and the lower. A broken line is *yin,* a solid line is *yang*.

Back in those days, it was only an entertainment, a pastime, an alternative to alcohol or dope or sex.

A line of Gambel's quail interrupted my concentration. Unusual for them to parade at midday, usually they'd head in one direction in the morning and come back in late afternoon. Something had startled them enough to move on. Strutting in single file, not even bothering to check for insects, *cha ca go go* on their way, half of them adults, I loved their waddling pace. A black head piece, the shape of a large apostrophe, wobbling back and forth from the rusty tops of the head, below a white stripe and black face, the younger quail with no head piece yet.

Turning back to the yarrow stalks, I realized I'd forgotten my question.

If the *I Ching* is to have any true meaning, you must concentrate on a central question and seek instruction and insight from the final ideogram.

I had so *many* questions in my head, I had to run through them all again, as I did before starting. Not about Nathan, not about our relationship. Not about Spider? No, that troubled me, but my daughter and I hadn't worked to any severe impasse.

My gun.

Or my reliance on guns, yes, a dilemma.

Five separate incidents, over the past five years, all ending in violence and death, all involving in some way my shooting a gun.

Yes. That was my question. Must I rely on weapons?

I worked through the second trigram, and when I looked in the book for an interpretation, the total result staggered me.

Water over water.
One of the worst of all the trigrams.
The pit, the abyss.
Darkness.

I crushed all the yarrow stalks, threw the twiggy fragments under the bench, left the book on the table and drove to Casa Grande.

24

He came by at two-thirty, clumping an aluminum walker down the curving pathway toward our shaded bench. Alone, without Nathan, but this had to be Bob Good Fellow according to Nathan's verbal picture. Several Rufus hummingbirds buzzed Bob's head, momentarily fooled by the bright red bandanna he wore tight around his scalp like a gangbanger's do-rag. A big man all around. Tall, chunky, muscled, with leathered skin below the do-rag. Sport coat hanging open, his Woody Woodpecker tie flopping over the checkered walnut grip of a Colt Python .357. He straightened the tie, didn't bother covering up the pistol.

A tour group of two dozen seniors, intent on hearing the history of Casa Grande Monument, shoaled apart just enough for Bob to slip through. Ninety-one degrees, surprisingly mild for late July, with breezes touching us in spurts.

He hesitated in front of me. "Bob Good Fellow," he said.

"Laura Winslow."

"Nathan tell you how long we've known each other?"

"Told me very little."

"That'd be his way. You know I'm with the Navajo Tribal Police?"

"Yes."

"Hope this pistol doesn't bother you. I feel naked without it. Moving so slow, I can't outrun anybody anymore."

"No problem," I said. "I've got a Beretta nine mil behind me. Nathan, now, he's probably already said something to you about the gun."

"Enough of the killing ways, what he said. You use a belt holster, clip-on, nylon, what?"

"Bent a coat hanger around it, slip that over my belt. I'd show you, but people with guns might freak out some of these seniors."

Bob cut his eyes to me, said nothing. The tour group drifted past us, the park ranger patiently herding them into the blazing sun. An old lady tripped slightly, which caused her to look our way, eyes opening wide as full moons when she saw Bob's pistol. She clutched a man's sleeve, but he shook off her fingers with an irritated husband's frown. Without missing a beat in his lecture, the ranger slipped backward through the group, gently guiding the lady away from us.

"Nathan did say you were, uh . . . injured. Just happened?"

"Souvenirs from one of Charley's AK-47s. Known Nathan long?"

"A year."

"Know him well?"

"I love him dearly," I said. "But I still don't know him well."

"Guess I'm not surprised he doesn't talk about me. Vietnam and all."

"Nathan has a lot of secrets."

"Mmm." Bob settled against his walker.

"Where is he?" I said.

"Up in the monument. Astro something or other."

"It's part of what he's going through. Learning the old ways."

"Struggle with that myself."

"Nathan is fascinated by archaeoastronomy. There's a hole up there, a window in that thick wall. Every summer solstice, the sun aligns perfect with the edges of that window."

"Time to plant. Helluva wonderful place here," he said. Casa Grande. The Hohokam. Seven centuries old."

"I know you two go back to Vietnam. Did you know Nathan on the rez?"

"Yup, but a really long time ago. Here he comes."

I popped the cap of a two-liter bottle of spring water, sipping to keep myself busy as Nathan hugged Bob, helped him get settled on the bench. Bob took his time folding the walker, laid it behind the bench as he twisted awkwardly to smile at me.

"Did you get a copy of the note?" Nathan said.

"I did." He slid a folded fax sheet from an inside jacket pocket.

"What is that?" I said.

"Leon Begay left a suicide note." Nathan took the fax sheet, kept it folded, running fingers along the creases. "Old crazy Leon."

"Old crazy sergeant."

"Damn," Nathan said. "Didn't we have some fine times together?"

"All three of us. Damn good times."

Bob shifted on the bench, his weight moving the oak slats and they rippled against my bare thighs. I drank some more water, feeling the two men bond tightly and slip away from me. Neither of them seemed in any hurry to read the fax sheet.

"All three of us go back to Nam," Bob said. "Leon was crew chief for Nathan's chopper. I was a waist gunner. After Nam, Leon and I worked for U.S. Customs. We both quit, moved to the rez, where I joined the Tribal Police."

He started to tell me more, the words never came to his lips. Nathan held up the folded fax sheet, still creased tightly.

"I don't buy it," Nathan said. "Not the murder, not the suicide."

"Me neither."

"What do you two know that I don't?" I said.

"Pima County sheriff closed out this morning, murder-suicide all the way. They'd been holding back a suicide note. Leon'd been drinking earlier that night at the Grubstake bar down in Arivaca, then the old Longhorn bar in Amado. Drove home when that place closed, put in a call to the Green Valley sheriff's station, said he'd just shotgunned his girlfriend and had the barrel in his mouth. Hung up the phone. Sheriff volunteer gets there after the gunshot, both people dead. I figure, somebody forced him to make that call."

"I figure that, too," Nathan said. "But why'd he actually do it?"

His fingers worked at the fax sheet, starting to unfold it. Both men were oblivious to my sitting beside them. I stood up with my water bottle, Nathan staring at me with tears in his eyes. I sat beside him, laid my head against his shoulder.

Bob gently pried Nathan's hands off of the fax sheet and unfolded it.

can't do this any more sorry about the girl, wrong place wrong

The writing ended without finishing the thought.

"His blood alcohol was point two four," Bob said. "There's more. Sheriff lives down there, knows the drug scene up from Nogales, on the Arivaca road, all the marijuana and tar heroin coming through these days. Sheriff told me there were unconfirmed rumors that Leon was dirty."

"Don't believe it," Nathan said. "Not having that young prostitute around, either, she was no girlfriend, we know from Antoinette Claw. She says Leon buried his wife Michaela not many years ago, he loved her still. Wouldn't have been fooling around with somebody young and frisky."

"So where do we go from here?" I said. Both of them so deep in their own thoughts they started at the sound of my voice. As one, we stood up. Bob unfolding his walker and leaning gratefully on it.

"I'm going back to your house," he said to Nathan.

"How you feeling?" Nathan said.

"Never better. We'll talk later. When this fax came in, thought you'd better hear about it from me."

"I'll find out if there's anything on Leon's computers," I said. "But there may be nothing to help us."

Bob maneuvered onto the curved walkway, trying to get inside the headquarters building ahead of the approaching tour group. "Another thing the sheriff didn't tell you is why only a volunteer was available that night Leon died.

"Sheriff got an emergency call twenty minutes earlier. Three youngsters, pumped on crystal meth, one of them with his dad's .30-30 lever-action Winchester, tried to hold up the gas station at the Safeway on Duval Mine Road. Another driver pulls into the station, sees the kids and the rifle, pulls out his Desert Eagle, and, hell, one kid gets shot right off, the cashier gets shot, kid with the Winchester blown apart, another kid runs off into the bush, and sheriff calls in all his regular people."

"Might be nothing," Nathan said. "Things fall that way, sometimes. I just, I mean, I just figure I owe Leon. To look at it one more time."

"It?" I said.

"The suicide. Leon handled guns all his life, but putting a barrel to his own head? I don't see that ever happening."

"People commit suicide everywhere," I said. "Anywhere."

"Suicides are never good," Bob said. "People get edgy when somebody swallows his gun. Hard to shake off trouble like that. A few weeks after I got shot up in Nam, pain nearly intolerable, I didn't want pain pills or marijuana or booze or even smoking an opium pipe, I imagined myself in a wheelchair for life, that's when I was on the edge of thinking suicide. I'd never go there, but I saw into it. Up on the rez, suicide is an answer for some. I've seen my share."

"You always hear these stories about suicide," Nathan said. "Like a mythology committing suicide, *hara-kiri,* that sort of thing. Like, there's a certain kind of weak person who worships suicide as the way out. Some people plan it out for months, even keep a suicide diary. You can go on the Internet, find all kinds of ways to kill yourself painlessly. Those websites say, I dunno, to me, *any*body can get to the edge of suicide and then it's just a matter of do you want to step back or jump off."

"So what's the sense in this business?" I said.

"Looked like suicide," Bob said. "Sheriff leaned to suicide, coroner was in too much demand, what with the gas station shootout, so he signed off quick on suicide."

The tour group returned, flowed past us quickly, the old lady who'd seen Bob's gun ducking her head at him, eyes crinkled in smile lines.

"Before we leave," I said. "I need to know something else."

The tour group entered the main building, leaving us alone in the shade of two overlapping palo verde trees. Beyond the trees, a huge anvil-shaped cloud, a perfect thunderhead formed many miles to the south, winds picking up down there, other clouds racing by in ragged formation, long strings of moving clouds, huge bubbles and triangles in long geometric rows, like a fleet of *Federation* battle cruisers.

They both turned to me. Distracted, I'd momentarily forgotten where I was.

"What do you want to know?" Nathan said.

"Tell me about skinwalkers."

·

25

"These are my best thoughts on what you ask," Bob said. "These thoughts came to me when I moved back to Dinetah, back to the reservation. I may not believe in the reality of skinwalkers, *chindi* ghosts and how we Dineh view life and death, good and evil. Everything is in balance, I had to relearn that from the beginning.

"Navajo witches are called skinwalkers. Nobody really wants to talk about them, especially to an outsider, so for months it was difficult to hear anything since we don't care to discuss the powers of the dark side. I know, it sounds like *Star Wars*. But it's real. We're careful because we don't know for sure. So in case there's a retaliation toward us, for what we may say, the elders caution us not to talk about witches or skinwalkers. Of course, everybody does."

"If somebody finds out that you're talking about witches," I said, "are you also saying, if anybody finds out you *are* talking, the witches will come? This is the twenty-first century, Bob."

"We're afraid of witches," he said. "For centuries, we've done our best to live in harmony with our surroundings. We don't kill animals or humans just to kill, just to destroy something. Animals and every other living thing have the same rights to exist as we do. Coyote and other animals show up everywhere in Navajo creation myths about how we find our way from one world to the next."

"A coyote ran into me," I said. "In the dark, I was out running and startled a coyote, I thought for a minute it was, I don't know what I thought."

"Coyote, he's a trickster. Always making trouble for other living beings. But Coyote isn't a skinwalker. Coyote's just having fun, looking to get by with as little trouble as possible so he doesn't destroy other living beings. Skinwalkers and witches, they want to hurt people and animals. They're not interested in making jokes, they just go for the kill.

"You've got to remember, the *Dineh* is the biggest Indian nation. Almost two hundred thousand tribal members. A lot of them leave the rez for the outside world, not many come back like me. And because I'm in the Navajo Tribal Police, I know that even those people who stay on the rez aren't all good people. Some go to the whiskey towns at the edges of the rez. Gallup, Flagstaff, places where there might be an odd job, or an honest place to pawn old jewelry. But some people are just plain bad. And some people are said to be witches or skinwalkers. They hunt at night, sometimes a story tells about a skinwalker wearing a wolf skin, but for those who are most afraid of skinwalkers, wearing a skin doesn't matter, the belief is that the witch has powers beyond what is human, including the power of any animal they choose, even if they're not wearing the skin. These people are witches."

"Are they like werewolves?" I said.

"You know," Bob said with a laugh. "When I was a kid, some traveling library van would bring an old movie project and screen, show us ancient movies in the dark, some of them so old they were silent movies. Or the sound system wouldn't work, so even a talkie would be silent. And we saw a werewolf movie, one night when I was about eight years old, holy moly, that scared the shit out of me. People talked about skinwalkers for days and the library people never came back, they were told not to bring evil ever again into our village. An uncle of mine, he told me that the movie projector was a witch bundle, that everybody who heard the motor was cursed by this powerful witch hex."

"Do you still believe that?" I said.

"What I believe isn't the point," Bob said. "Other people *do* believe. Werewolf? Witches can be *any* animal. They're . . . how would you say it, they can change what they look like?"

"Shape shifters," I said.

"Yeah," he said. "That's good. Where'd you get that phrase?"

"When I'm afraid of something, I try to meet my fear by making myself somewhat aware of what's terrifying me."

"That's what good policemen do. That's how I have to talk to people on the rez. Have to be patient, have to listen between words, people don't outright lie most of the time, they just have their own way of telling stories, what's most important to them can be totally irrelevant to me. You had enough of this talk?"

"Does it make you uncomfortable?" I said.

"Well, I'm not used to such direct talk. On the rez,

anybody asking direct questions like you could actually be a witch, a skinwalker, so people are very careful how they answer, to avoid being witched. And it's not a big thing, you know, people don't talk about witches all the time. Most talk is about what happens day to day, who's born to and for which clan, sheep, the weather."

"And ghosts?" I said.

"What Nathan did, that bothers you?"

"Smashing up a man's possessions when he dies, I'm not used to that, I'm used to traditional ways of inheritance, of passing goods along to the family."

"When somebody dies," Bob said, "a *chindi* is expelled into the world with the person's last dying breath. *Chindi* can be powerful, you don't want to go looking for this evil force, you might get sick or have incredible bad luck, your sheep could die, your hogan burn down, something dangerous and terrible.

"It's the opposite of when we're born and the Holy People put breath into you. When you die, this breath comes out, it's *chindi* and it's evil, unless you're either a newborn baby or somebody really, really old."

"And what if I contact a *chindi*?" I said.

"Ghost sickness comes into your body."

"And how do I cure that?"

"We have sings. We get a shaman, get a singer to perform ceremonies like the Blessing Way."

"I don't understand," I said. "But I guess, maybe I shouldn't even try?"

"It's a matter of what you believe."

"Ghosts? Skinwalkers? I don't know *what* to believe. And you?"

"As I told you at the beginning of these thoughts," Bob said, "I don't necessarily believe in them myself. But also, as a *Dineh,* as a Navajo, I can't choose not to believe."

gary cooper

26

"Why?" I said. Bob didn't understand. "They've got television up there. On the rez. TV, magazines, the Internet, email . . . why do they still believe in witches?"

"Not everybody."

"*Powakas*," I said.

"Sure. Hopi witches. Hopis believe in witches. Just a different name."

"I don't understand it."

"You've read the books, you've seen the movies. Navajos, spiritual, a life of balance and harmony."

"*Hozho*," Nathan said.

"I've been up there," I said. "I married a Navajo. Don't tell me about harmony, I never saw harmony, never . . . no *hozho*, no life in balance."

"Doesn't mean anything," Bob said. "It's there. White people, they suck up the mysticism, they've got their Halloweens, their ghosts, their own demons. Jason and Freddy."

"The devil," Nathan said. "Satan. It's no different for us, he's just got a different name."

"That's just crap."

"Maybe," Nathan said finally, "maybe . . . we should drive up there."

"I don't want to go back," I said. "I want to know what this whole thing is about. You two, you've got some agenda, and I'm not on the committee."

"You're right," Nathan said. "You have a right to know. Our problem is, we don't know *what* we know. Leon Begay's father died of a self-inflicted gunshot."

"Suicide?"

"Up there, with the circumstances, with the . . . tradition of skinwalkers, many people believed he *did*n't commit suicide. That it was a witch, a skinwalker. In the past weeks, almost everybody in that Begay clan family have died. Some of these deaths were so outrageous that people say it's the work of skinwalkers."

"And you?" I said. "You don't really believe that?"

"We think," Bob said, "that one of the two surviving members of the Begay clan is somehow responsible for these deaths. The brother. Vincent Basaraba."

"Get out," I said. "That's too much of a stretch."

"He travels back and forth to the rez. He's supposedly got this huge dog."

"I've seen it."

"You've seen the dog?"

"Yes. He does have a black mastiff. Must stand over three feet high, weight I could only guess about. Huge, heavy, but really friendly."

"That dog has been seen running around at night," Nathan said. "People talk about animals like that, especially when they're only seen at night."

"But *why*?" I said. "What does Vincent have to gain?"

"Vincent?"

"Well, I'm having dinner at his house tonight, Nathan. He asked me to call him Vincent. You've got a lot of people dead, you've a man, a rich man, who owns a black dog. Tell me there's more."

"We don't know," Bob said.

"We feel it's true," Nathan said. "We just don't see why."

"Alex is checking out his financials," I said. "Off the top, she says he drives a four hundred thousand dollar car, his house must be worth two million. He's the front man for a casino, okay, and he's got a weird security manager working for him, okay. But what else? Money? He's got money. He's even got enough money to produce a movie."

"A movie?"

"*Man of the West*. An old Gary Cooper movie."

"What does it cost to make a movie?" Bob asked.

"Millions. Depends on the salary structure of the actors, I guess I don't have any real idea."

"So during dinner tonight," Nathan said, "ask him. Where's the money coming from that will finance this movie?"

"Do you think that's a motive? For what?" They both shrugged. "I'm going to this man's house, but you're telling me he's responsible for how many deaths?"

"Six."

"You're freaking me out, Nathan." I said. "Should I not go?"

"Yes. Go. There's one other possibility we're working on. Leon might have been working with a Nogales drug cartel. I'm going across the border tonight for a meeting with a DEA agent."

"Drugs?" I said. "That's even more of a stretch."

"Depends on what you find on Leon's computers.

Listen. If you feel in any way troubled about being at Basaraba's house, don't go."

"I'm going," I said. "If he's got a lot of money, it may be the best meal I've ever had in Tucson. Something else is really bothering me," I said. "My husband, my ex-husband, was Jonathan Begay."

"You're wondering," Bob said, "if you're related?"

"It's probably not so, but . . . yes."

"Did you know his family?"

"I lived in Hotevilla. On the Hopi mesas. Jonathan met me there, most of the time. Or I'd hitch a ride into Flagstaff and hook up with him."

"You don't know his clan name?"

"No."

"That makes it hard," Bob said. "Navajo babies are born to their mother's clan, they take her clan name."

"Not the father?"

"You're born *for* the father's clan."

"Is Begay a clan name?"

"No. I was born to *Dichin Dineh,* the Hunger People clan of my mother. Born for my father's clan, *Gah Dineh Táchii'nii.* The Rabbit People of *Táchii'nii.*"

"And Leon's Aunt Sadie? Who's staying with you now. Isn't she a Begay?"

"Yes, she might be able to trace back the name Begay. But she was born to *Jaa'yaalóolii Dineh,* the Sticking-Up-Ears People, and born for *Honágháahnii,* the One-Walk-Around Clan. It gets complicated really fast, but any Navajo can trace lineages back through their parents' clans and their respective grandparents' clans."

"I guess what you're saying, anybody named Begay

could be related somehow to half the people on the rez."

"It's complicated, it's really a complex interrelationship. Sadie, now, she's down here in a strange place, she's already calling around, checking on relatives so she feels like home. If Nathan hadn't offered us a place to stay, Sadie wouldn't take more than a few hours to line up rooms, food, whatever we needed."

"Why are you bothered about this?" Nathan said.

"Because I never thought of it before Leon's murder."

"Has your daughter been asking about her father?"

"Spider hasn't been home in almost three days," I said. "I don't know *where* she is, but it's unlikely she's concerned about either of her parents."

"I'll ask Sadie," Bob said. "Tonight, she can draw up her lineage. Will that help you?"

"Maybe. Something else. Tonight I'll work on Vincent Basaraba." Nathan's eyes widened. "There's some connection between these brothers, I can't work it out. And Alex still hasn't called me about Leon's computers. Maybe it's nothing."

"You're not starstruck?" Nathan said, stroking my arm.

"Hasn't made a movie in decades. Just think of my having dinner with him as a way to sharpen my people skills. That okay?"

"You'll come back to Casa Grande afterward?"

"Yes, sweetheart," I said. "There's nothing in my having dinner with an old movie star. My biggest problem will be figuring out what to wear."

"Won't matter. You're a sexy devil."

"You ought to see me in a blue dress. I'll be there to spend the night. In fact, I'll have a movie for you to watch."

"One of his old movies?"

"Gary Cooper. I'll see you sometime between ten and eleven."

"Laura? Laura, you there?" Spider's voice on my answering machine. "Pick up."

The message two hours old.

"Okay, you're *not* there. I'm in Mexico."

My only thought was that she'd run down there to marry Carlos.

"This is the first working phone I've found in two days. Don't worry about me, Laura. I'm in, I'm just a few miles north of Puerto Penasco. Rocky Point."

Don't worry, I thought. *What a stupid, stupid thing to say.* And she had to call me Laura, she rarely said Mom.

"I came through Sonoyta, and tomorrow I'm driving to Caborca."

Using the singular pronoun, *I, I've, I'm* . . . so is she alone?

"I'll call you somewhere on the road, I think I didn't put enough *pesos* in this pay phone, don't worry about me, Laura, I've got to do this thing, I've got . . ."

A dull *tonk* over the line, the connection severed. Since she'd called outside the U. S. I couldn't use star-six-nine to find out her number, and if it was a pay phone, by the time I might've discovered the number, she'd be gone.

I played the message five times. At least she'd left a

message, at least I'd heard her voice. Running through all the clothes in my bedroom, I tried to put her call out of my mind, hard to do every time I held a dress or blouse in front of the mirror, no idea what to wear, hardly noticing what the clothes looked like since my eyes kept straying from the mirror to Spider's picture in an old plastic frame. Tall, model-slim and model-beautiful at the time, the picture I'd found in Jonathan Begay's abandoned trailer at the Cocospera mission.

Now I was thinking of both my daughter and my ex-husband. Too much. I shrugged out of my lacy bra, the only fancy bra I owned, and got into a familiar white sports bra. Tugged on an almost new pair of tight-cut low-rider jeans, a one-inch black belt I fastened an inch loose, tucking my Beretta inside the small of my back without thinking, removing the Beretta to hold it in my hands, not a pose for the mirror, just looking at its mirror image. I checked the clip, snugged it back into the handle, stuck it behind my back again and got into a short-sleeved, ribbed, and very lightweight cotton mock turtleneck pullover.

Before leaving, I played Spider's message one more time.

Outside the casino, a parking lot, I backed the Cherokee into a slot, kept the engine running while I lifted back the driver's-side floor mat, and unlocked the gun safe to leave the Beretta behind. Closing things up, I turned off the engine, the final bolt of the gun safe sliding into place. Twenty feet from the Cherokee my cell rang.

"Laura, it's Alex."

"Yes?"

"Those computers. That disk-erase program on both hard drives?"

"A serious erase program?"

"No. A weak one. It only made one pass over the hard drive, scrambled some of the data sectors but left a lot of information."

"Telling us what?"

"Not much so far. We just finished the defrag program and I ran a few keyword searches, see what might pop up."

"You found somebody's name," I said.

"Fragment of a name. Four letters. Vee. Eye. En. Cee."

"Vincent Begay," I said, heading back to the Cherokee.

"Since it appears over a dozen times, I'd say that's a good guess. Where are you now?"

"About to have dinner with him."

"You said, I think you told me, Vincent and Leon hadn't seen each other for a long time, right?"

"Right."

De-arming the Cherokee, I switched on the ignition, cranked the engine over, retrieved my Beretta from the gun safe.

"I wouldn't get too excited about this, Laura, we've got a long night ahead, making sense of what readable data we're able to recover."

"Not a problem," heading back to the casino, "just call my cell if you find any meaningful data."

"Ten four, good buddy."

27

Xylophone music rolled out of the casino, swelling every time the automatic doors opened. Unsure where Vincent could be waiting, I moved inside, hit by a blast of refrigerated cigarette smoke.

In a lounge opening off the main floor, seven women flailed wooden mallets at all kinds of xylophones, some no longer than three feet, two bass 'phones longer than pool tables. A young woman in a cotton print sundress and hi-tops jumped up and down on a platform behind the largest bass phone, raising herself on tiptoe at the top of each stroke, hopping onto the other foot when the mallet struck.

Crowds moved back and forth at the slots, few people taking time to listen to the band as they switched from a slower tune with an African beat to some salsa. I went to one of the cashier cages to ask about Vincent. While waiting, I watched a young man whoop as a blackjack dealer paid him in stacks of red and blue chips.

The dealer swept cards out of the shoe without looking at them, pitched them over in a fluid motion to the three older, bored men slouched down near third base of the table. The dealer a young kid, neutral features, expressive smile, talking to all the players but looking more like he belonged surfing a California beach. I kept watching the pit boss, an Indian woman somewhere in her midtwenties, skin almost cliché color brown sugar or molasses, and row-of-dominos smile, she glowed without making any effort, checking all her tables in a continuous, easy flow of her head from side to side. Her nametag said OFELIA.

"Ever wanted to deal blackjack?" Vincent said in my ear.

"Hello. No, I don't even know the game."

"Wish I could say that. My car is outside."

"I'm surprised, I didn't know that dealers could talk to players."

"The dealer chats up the players, but not much. Mostly, he deals, and he listens, stays pleasant so winners will tip him. The players, a lot of them don't talk."

"Why? I thought this was fun."

"Bill and Sally St. Louis, they come here expecting to lose a few hundred. They talk, they laugh, they give us their money and we show a good time. Some players come to take our money. Most of them don't talk. Trying to pick up something."

"Pick up what?"

"Dealers are just . . . *there*, you know? In the background, like a waiter, a service person that mainly exists to do something for you. People talk all around them, like they don't much exist except to provide the service."

"Talk about what?" But I could see him working the possibilities.

"Well. They're all looking for an edge. Once in a

while, they're not even gamblers. Keep their money, check out the winners. Money winners like to whoop and shout, let everybody know they've hit big. And their possessions talk. What kind of jewelry, is that a Rolex Oyster, real gemstones in the necklace? Say their room numbers out loud. They just play their cards, bet the dice, they don't know what they're telling you about themselves."

"It's a long shot," I said. "I'm sure it happens, but it's too random. Almost too petty. We're not after some cat burglar, has a digital master key to all the rooms."

"Agreed. Plus, there's no real systematic connection between gamblers and stealing their money. Or jewels, or credit cards. It's a random payoff. Anyway. Let's eat. You hungry?"

As hot as it was outside the casino, at least the air was fresh. A few people smoking cigarettes never had bothered me, but the reeking miasma inside the casino, no matter how powerful the ceiling aircons and fans and air scrubbers, the smell remained on my blouse. On either side of the automatic doors, two huge leaden trays suspended on top of fake marble pedestals, the trays full of sand and cigarette butts.

Chavez Sliding opened the rear door of a car entirely different from anything I'd ever owned. From the front, the grill looked like a Lincoln, but without the familiar Lincoln ornament. Long and huge, both front and back sloped down in a deep silver exterior finish, polished so exact that the car glowed in the entrance-area lighting.

I slid into a supple cream-colored Italian-leather

seat, not even a bench seat in the back, but as luxuri-
ous as any first-class seat on any airplane. Chavez shut
the door, no *thunk*, just a soft click. Vincent got in the
other side, pressed a few buttons, and his seat
stretched out slightly.

"Go ahead," he said. "It reclines, you could even
sleep back here."

As Chavez Sliding got behind the wheel, I realized
that somebody was sitting in the other front seat.

"Marvin," Vincent said. "I'd like you to meet Miss
Laura Winslow. Laura, this is Marvin Katz. My Hollywood agent, my manager."

"How do you do?" Katz said. An elderly man, probably in his seventies, wearing a light green polo shirt,
no tie or jacket. He swiveled awkwardly around to offer me a hand. I scooted forward on the seat so I could
reach the hand.

"Do you live in Hollywood?" I asked.

"Oh, lord, no. I'm retired, moved up to Santa Bar-
bara."

"Marvin came out of retirement to help me set up
the movie," Vincent says. Marvin shrugged, turned
around to fasten his seat belt. "We're talking to a few
people for the other leads in the movie, I'm not saying
names yet."

"Please," Marvin said, raising his hands, "let's not
go saying names."

"Are you joining us for dinner?" I asked.

"Lord, no. I eat early, go to bed early. Had the buf-
fet dinner at the casino. Now we're going home, wher-
ever that is."

"He means the Arizona Inn," Vincent said.

"Are you here long?" I asked.

"Long enough," Katz said. "This rain, this humidity, forget about it."

On Sunrise Highway, headed east to the foothills, the night lights of Tucson spread out for miles, black patches from the older neighborhoods without streetlights, orange-yellow low-glare street lighting along the major north-south and east-west routes. Vincent pressed a button and the roof suddenly *disappeared*.

"How did you *do* that?" I said, moon hovering faintly above us.

"An electrotransparent roof. LCD crystals, either artificial or natural lighting." Flipping another button, he slowly rotated a dial with his thumb, the moon disappearing, artificial lighting now flooding the back of the car. Leather covered almost every square inch, except for smooth paneling. "Amboyna," he said.

"My Jeep has plastic wood grain. I've never heard of amboyna."

"Champagne?" A panel slid back, a tiny refrigerator opening between the two rear seats, just big enough for a bottle of Moët and two crystal flutes.

"I once drove a Mercedes," I said. "Finest crafted car I've ever seen, until now. What *is* this?"

"A Maybach. Actually first made by Mercedes-Benz in the early twenties. This is brand new, took nine months to deliver once I placed the order." He uncorked the Moët, held both flutes in one hand and poured the champagne.

"I'm not going to ask the price," I said.

"Four hundred thousand." He clearly enjoyed the luxury, but just as clearly took it for granted, not showing it to me like a toy as most boys would. The

car turned at La Paloma Estates, wound through a divided two-lane road and stopped at the front door of a
restaurant.

"Janos," Vince said. "Have you eaten here?"

"Not before the restaurant moved from downtown."

"You have your choice of two restaurants. Chavez,
we'll be an hour and half. Check on those issues."

The Maybach slid away from the entrance and Vincent led me to the huge wooden door, completely un-
pretentious. Inside, he gestured to the right and left.

"Fancy, this way. But I actually like the bistro.
Latino-Caribbean food in both places, the bistro is less
froufrou."

My cell rang. "Excuse me," I said. Flipping it on to
take the call, hesitating with uncertainty who was calling about what, but unable to read the caller ID.

"Bistro then. I had tables reserved in both places."

"Yes?" Twenty feet from the front door, sitting outside on a stone bench.

"Recovered some more data," Alex said. "Vincent
Basaraba. His name's all over these hard drives."

"Yes?"

"Somebody listening?"

"I'm not sure."

"Doesn't matter, nothing of serious interest. I'd
guess, and it's really my gut that's guessing, not my
head, Steffi agrees with me, I'd say this Vincent is in
hock up beyond his doodah."

"I just rode in a car, the roof can be transparent."

"That is so cool!"

"It's a Mayfly, no . . . Maybach."

"Hold one." She chattered at somebody. "We're

Googling . . . hey, that's reaching up to half a million. We'll check to see if he owns or leases."

"My guess, it's a lease. He's used to Hollywood, catering to stars, I'd guess he uses it to quietly impress actors he wants for his movie."

"Where are you now?"

"Janos."

"Fabulous bistro. And after that?"

"I don't know."

"We're looking up his financials right now."

Vincent appeared at the door, smiling. "All right, Pete," I said, loud, "just go to the office, they'll have contractual stuff, somebody will take care of you."

"Wow," Alex said. "Wait until you see his house."

28

Rich people move to the Tucson foothills, underneath the southern slopes of the Santa Catalina Mountains. The somewhat rich houses lie along the lower edges of the foothills, the fairly rich own more or less land but are higher up. The super-rich, those whose money is managed by others, live up in the canyons. During the disastrous Mount Lemmon fire two years before, firefighters drew their line in the desert when fire-fingers came down Ventana Canyon and threatened multi-million-dollar homes. Not that these firefighters valued property, the fire had burned too long, destroyed too many homes to allow it to continue. By chance, the richest homes in the path of the fire lay south of the fire lanes.

I'd driven along some of these roads, seen the houses from the road and thought little of their value. Ten miles farther south, a million-dollar home might bring only a few hundred thousand. But I wasn't prepared for Vincent's hacienda.

Somewhere off Sunrise, east of the restaurant, we turned south on a foothill road, lights from Tucson glinting in a one-hundred-eighty-degree panorama that disappeared momentarily as we dropped into a

wash and to a cul-de-sac with four mailboxes. Cruising slowly up the far left drive, we came to a wrought-
iron gate set between two massive stone pillars, an
iron-bar fence stretching in both directions away from
the gate. Vincent pushed a button near his seat and the
gate swung open. We wound around and uphill, ending on a wide paved lot fronting a five-car garage.

At the back of the house, Chavez Sliding stopped
the car and opened both our doors before going to the
heavy oak doors where he punched a code on a digital
keypad and opened a door for us, but I'd already
turned toward the lights of Tucson.

"This is a serious view," I said.

"Pools, gardens, a spa my housekeeper calls the ro-
mance puddle."

"I've never seen a view like this."

"During the day, if it's a clear day, you can see almost to Mexico, sixty miles away. This time of year,
the monsoon season, I could stay outside all night trying to photograph lightning. Up on the roof. There's a
sundeck, right at the edge of the house, you sit up
there, can't see any of the house or any other houses
nearby. A clear shot at lightning."

"Tricky," I said.

"Pure chance. I set up four cameras, run the shutter
cables between fingers of both hands, punch the
shutter-release buttons with my thumbs. I've taken
over five thousand pictures of lightning, only a half-
dozen are worthwhile. Shall we go inside?"

An alarm *ooga ooga* just after I stepped over the
door sill and there was the mastiff, no paw extended
this time, lips back over his enormous yellowed teeth
and his head about the level of my shoulders and only

three feet away. Chavez Sliding appeared behind me in an instant, a hand on my shoulder. I froze.

"Do you have something metal on you?" Vincent said. "Heavy, maybe a small camera in your handbag?"

"Belt level," I said slowly. "In the back. It's a Beretta."

"Really."

Chavez Sliding lifted my ribbed cotton pullover, removed the gun and handed it to Vincent, who held it in both hands.

"I'm a private investigator," I said. "Sorry. Habit."

"You thought you'd need this? Tonight?"

"It's habit. Really. I wear it all the time, I sometimes forget I've got it."

"Nobody forgets they're wearing a gun," he said.

"Actually," I said, "the only time I think about it is when it's not there."

"Really. Come into the living room. Roger. Bed."

Tail thumping, the mastiff trotted off into another room.

"Roger?" I said.

"Named him after Roger Rabbit. He hunts the grounds here, keeps the jackrabbits away. I only wish he'd develop a taste for pack rats. In here."

An off-white sofa, nearly eight feet long, buttery soft leather with almost no creases, I couldn't understand how leather might be stretched on a sofa frame so carefully. Two heavily stuffed armchairs upholstered in the same leather, the chairs sitting on the other side of a massive oak coffee table with an inset marble top.

Vincent gestured at the sofa, but I sat in one of the

chairs. He chose the sofa, carefully pinching his linen trouser legs, one at a time, as he sat down.

"What's this wire thing?"

"Half a coat hanger."

"Why not a holster?"

"Too big, mostly, too hot. I tried leather, nylon, all kinds of rigs, they always made me sweat. I saw this picture of a New York City detective, he had a wire thing like that, so I bent it and . . . well, it's a habit. I shouldn't have carried tonight."

"No problem." He laid the gun on an elaborate coffee table, three square feet of glass nestled into a frame made from carved mesquite. "Do you like guns?"

"I've been wrestling with that."

"Do you shoot them?"

"I qualify every three months on the U. S. Customs range. Down in Nogales, I've got a friend who's a customs inspector."

"Wait here." He wandered through an archway, returned a few moments later carrying a revolver. "I don't collect guns, I don't shoot them. This belonged to my father. He got it from Henry Fonda, my father was an extra on *Fort Apache*."

An old army Colt.

"A replica. But it fires. My father killed himself with this gun."

"Excuse me?"

"My father and my brother Leon. Both shot themselves. I'll never begin to understand why."

Later touring some of the house, he showed me two lithographs in gorgeous bold colors. Heavy, voluptuous Indian women, one clearly Mexican, and the other vaguely generic, the lithos arranged so that they both faced toward the other.

"Zuniga," he said. Lifting his head slightly toward the Mexican woman. "And R. C. Gorman." Head to the other. "Most people would say it's scandalous, pairing a Zuniga with a Gorman. But the colors, no? Of their dresses? The reds, the faint yellow and sapphire edgings at the bottom. Who cares which is which, I just love these two women. Which one do you like best, Miss Winslow?"

"I don't have much of an eye for these things."

"Just look at them. Zuniga's woman, she's got a pitcher of water, she's going to carry that pitcher from the stream to her small *casita* and pour it out for her family. Classic lines, except for the bunched hair, she could be a European peasant, Russian, working class, probably poor. And the Gorman. The colors, do you know the Fauvists, Miss Winslow?"

"Ah, no."

"A school of painting, a century ago. When everybody in Europe was crashing into new dimensions of color, shapes, styles. Fauvists used only prime colors, so a roof might be brilliant red or blue or green. See the reds of the Gorman woman's dress? He mainly drew the figures, then worked with a printer who selected the colorings, ran the number editions of these lithographs. But she's not really a party girl."

"Vincent," a man said from a doorway.

"David." Vincent stood up, buttoned his jacket. "David, please, let me introduce Miss Laura Winslow. Miss Winslow, this is David Schultz. My museum curator."

"Miss Winslow." He tucked his head toward her neck, a broad smile. Like Katz, also in his seventies, impeccably dressed in a gray nubby-silk suit, light blue dress shirt with a white collar, and an off-turquoise tie. A courtly gentleman, probably the perfect host. "Vincent, have I intruded?"

"No, no." Gesturing to me. "Please, come, come."

"I can wait," I said.

"No. You should see the museum. And David brought me goodies."

We followed Schultz out of the apartment, through some private hallways of the casino and into an office, windows looking out onto the desert. More of a study than an office, maybe a library, bookshelves on two walls, floor to ceiling, and the third wall lined with wide drawers not more than a few inches high.

"David." Schultz stood at a large oak table that held a large leather portfolio, at least two by three feet. "So, what have you got?" For the first time tonight, he bubbled with enthusiasm and delight.

Schultz touched the portfolio's two brass clasps, almost stroked them, I could see he was good at selling, but he didn't let his hand linger there, just a beat then he snapped the portfolio open and spread his arms across a stack of acid-free protective pages.

"Can you take them out?" Vincent said.

"Of course."

Pulling cotton gloves from his suit jacket, Schultz put them on and removed a large poster, the back of it toward us until he laid it out on the table.

"Amalia Aguilar," he said. "*Amor Perdido*."

A movie poster.

"The golden age of Mexican cinema," Vincent said.

"Midthirties to midfifties. The posters now collectibles. David, tell her about the AgrasAnchez Film Archive."

"A major repository of Mexican film goodies," he said. "Twelve thousand lobby cards, over sixty thousand still photos, many posters, like this, and of course, movies. Maybe fifteen hundred. From the period."

"And you have?" Vincent said.

"I've got seven original posters. The lust movies, I call them. So. First, I've got this one you're looking at. *Amor Perdido.*" He took out another poster, laid it carefully on the table. "Here is Rosa Carmina in *Amor Salvaje.*"

Vincent slid open a narrow drawer in the table, took out a jeweler's loupe. For a moment, I thought he lingered on Rosa Carmina's face, tilted up, mouth open and eyes half shut, about to kiss Victor Junco. But I realized he was only checking what looked like a small scratch on the poster, he pulled back, smiled, looked at me to duck his head in a silent question, and I saw the lines of Carmina's face, her plucked eyebrows, a strong nose tipped up slightly, upper lip full over her teeth, almost an overbite and, yes, I saw the resemblance to the Zuniga and Gorman faces.

"What else?"

"Okay. Savage Love. Lost love. Here's a few more of the bad girls."

La Adúltera with Silvia Pinal. David Felix in *Doña Diablo,* almost a Joan Crawford face on a forty-five-degree angle, hands pushing back her hair on both sides of her head. *Cortesan,* Mercedes Schultz, and *Susanna,* with Rosita Quintana in Jane Russell pose just like *The Outlaw,* right down to the thrusting breasts cantilevered in what had to be the same kind of bra that Howard Hughes designed.

"And this is my favorite," Schultz said. "And, the most expensive."

Dolores del Rio and Pedro Armendáriz, *La Malquerida*. In full color. But in the lower right of the poster, in a faint sepia, another woman turned in profile, hair pulled back severely with two checkered ties. The three of them seemed to be waiting for something. I looked closer, looked at David Schultz.

"It's del Rio?" I said.

"Yes," Schultz said. Her head in profile, matching the figure on the poster. Peasant blouse down at the neck, showing all of us, probably showing herself mostly the collarbones, almost horizontal. I immediately thought of Gloria Swanson, *Sunset Boulevard*. Down the staircase, mad, she's just shot William Holden but she thinks that Cecil B. DeMille has just come for her.

"Very difficult, finding this one," Schultz said. Watching Vincent carefully, seeing him look from Schultz to the poster and back.

"I'll take them all, of course," Vincent said. "I'll have a space cleared in my office. You'll get them framed, you'll take care of all that?"

"Of course, Vincent. There's just one thing."

"Yes, the cost. The casino will take care of it."

"I only ask because . . . well, there's an outstanding amount due for the last items. The still photos, location shots from the Cooper movie."

"David. If you like, please, take these posters home with you until I have a cashier's check."

"No," Schultz said. A careful smile, a deliberate decision. "I'll trust you."

"Are you driving back into the city?" I said.

"Yes."

"Can I hitch a ride?"

"No," Vincent said. "We're just started, I wanted to take you to the warehouse, show you some interior sets for the movie."

"Maybe another time. I've promised a friend, I've got to feed her dog."

"My pleasure," Schultz said. "I'll be glad to drop you off."

"May I call you?" Vincent said. "You so loved the poster, I'd like to get your opinion of how I plan on remaking *Man of the West*." I gave him a cell phone number, not my regular phone, just something that rang to voice mail and was untraceable. "I'll set up a tour of the sets. If you like, I'll drive you down to the location, kinda messy with the monsoons, it's off a dirt road, but I've leased a Range Rover and can get us off-road with no problems."

"Where *is* the location?" I said.

"One of the last true ghost towns. Ruby. Surrounded by mountains, desert, a beautiful valley just over some hills toward Arivaca. I've leased two acres."

"Ruby."

"You know the place?"

"I've only heard the stories. Buried gold, silver, the treasure of the Jesuits, of Father Kino. And the vortex arch."

"My word," Schultz said. "Whatever is a vortex?"

"A gateway to . . . I don't know what. Vincent, you'll have to tell me more about the movie, I'm a total movie freak and I've never been on a set, or a location. I don't even know what producers do."

"We're the money men," Vincent said.

"Oh. I didn't realize. You're producing the movie?"

"Been a dream for twenty years."

"How do you raise enough millions to make a whole movie?"

"You save and save and save," he said. "You have an excellent financial manager who squirrels away your money, invests it for you. Marvin Katz, you met him earlier tonight. He's executive producer. Enough of this money talk."

"Are you ready?" Schultz said to me.

"Yes."

In the living room, Vincent handled my Beretta for a moment before giving it back to me. I dropped it in my handbag and left with Schultz.

29

The thing is, I liked him. Who isn't fascinated by movie stars?

Once David Schultz dropped me at the casino parking lot, I leaned against the hood for some endless time, working on this fascination with movies, movie stars, also working on the reality of the man, the unsuspected realization that I liked him, liked his enthusiasm for movies, his collections of posters and other memorabilia giving him far more satisfaction than the expensive car and house.

At the same time, I had trouble with his seeming abandonment of caring about his brother Leon. Instead of family grief at a suicide, a most potent loss for any family, Vincent's concern about Leon didn't seem much more intense than his love of the Maybach's electrotransparent roof panel. It was there, an opening to the skies, but at a flick of the switch it shifted from transparent to opaque.

Like shape shifting.

The huge casino parking lot was only half full, yet it was a weekend evening, an hour to midnight, and after tossing things in my mind, I thought of the half-full parking lot as half empty and wondered about the casino's profit and loss. I went inside, moving along the outer walls to avoid some of the cigarette smoke that lingered despite the huge exhaust fans sucking air into ceiling scene scrubbers. Stopping at the first cage, I asked where I could find Clive Davis.

"Managing the gambling floor can't be easy," I said.

"With enough people, it works." Wary of talking to me, yet cooperative once he recognized me from our brief meeting in Vincent's office. "Regular gambling, that runs by hiring the right people. The slots run themselves, we circulate coins and casino cards, always greet big payoffs with smiles and very quick cashing out for those people with sense enough not to feed their winnings back into the machines."

"And the card games?"

"People skills. We start with the dealers. They're certified, checked for criminal records, sometimes checked for health, financial, or marital problems. It's a manageable system. Dealers, shift bosses, pit bosses, section managers, me. Almost everybody working here tonight has been with this casino for months, some since it opened nearly two years ago. Why are you asking me, or, *what* are you asking?"

"Curiosity," I lied. "I like Mr. Basaraba, I've never known a casino manager, I hardly ever go into a casino."

"You like Vincent," he said shortly. I couldn't read his face or his tone. "And what do you like about him?"

"It's personal."

"Miss Winslow. Uh, if you're trying to find problems with casino staff, I can tell you honestly, there *are* no problems. If, say, Vincent has hired you."

"Hired me?"

"You're a private investigator," he said. "I'm assuming Vincent has some motivation to hire you, something not right here in the casino."

"Nope. Just curiosity."

"Curious."

"That I'm here?"

"That you're curious about something. This can't be idle conversation."

"Mr. Davis. Trust me, Vincent hasn't hired me to look into casino operations. I wouldn't even know how to do that, other than security. And that guy McCartney seems to have all security under a really tight thumb."

His walkie-talkie beeped. "Davis."

"Sandra, cage two. We've got a seventeen-thousand-dollar winner, from the Texas Hold 'Em table. Doesn't want to sign the IRS form, doesn't want us to declare his winnings. Doesn't want to show me any ID."

"Hold the winnings until you see valid ID. Inform the person that we'll send in the IRS form with or without a signature."

"Ten four, good buddy."

"That's our staff," Davis said, a wide-open smile. "Random problems, nothing but confidence and good humor in their work. We done here?"

"What about people who *lose* money?"

"They lose, we profit. Look over the slot rooms. Lots of people come here expecting to lose anywhere up to a few hundred dollars."

"And when they lose a few thousand?"

"Is this just curiosity? Or something more specific?"

"The person who jumped, the suicide. Had he lost a lot of money?"

"Is that why you're here?"

"I'm just . . . wondering, it's my curiosity about casinos. I don't much understand gambling for money. Risk, I know about personal risks. But money?"

"This is a strange conversation," he said, making an internal decision. He clicked a button on the walkie-talkie. "George. I'm in the main restaurant for the next twenty minutes or so."

"Copy that."

Davis led me through several card rooms to a restaurant with at least one hundred tables, most of them empty. "Floor show ended half an hour ago, they're setting up for the midnight show. Sit. Here. Can I get you anything?"

"How are the margaritas?"

"Over a hundred kinds of tequila." He called a waitress over, ordered a margarita for me and a Perrier for himself. "I'm going to tell you something." The drinks came, he sipped the Perrier, watched me run my tongue over the salted rim of the margarita glass after tasting the drink. "That's my favorite tequila. It's okay?" I nodded, couldn't say anything while tasting more of the drink. "You work on computer crimes?"

"Yes."

"Identity theft? Credit card theft?"

"Yes."

"Let me tell you about my son."

"Mr. Davis, do you want to hire my company?"

"My son is dead."

"I don't understand."

"Seven years ago, he killed himself."

"I'm so sorry," I said, not in any way sure where this was going.

"It's okay, it's okay. We've dealt with it. My wife and me. My ex-wife. She wanted to . . . I guess, she needed a whole new life, away from family, away from the house. That's okay, it happens. Very hard for families to deal with a child's death. But that's not what I really want to tell you."

"Uh," I said. Toying with the margarita glass, wetting a finger to run across the rim and licking the salt off my finger.

"You were asking about people who lose a whole ton of money here."

"How *much* money?"

"Hundreds of thousands. Occasionally seven figures." He stopped talking, a hand inside his tuxedo, fingering something in a pocket while watching my face light up with understanding.

"Suicides?" I said. "Are we talking about suicide over gambling losses?"

He pulled a folded sheet of paper from his pocket. "A serious problem, all over the country. Gambling addicts, mostly. People who get in so far over their heads they've got no other way out." He opened the paper, folded it shut, ran the creases through fingernails, I couldn't tell if he wanted to show me the paper or not. "Fortunately, this casino has never had a jumper. Suicides in the rooms, mostly."

"Mr. Davis. I'm totally lost here." He unfolded the paper, slid it to me. Seven names, addresses, and a variety of personal and financial information. And a date. "On this date," I said. "Did the person commit suicide?"

"Yes. But that's not what's significant."

"Mr. Davis. We're crossing over into a zone here, I have to know what you want me to do."

"That's just it. I don't know. I've had this list for several weeks. One of the things I do, when I'm off work, I read online editions of newspapers. New York, D.C., L.A., eight or ten in all. Just over three weeks ago, a front page article in the local section, I don't even remember what paper, but the article was about a millionaire who'd committed suicide because of gambling losses. Almost three million dollars. I recognized the name. He'd been here, dropped just over a million in a fourteen-hour period. Because of his financial status, we agreed to hold a signed lien on one of his properties. We checked, discovered that all of his properties were mortgaged to the max. But even that . . . he had no survivors. Absolutely no family at all, nobody to leave his estate to."

"And the other names on this list?" I said.

"Same."

"And?"

"Whales," he said. "We call them whales."

"Excuse me?"

"Gambling addicts who've got a whole lot of money and very little skill. We know we're going to take them off. We comp them to the hilt. Free limos, our best suites, our best food from our best chef. We lay out a thousand a day, they lose a hundred thousand in an hour. Whales, it's just, I don't know where the term came from, but they keep us in the black."

"And without them? Would you be in the black?"

"I'm salaried. I deposit my paycheck every week."

"And the casino?"

"Barely afloat."

"Is that what this conversation is about?" I said. "Is the casino losing money? Does Vincent have something to do with this?"

"I showed the list to Wes McCartney. Said I was concerned about the casino's losses. He told me to forget about it, that he personally knew of the list and that he and Vincent had worked out arrangements with the estates."

"And? I just don't see where this is going."

"Where *could* it go, Miss Winslow?"

"I had a case," I said. "Three years ago. People who'd died, with no survivors, no family, their identities were used to take out all kinds of loans. To buy houses, buy property, expensive jewelry. All of which were refinanced by a third party within days of the purchase, sometimes within hours. A massive fraud, actually the first serious case I ever had with identity theft. Do you suspect that?"

"My son died seven years ago," he said shortly, pushing back his chair, standing up after checking his wristwatch. "Suicide is very much on my mind." Holding out his palms at my startled expression. "Not me, no, I'd not do that."

"Are you asking me to run checks on these seven names?"

"I'm telling you about what happens after a suicide."

"Is the casino involved?"

"The casino?" he said finally. "No."

"McCartney?"

"Thank you for listening, Miss Winslow. I've got to take over my station."

"Does the casino make money? Lose money? Does the casino need money?"

"Please have another margarita. If you want. Or a late dinner. On the house."

"Is Vincent involved?"

He folded the list over and over, compressing the sheet of paper into a tight square wad, poked it into my handbag, and left me alone.

Whatever do I do with that whole conversation? I thought, driving on I-10 back up to Casa Grande, Picacho Mountain ahead and to the left, a pronged horn against the night sky. I played back the evening with Vincent, found nothing to change my feelings about him. I liked him, I . . . liked . . . *him?* Or that he was a movie star.

30

Once upon a time, a long time ago, I swung open my front door and found a live five-foot diamondback rattlesnake. Nailed to the back of the door. Ever since then I've looked at doors, doorways, everywhere, checking for snakes. Always carried a flashlight, coming home in the dark, swung the light in front of me like a blind woman's white cane. Back and forth, back and forth. All the way to the door, open the door and light up the back of the door.

It's an old habit. We've got these habits, you and I, like we're on automatic because of something that's happened in the past, our semiconscious programmed with habits. See an octagonal sign, red with white trim and letters, we stop. ATM asks for a PIN, we've got it memorized in our fingertips.

But some times, some *emotionally* loaded times like now, coming from the casino, head swimming with possibilities as supercharged as becoming a mother again, these are times, I tell you, when we're never thinking of snakes until we get inside the door.

The house was dark, but I heard the TV playing. Saw a flicker from the living room, I wondered about that, Nathan rarely watched TV, but he could be watching anything. I sighed, dead-bolted the front door, and went toward the white leather chair, seeing a man's figure laid out against the headrest, feet propped up on the coffee table, he knew I was almost in the room and muted the sound. I grabbed the bottom of my pullover, lifted it off my sweaty torso and back, dropped it on the floor, glad that Nathan was by himself, Bob and Frank must be in bed.

"Hey," Wes McCartney said. "You got a dynamite DVD collection here."

"God!" I said. Throat constricted, I had to grab for air. Said, "What are you doing in here?" as I backed against the front door, reaching for my Beretta nine, it snagged on the edge of a belt loop, I ripped it loose and racked the slide.

"I *heard* that," Wes said. "C'mere. C'mon in here. *Look* at this."

He unmuted the system, ramped up the surround sound system. Tires screeching, action-movie soundtrack blaring underneath roaring engines. Moving toward the sofa, alert in the Weaver stance, left palm supporting my right wrist until I rounded the sofa.

"*Ronin*," he said. He muted the sound. "Middling DeNiro, David Mamet screenplay blah-blah, but the most incredible car chase scenes on film. They put cameras out-board on those cars, I mean, *look* at this. Stellan Skarsgård, in back of the van, working the computer mapping software."

"Turn it off," I said.

"Oh." He pressed several buttons on the remote, turned the whole system off. Slowly flopped open both

flaps of his jacket. "I'm not carrying." Holding out his
hands, *he wore latex gloves*. Why didn't he want to
leave fingerprints?

"What are you doing here?"

"Vincent asked me to check you out," he said. "In
your world, you'd turn on a computer, look at some
databases, find out everything about a person you can."

"What are you *doing* here?" I asked again.

"Working," he said. "I love those sports bras.
Woman your age, they shape up your breasts nice and
round, gives you tightness, I like that in a woman."

"For *Vin*cent?"

"In a way. Yes."

"In *what* way?"

"Can you put the gun down?" I hesitated. "Laura,"
he said in an entirely different voice. "Seriously, no
more kidding around. If I was here to do you any
harm, I'd've already done it. Right?"

He moved his right hand inside his jacket, froze.

"I'll do this slowly. It's just paperwork."

Pulled out a single sheet of crinkled paper,
smoothed it on his knee.

"Got your whole history here. Especially the last
four years. Audrey, the woman in the kitchen. Your
friend Meg, your time down in San Carlos, rescuing
Meg, and she killed the guy on the boat. Lot of violence in your life, Laura."

"What. Do. You. Want."

"I'm here strictly looking out for Vincent," he said.

"Vincent?"

"My boss. Vincent Basaraba. The movie star. Well,
the one-time movie star."

"I want you to leave right now."

"Music," he said, and I realized that was his interrogation pattern. Jump subjects unexpectedly, trying to throw people off balance. It was a tell, a major tell. And like most tells, he didn't seem to be aware of what he was doing. "Theme music, movies and TV shows. There's just, I mean, these signature pieces of brilliance. Like that *chaCHING* sound in *Law and Order*. Brilliant. Or those Angelo Badalamenti scores that David Lynch uses. Theme of *Twin Peaks*. What kind of music do *you* like, Laura?"

"Flutes."

"You got quite a collection here. I tried a few of them out. Ah, I don't know, I love music but I can't play anything but a jukebox." He leaned toward me. "Can I cut the crap, here?"

"Uh," I said, "uh, you're really freaking me out."

"I know. You come home, you think you're alone, bada bing, you're not. Do you know how much Vincent is worth? His casino, I mean, not just his personal assets, but all the money he's got sunk into the casino, into this movie he thinks he's making? Trying to make a go of it, trying to, like, suc*ceed* in the gambling business while he reinvents himself as a movie. A ton of money coming in and going out. More than I've ever had. He pays me well. Six figures, my salary. Well, low six figures. But I'm his security manager. Mostly, I keep women away from him. Women want his money. I see you visiting him, once, okay, that could be business. Twice, I'm his man. I've got to check out these women. I've got to check *you* out. What are you after with him?"

"Nothing," I lied. *He's asking if Vincent has hired me*, I thought. *And if he's asking that, he doesn't* know *why I had dinner with Vincent.*

"Go on."

"Vincent. Me. We don't know much about computers. We *pay* people who know how to work computers. Me, I favor the personal touch. Chitchat. Look you in the eye. I work for Vincent Basaraba, Laura." Serious again. "He's, uh, the casino, like I said, there's a lot of money floating around here. Lots of people, lots of *women* trying to get inside Vincent's good behavior. Trying to out-act the actor. Get to some of his money. I'm just here, as a favor to Vincent. See if you're out for the money."

"I'm not."

"Good. Hey." He stood up. "That's all I wanted to know."

"Okay."

He turned the TV back on, cranked up the speakers, started the final chase scene of *Ronin*. I wrapped my thumb around the hammer, eased it down, and released the clip. I laid the Beretta on the coffee table and just as I took my hand off it he reached underneath the back of his jacket and pulled out a chrome-plated Llama .40 and shook his head. Stunned, I sank back into my chair, but he laughed, and stuck the Llama in his belt.

"That was *stupid*," he said. "Trusting I didn't have a piece, that was really stupid. I didn't figure you for being a dumb sucker like that."

He worked the remotes, changing from the DVD player to the digital TV channels, pressing the Guide button and flicking down the channel listings. 11:00. The only thing I noticed, the time, figuring Nathan was at least half an hour late getting home.

"Look at this." He punched buttons to one of the

HBO channels. *The Making of Tomb Raider*. "Some people see Angelina Jolie playing Lara Crap, they think movie roles for women can't get any worse in terms of sexual exploitation. Are those breasts real or inflated, I mean, come *on*. Me? I think that's what Hollywood's all about. Exploitation. Women, niggers, spics, queers, teenage sluts, anything they can make money from. Personally, in terms of exploiting women? I mean, Geena Davis in *The Long Kiss Goodnight*. Can you imagine anything dumber than Geena playing an amnesiac company hit woman, driving a semi tanker near the end, where she crashes across the border into Canada and says, honest to God, if you've never seen it, she actually says 'Suck my dick!' I mean, she was *so* great in *Thelma and Louise*. I remember, I first saw her in *Tootsie*. She shares this dressing room with Jessica Lange. She's really young, got this great body, Dustin Hoffman comes into the dressing room, there's Geena in her bra. And *Earth Girls Are Easy*. Geena loved showing off her body. But really, to actually condescend to a director and say Suck my dick? Shows you the absolute power of the adolescent sexual fantasies of those men that run Hollywood."

You're nowhere near as smart as you think you are, I thought. Trying to keep my eyes neutral, my face muscles composed. But he saw something, bent over to look into my eyes, he'd caught me looking at my Beretta and noticed that while he'd been talking I'd inched forward so I could dive, grab, roll, and fire.

"Chicks with guns," he said, taking the Beretta and ejecting the shell still in the chamber, sent it tinkling against the tile floor. "Thought I'd forgotten about that live round in there, didn't you? What movie was that, chicks with guns? Oh, yeah, *Jackie Brown*, where Sam Jackson's got the TV on for DeNiro, showing these bodacious babes wearing not much more than automatic weapons. Tarantino. His first three movies, he let the guys do the slaughter. *Kill Bill*, now, wow, all different shades of blood whooshing out, those swords and stuff. Times have changed, haven't they, women in movies now kill like men."

Why is he still talking? I thought. *What is he waiting for?*

"You know where it really started? *La Femme Nikita*. Or *Nikita*, in the original French version. Anne Parillaud, *gorge*ous body, she must've been a model and a dancer, she's deadly. You do any of that, you being a PI and all? Oh, yeah, I've read up on you, about once a year, you get involved in some kind of gunplay, some people die. Tarantino understands what's happening these days, give women the power to kill. Uma Thurman, now, I always thought she was icy looking, but in *Kill Bill*, she's like old Charlie Bronson in *Death Wish*. Wants revenge for her lost family, the avenging angel. Talk about a movie you could lose your head for. Takes slice and dice to a new level, women don't just lie there for sex and slice, they *whoosh* off other women's heads."

I heard a faint rumble and relief must have flickered in my eyes.

"He's coming home," Wes said.

So that's what he was waiting for. "Stick around. He'd like to meet you."

A mile away, I thought. *At least a mile.* Nathan had replaced the exhaust system of his 1500 cc twin-cylinder Suzuki Intruder, installing straight pipes, hollow chrome tubing with absolutely no noise-dampening capability.

"Didn't know your man was a biker. Okay. I'm outa here."

McCartney left quickly. I heard an engine turn over, a car drive off. Minutes later, Nathan turned off the main road, the Suzuki's pipes *blatblatblatting* up the driveway, but instead of parking in front of the work shed, he stopped, revving the bike. I turned on the outside lights and he switched off, looking back down the driveway as he got off the Suzuki, removing his helmet.

31

"Who was that?" Nathan said when I ran to hug him. I couldn't talk, buried my face against his neck, trembling. "What's wrong?" Disengaging his right arm, touching his holstered Glock nine. "You're only half dressed, what happened? A coyote, some animal in the brush startled you? Where's Bob and Frank?"

Still holding me, he leaned back, brushed my hair, touched my nose.

"A man from the casino," I said. "Security manager."

"Did you know him?"

"Met him yesterday. Wes McCartney."

"You invited him here?"

"No. When I arrived, he was watching a DVD. Caught me by surprise."

Shifting me to one side, left arm around me while he drew his Glock, thumbed back the hammer, I always hated that he kept a live round in the chamber, with no safety on the Glock.

"Anybody else?"

"No. Where have you been?"

"Get my flashlight, left saddlebag on the bike." I got it out, a four-cell Magnalite, turned it on to flood the pathway. "Had to clear my head, been out riding for an hour. Let's go inside. What's that?" The flashlight picked up the latex gloves, lying beside the path on a large rock, one carefully placed on top of the other.

"He wore those, he didn't want to leave fingerprints."

"Then why leave the gloves? We can turn them inside out, use crazy glue or whatever to raise prints from inside. Doesn't make sense. Where are Bob and Frank?"

"I thought they'd gone out."

"Bob's pickup is here."

"I never saw them."

"So where are they?"

"Sleeping, I guess."

"Did you look?"

"No. He kept me in the living room all the time, I think he was just waiting for you to come back."

Taking the flashlight in his left fist, tucking the fist under the butt of the Glock, he opened the door and jumped inside. "Bob? Frank?" Nobody answered. "Stay here," he said, duckwalking across the room and moving slowly down the hallway to the bedrooms. I stayed at the door, keeping it open, not knowing what I should do and then Nathan shouted or screamed, I didn't know which, not saying a word just making a long drawn-out horrible sound.

"Nathan? *Nathan!*"

Appearing at the entrance to the hallway, supporting himself, propping himself up with one arm leaning heavily against the wall, not carrying the Glock as he staggered over to the sofa and slumped, head forward into his hands.

"What?" I said, kneeling in front of him. "What's happened?"

"Call 911."

"Are they hurt, what, do we need an ambulance?"

"Get the sheriff's office."

"Nathan, what's back there? Where are Bob and Frank?"

"Laid out on my bed."

"Laid . . . laid out? What do you mean, laid out?"

"They're both dead."

"Twenty minutes," I said, hanging up the phone. "A deputy will be here in twenty minutes." I hadn't gone into the bedroom, didn't *want* to go into the bedroom.

"I've got to ask you to do something."

"What, Nathan?"

"Take pictures." I bit a knuckle, sucked my breath in. "I don't trust anybody else to take pictures. Can you do it?"

I'd never met Frank, I'd never asked him about family lineages, about the Begay name and any possible connection to Jonathan Begay. Frank, I could maybe take his picture, but Bob Good Fellow, I'd just met him, he carried bullet wounds from thirty years before, how could I take a picture of his body, not thinking too clearly about any of this except thinking I really didn't want to do it.

"You've got to, Laura. We're going to find whoever did this. Pictures might help. Once the crime scene techs get here, they'll want us out of the bedroom, out of the house, out of *our* bedroom and *our own* house. We'll never get another chance. After the screwup at Leon's place, I want to be sure we've got pictures of everything we can see, things we might not even see when taking the pictures."

"All right," trying to ready myself, "first I've got to see them, I can't just go in there and look them over through my viewfinder, I have to see their faces with my eyes so I can, like, prepare myself, god, I never thought I'd have to take photos of a dead person that I knew."

"I'll come with you, I'll be beside you when you see them."

Fully clothed, Bob and Frank lay side by side, Frank on his back and Bob propped over halfway on his left arm, right hand clenched around his pistol, which lay across Frank's chest, pointing at his head.

What was left of his head.

Both of them shot once, probably twice, all in the head.

I grimaced, turned partly away, the room overlaid in shadows since only the bedside light was on. In this dim light, I couldn't really see much of the bullet damage, I knew it was there, knew it had to bleed, those dark stains all over their bodies and the pillows and sheets.

"Can you do it?" Nathan said.

"Yes," turning my back on them, "let me get my camera."

One of my last sets of crime scene photos happened by accident. Nathan was driving us back from a beach vacation at Rocky Point, we'd just passed through Sells on the Tohono O'odham rez and were some fifty miles west of the Baboquivary mountains. Lots of

flashing cherry and turquoise lights ahead on Highway
86, all kinds of Law gathered where a drug smuggling
bust had gone bad. Three drug mules were dead, all
young men barely out of their teens. One Border Pa-
trolman dead, another wounded. When a CSI unit got
there from Tucson, their Polaroid didn't work, nor did
a drugstore throwaway Kodak. Disgusted, the bodies
going into rigor, Border Patrol wanting to claim one of
their own, Nathan told me to drive as fast as I could
with an Arizona Highway Patrol car leading me, flash-
ers and siren blaring.

I'd just charged two sets of batteries for the Fuji S2
and Nathan had me shoot several hundred pictures.
Don't look at them as real people, he kept saying as
he'd clamp his hands around mine to stop them shaking, *I really need you to get these photos, to help me
identify these men.*

Autopsies, I wouldn't participate while the saws and
knives worked. Taking pictures before and after, that's
all I could do.

"Laura, I really need you to get the head," he said.
"Full frame. The whole head, the face. Straight on and
whatever angles you can shoot. You ready?"

I held the Fuji to my right eye, closed the left eye,
nodded. I can pretty much deal with it, you see, if I
look at it through a lens. A distancing kind of thing, I
really tried not to think about it much.

Nathan and the coroner stood back against a wall,
but the room was small, I had to twist and bend a lot.
The tables were fixed to the floor, with barely a foot
between them so I had to squeeze sideways, facing either table, bend from the waist to take pictures. At one

point, as the flash batteries wore down, the camera
recharged slowly with a loud whine, *wheeeeEEEE*.

"That's enough?" I said. It wasn't really a question.

Thirty minutes later, when the deputy still hadn't arrived, all pictures taken that I could bear, Nathan decided to go out to the main road and keep the patrol
car there to avoid contaminating any possible tire
tracks or footprints left by McCartney. I reheated
some chicken breasts, nuking them while emptying a
bag of store-bought salad greens into a wooden bowl.
Poured on some Paul Newman's Italian dressing, *All
profits donated to the needy.*

We ate on the patio. In the dark. Nathan picked at
his food, finally gave up. I tried to kiss him, our lips
greasy from the chicken, but neither of us was in the
mood at all. I took his hand and we walked down the
road for half an hour and then walked back. Three
jackrabbits ran across the road, long ears erect in the
moonlight. Mourning doves *hoohoohoo*ed when we
flushed them, and a sage thrasher squawked continu-
ally until Nathan threw a small pebble into a bush, not
meaning to hit the thrasher but just make it fly away.

One of his dark moments. I never knew what to do
with them, but at least I wasn't terrified anymore. The
first time, he came back from somewhere in the Sonoran desert, dirty, cleaned his Colt .44 magnum at the
kitchen table, then brought out a Smith nine and
cleaned it also. Didn't say a word for two days, slept
no more than an hour at a time, I'd turn, wake in the
dark room, feel across the sheets, looking for him, the
sheets not even warm, he'd been gone so long. Once, I

heard him playing his shakahachi flute. I went outside, tried to find him, but he stopped playing, made no sounds, didn't answer my shouts.

He called the Arizona DPS, the Coolidge police, even the Casa Grande Monument rangers' office, all of them involved with a seven-car smashup on I-10 because a milk tanker truck overturned and the cars slipped and skidded in the hundreds of gallons of white milk and caused at least five deaths.

This time, when he let go of my hand to throw that pebble, he didn't take my hand again, and I left him sitting on the patio. I went through my DVD collection, looking for one of Vincent Basaraba's Westerns, couldn't find any of them, spent half an hour online ordering every single DVD and VHS available. Not that many, two on DVD and three more on VHS. Back at the TV, I found my John Wayne collection, put the *Fort Apache* DVD into the system, muted the sound, and watched the entire movie looking for Vincent. I isolated all of the DVD chapters that had lots of Indians, began looking at the children. I paused the DVD finally, wrote down the exact play time, and took the DVD to my G5 computer. I brought up the movie scene, froze it, cropped and cropped and finally was able to save a frame that I could print.

Vincent and Leon. With an older Indian, probably their father. Vincent couldn't have been more than five or six, Leon noticeably older. Vincent flashed a grin toward the camera, Leon's head was ducked partially away.

I set the printout on the kitchen table and sat outside until the deputy finally came and the long night of floodlights and crime techs took away any chance of sleep.

And then Alex called, and we caught our first real break.

32

"This is both simple and complicated," Alex said. "We've finished sucking every last data byte out of those two hard drives."

"And?" I said.

"I've got no news, good news, and bad news. How do you want it?"

"In that order."

"No news, meaning, there are *no complete files* on either hard drive."

"That's mostly bad news."

"Just wait. Whoever cleaned these drives, whatever software program they used to scrub data clean, Steffi and I figure that software made four passes."

"I'd use thirty or forty."

"Exactly. That's a part of the good news. Except . . . the scrubbing was good enough to fragment all the data chains. Most of them are garbage. We've used every funky trick I know to recover the data, probably tricks you haven't even heard of, since I wrote them myself in the last few months."

"So, no news means, nothing useable?"

"Didn't say that. Nothing complete, that's what I

said. But what *was*n't on those hard drives tells us a lot. I'd say that both computers were very new, that little more than the original operating system software was installed. Panther. The last upgrade Apple wrote for these Mac G5s. We didn't even find traces of a sophisticated word processing program."

"That's not very good news," I said. "There's nothing useable?"

"Back up. That's the last of no news. Good news. First, this is skimpy. We found fragments of the name Vincent."

"You told me that."

"We also found this connective, has to be the same file, the name Vincent is linked to the name Ruby. Is he married?"

"Ruby, Ruby," I'd heard that somewhere, but where, "it's a ghost town."

"Cool."

"Down near the border. An old mining town, prosperous as late as the twenties, fell on hard times, now you pay ten or twelve bucks to get a tour."

"How do you know this? You been there?"

"Not exactly."

"Don't give me a Hertz ad. Listen, here's the rest of the good news. You know that any Mac can set up a public space, part of the computer that can, if the owner sets it up that way, this space can be accessible by anybody who has some simple log-in stuff."

"Somebody else is involved? Another computer?"

"Another person, no. Another computer, yes. He wasn't receiving data into his own computer's public space. He was sending to another computer. What's

good news, ex*treme*ly good news is that we've recovered almost all of that log. Enough to show that it's
another Apple computer."

"Where?"

"Well, shit," Alex said. "That's the bad news. I have
no idea."

"He didn't use the standard ways of sending data?
File transfer protocol?"

"No. Very simple. To another computer's public
space."

"And where is it?"

"No idea."

"Could be anywhere in the world," I said finally.

"Could be two hundred yards away. Don't have a
clue where. But, Steffi has this idea that maybe our
Leon Begay had another computer set up in a rented
space somewhere in this area, maybe here in Tucson,
quite probably in Arizona, although it could be as far
away as the Navajo reservation. Steffi's checking
Tucson."

"You'll let me know?"

"Yes. Where, uh, are you going back to, uh,
Nathan's house?"

"It's a crime scene. We've moved down here for a
while, moved into my house. Nathan feels, we both
feel, two people killed in our bedroom, killed in our
bed, it doesn't matter what cleansing rituals we go
through, we'll never be able to live there again."

"I'm just, I don't know what to say." Unusual for
Alex to be tongue-tied. "I've never seen, I mean, you
know, dead people. I can't imagine . . ."

"A sacred place for Nathan."

"Laura. What, I mean, like, what *hap*pened up there?"

"Don't ask."

"Are you going to stay here?"

"If you find that other computer's location, I want to know."

"Ghost town?"

"Ruby? Yes. It's well known. Treasure hunters pick around there, looking for lost Jesuit gold or silver."

"Small world," Alex said. "So. Want to see a movie?"

"No, I'm, like, I want to stay here."

"Yeah. I've rented a movie. Special delivery from Chicago, cost me extra."

"No, Alex, no TV, no movies."

"You told me about this movie?"

"Told you?"

"Yeah."

"What movie?"

"The one I rented, you gave me the title."

"*What* movie?" Exasperated, frustrated, itchy, edgy, anxious.

"*Man of the West.*"

"That is *so* not a great flick," she said. An hour later. We'd fast-forwarded through a lot of it, unable to watch half of it.

"I used to like it. Thought it was an epic Western."

"Give me a break, Laura. Gary Cooper, come *on*. He's a hundred years old in this, walks like he's got arthritis, talks like it's causing him pain and he's got to bite his lip, keep in control."

"You're right."

"And Julie London? I heard she was a great singer, but an actress? Why does this guy, Vincent Basaraba, tell me why he wants to remake this movie?"

"I only know he does."

"Ghost towns, right? That's the connection? Movie town named Lasso, real ghost town named Ruby?"

"Has to be a connection."

"Probably just a good movie location. They're hard to find, good locations. Ghost towns are dying everywhere."

"What time is it?"

"One of these days, Laura, you'll start wearing a watch. Here. I'm wearing three, take one."

"Noon," I said, strapping on a lime-colored Swatch. "Time for lunch."

ruby

33

Marvin Katz squeezed a few drops of lemon on the plate of oysters Rockefeller, offered them to me again, and when I said no he manipulated the small fork to slide meat off the shell and into his mouth.

We sat on the open patio outside the Arizona Inn's main dining room. Very hot at twelve-thirty, the humidity unusually high because of the monsoons, but Katz claimed it felt just like Miami Beach.

"Why should we be talking?" forking in another oyster, "I'm just wondering that to myself."

"It's just routine," I said. Dominique set a mixed green salad in front of me, light vinaigrette dressing on the side in a delicate china bowl.

"You'll excuse me," reading my business card again, "Miss Winslow. My life is a routine. My wife and I get up in the morning, bagels and lox and sometimes onions and tomatoes. We go to the beach, she goes shopping, I read the *Sporting News* and the Miami dailies and the trades, like *Variety,* and every day it's just like that. Me talking to you about Vincent, I don't even know you, there's nothing routine here at all."

"You know why people use lemon on oysters?" That stopped him for moment, finally cocking his head and gesturing with one hand, bring on the answer. "They're not quite dead yet. The lemon juice stuns them."

"Close enough for me. Once in Tokyo, I'm there as line producer for some weird *yakuza* shoot-em thing, there's this typhoon coming in so shooting's cancelled for the day and we take a train over to Kyoto for a *kaisecki* meal, don't ask from Japanese food, anyway, they got a lot of raw stuff, it comes and goes, I don't know what most of it is, except the squid, *ika* I think they called it, whatever. So these are just the appetizers, of course over there, almost everything seems like an appetizer. Now my Japanese host tells me, say, you ever been to Japan?"

Does he ramble out of habit? I thought, *or is he trying to deflect my questions?*

"No," I said. "But I like *sashimi*."

"That's the word." I was getting used to his way of gesturing, both elbows on the table, forearms straight up and palms flipped outward. "So, they bring the raw fish, excuse me, the sashimi, and the chef, he starts slivering off long, thin pieces for each of us. The only thing is, that fish is still alive. Until the eighth or tenth slice."

"I'm onto you," I said. "You just like the taste of lemon."

"Exactly."

"Mr. Katz. The other night, you argued with Vincent?"

"*Vin*cent argues, I'm too old for that."

"A money problem."

"His casino's doing good, no problems there I can see."

"Not the casino. Vincent's personal money problems."

"You've been to his house, you've tooled around in his four-hundred-thousand-dollar car, you've seen his collections. No money problems there." Savoring the last oyster, he stuck the small fork in his scotch glass and twirled the ice cubes around. "Old habit," he said. "First time I had money to eat good food, I kinda forgot to forget my old habits. I've got others, you should see me cut up linguini with a knife, I hate those long strings hanging out of my mouth. You gonna eat that salad?"

"About this movie."

"The movie." Snorting, inhaling two ice cubes with the last of the scotch. Dominique slid out of nowhere to take the oyster plate. "Another single malt," he said. "Make it a double. No water, just ice."

"Yes, Mr. Katz."

"This is a fine restaurant," he said. "Until nine, ten months ago, I'd never been to Tucson. Tried eating all over the city, there's a fantastic Jewish deli up on Fort Lowell, but too much mediocre Mexican food here. New Mexico, now, why is their Mexican food so much better than anything you can get in Arizona? Don't ask me about the movie until I get some more scotch."

I ladled some vinaigrette onto the greens, ate instead of talking. Through the open glass doors, I saw Dominique come up the stairs from the bar. I finished the salad as he realized the oyster fork was gone, settled for twizzling the scotch around the ice cubes for a full minute before he tucked into it with large mouthfuls and a grin after each swallow.

"Look at me," he said. "I'm Miami Beach. Got a

lime green polo shirt, avocado green slacks, tasseled Cole-Haan loafers, and stretch hose. I'm seventy-seven years old and all I want to do is eat my medium-rare filet. When it comes."

"How long have you been Vincent's manager?"

Elbows anchored, the gesture.

"Since just before *Billy*. Thirty years or so. I'm not going to have any more scotch, my wife'll kill me, my *stom*ach'll kill me. Where's that filet?"

"Mr. Katz."

"Please. Marvin, okay?"

"Okay. Vincent seems thrilled with this new movie."

For the first time, he narrowed his eyelids to half mast, saw me take in the change in his attention. He rapped his knuckles on the white tablecloth. "Back in my poker group, we had this one guy, youngish, he'd been to Atlantic City, he'd been up and down the coast to the Indian casinos, he watched World Poker Tour on the Travel Channel. We played nickel, dime, quarter, dollar raise once a night. This guy, always looking for tells. You know from tells?"

"Yes."

"All right. You've got my attention. Until the filet gets here."

"Vincent is going to make a new version of *Man of the West*."

"Vincent *thinks* he's going to make this movie."

"What are you saying?"

"Movies cost money."

"Mr. Katz, that's, uh, you're slipping around my question."

"So he gave you the whole spiel? From after I left? About how he's going to be Gary Cooper?"

"I liked that movie once," I said.

"I've never seen it. If the money ever falls into place, then, maybe I'll rent a videocassette."

"Money?"

"Look, Miss Winslow."

"Laura."

"Laura. What do you know about making a movie?"

"I just watch them. I don't know, I read *People* magazine. I get DVDs with those commentaries by the director or actor or screenwriter."

"But you never heard a producer talk about movies?"

"No."

"It's all money."

Behind him, Dominique drifted close with a large platter and a folding wooden tray. Snapping the tray open, she set down the platter, removed an anodized aluminum cover from the plate.

"Ah," Katz said. "Time to eat." Dominique laid a steak knife next to his spoon and set the plate in front of him. A spiraled, entwined tower of daikon radish rose above the small serving of green beans and carrots, next to swirled garlic mashed potatoes. "You're not going to go away, are you." Not a question as he sliced off a strip of the filet and quartered it, spearing a piece with his fork.

"Just a few questions."

"I'm gonna eat this right now. If I grunt, that means yes."

"Vincent's having money problems with this new

movie?" He chewed the first piece, forked another. "It's not about money?"

"It's *al*ways about money."

"Does he have enough to make this movie?"

"Not yet."

"Not yet?"

"You'll excuse me, I'm eating the filet while it's more than warm, I've got to talk while I'm chewing?"

"I'll settle for that, sure."

"In the movies, money means all kinds of different things. Desire to make a movie? Everybody wants to make a movie. So, first. Option a script? Money. Get a studio to commit? Different kind of money. Money is just like ducks in a row, but you gotta work all the ducks at the same time. These days, comes down to who's playing the leads. Got to have a current box-office earner for leads."

"Vincent hasn't made a movie in a long time. Does he have any box office?"

"Called the Q factor. A rating system, how well you're known. Vincent? Nobody remembers him."

"Last night, he wanted to show me the interior sets."

"Oh, he's got money for that?"

"He doesn't?"

"First I heard."

"Mr. Katz. I really don't want to bother you."

"So? Don't."

"But . . . if money's not the problem, what is?"

"You don't know from nothing about movies. Money." He grinned around his mouthful of mashed potatoes. "Hollywood is the prototypical American business. Everybody wants to make a profit. Movie with a leading actor whose last film was thirty years before? Maybe. If . . . *if* the actor takes a supporting role and the lead goes to a name."

"But Vincent said *he* was playing the lead."

"Yeah. Well. They're looking at Costner, I think there's a solid offer out to Scott Glenn, not the same Q factor, but established. How well do you know this movie that Vincent's trying to make?"

"I just watched it again this morning."

"Gary Cooper's the lead, he *is* the man of the West. Lee J. Cobb, playing Dock Tobin, second lead." Katz pointed a speared green bean at me, nodding. "I don't understand."

"With Vincent playing Gary Cooper, the movie'll never happen. Guarantee five to ten million up front to somebody with box-office clout, maybe."

"So we're finally talking about the real money?"

"Which Vincent says is coming in."

"How?"

"I get 25 percent of what Vincent gets, that's the whole baby, that's what motivates us both, eh, all right, so I'm a leech, all middlemen are leeches, you know, realtors, agents, lawyers, put us between two parties to settle out the money. Vincent says the money is coming in. Me? This southern Arizona, I like the heat, I always like heat, loosens up my arthritis, old story with old people. But I like humidity. I live in Florida. Where I'm going tomorrow."

Dominique appeared at my left side.

"Are you still working on the salad?"

"The lady's not having anything else," Katz said. Dominique smiled, took my salad plate and left. "Working. Where the hell did that come from, are you still working? Why don't they just say, Are you finished? Are *you* finished?"

"There's a Sean Connery movie," I said.

"Miss Winslow, enough already with movies."

"*Outland.*"

"*High Noon,* right? On some planet?"

"One scene where he sees one of the meth pushers on a video monitor, he takes after the guy, chases him all over the space station and into the kitchen, the guy has this reddish plastic bag, looks like a silicone breast implant, except it's red. They fight, the guy throws the implant into a bubbling cauldron and without hesitating Connery sticks an arm into the cauldron and pulls out the package."

"Ever hear of a log line?"

"No."

"The complete Hollywood concept. Pitch a movie in one sentence. *Outland*? Perfect log line. *High Noon* on a space station. So. You're a dog with a bone," Katz said. "Did I give you the right bone?"

"I'll look into it," I said. "Thanks. If I understand this right, Vincent thinks he's playing the lead, but he's not. Vincent does not *know* this. Vincent is raising money on his own, like an indie studio. Has he raised enough money?" Katz shook his head. "How much more money does he need?" Katz shook his head again. "So, Vincent has to keep raising money until somebody tells him the truth, that his movie will never be made until he's got enough money to interest Hollywood."

"You're almost there."

"Almost . . . *where*? Ah! If this movie gets made, would Vincent be cast?"

"Dock Tobin."

"The Lee J. Cobb part? He's a crazy old man."

"So now you got it," Katz said. "So now, I can eat the rest of this?"

"And Ruby?"

"Oy. Some cockamamie ghost town, he keeps wanting to take me down there, show me the locations. I tell him, you build the set, you get a line producer, you get the money, *then* maybe I'll come visit the location sets."

"You don't think they exist?"

"What do I know?"

"The warehouse? Here in Tucson, with the interior sets?"

"Haven't seen it. This filet's cooling down. We done here?"

"Enjoy," I said, standing. "Keep it working. Oh. The lemon juice, stunning the oysters. John Malkovich says that in *The Killing Fields*. I really don't know if they're alive."

34

I once *loved* to drive long, empty miles to nowhere.

More a man's thing, a middle-age thing, buy a new Porsche or Miata or BMW and take it out for a hundred miles after work, work out the aggressions and stresses and try to solve the mysteries. But I loved it. My last wonderful ride, five years ago, away from Cheyenne, Wyoming, from the famous rodeo where for the first time in my life I shot somebody.

So many things remained forever unknown after that time. So much life, gone and untraceable before I moved to Arizona. At that moment, only a few things were certain to me. I am the half-Hopi woman Kauwanyauma. Butterfly Revealing Wings of Beauty. I had forty-seven dollars in my pocket, a full tank of gas in a rental car I abandoned somewhere across the southern Wyoming border, at which time all I possessed was an unwrapped packet of cheese and peanut butter crackers, a twenty-ounce bottle of Diet Coke, a change of clothing, two pictures of my dead father, the memory of a lover's hand on my face, and a magnificent hug from a young friend to warm my spirit.

What more did I need at that time?

* * *

One thing about high-speed highway driving. There are these metal thingies, sticking up half an inch or so along the dashes marking the middle of the road. Every other dash had these thingies, so if you drifted too far to the center, your tires would strike them and make a soft *bopbopbopbop* sound, almost like a soft swish with a wire brush on a drum. I liked to time my moves across the middle line so my tires avoided the metal thingies. I was really good at it.

Another thing in Arizona, somebody had stuck blue metal reflector bumps in lanes, not in the exact middle, but offset to the right, as though somebody in the statehouse had once decided that drivers would learn to line up their cars to the right of the lane, at least, I couldn't think of any other explanation.

When I drove, I collected signs, but today I'd seen only two of my favorites, both of them on I-10 while still in Tucson.

WE BUY UGLY HOUSES

Whatever does that mean? Who's to say if your house is ugly? Maybe it's all you can afford, maybe it's a rich person's Spanish or mock-Greek monstrosity.

At least the other sign was plain enough.

JUNQUE FOR JESUS
DONATE YOUR OLD CAR

According to my AAA map, I had two ways to drive into Ruby. Either drive almost to Nogales, turning west on Rio Rico, or turning at Amado and on to Arivaca, then heading southeast. Both choices put me on the same road, marked in black dashes, some of it with squiggles that could only mean mountain switchbacks.

At Amado I made my choice, exiting quickly cutting across traffic, a horn blowing from some senior driver a hundred feet behind me but startled. I swung around the access road, turned left near the Longhorn, and headed into Arivaca. I knew this road, I'd been on it once before, this time I wouldn't stop at Sara's bakery for jalapeno muffins, I'd just push on.

From the front, the Longhorn diner looks like a cow skull with these fake long horns out either side. I think Paul McCartney used a photo of it on one of his Wings albums, I wasn't really sure, except with the new addition jutting out from one side it looked half like the rowdy cowboy bar it used to be and a freeway restaurant.

The Arivaca road dipped into a huge wash near the Mile 19 marker, swirls of dried sand across the road from a flash flood just a few days old. Instinctively, I looked to the south, saw black clouds roiling up from the border although drifting west of me. With monsoons, anything could happen, especially on gravel roads like the one my map showed from Arivaca to Ruby. I drove as fast as the curving road allowed, but when I came to the rest area at the Mile 3 marker, the road sloping down into Arivaca, the black clouds covered the entire southern horizon.

My cell rang and I pulled to a stop in the rest area, next to a white Border Patrol Jeep marked by a green line across each side, two men in the Jeep swiveling to stare out tinted windows at me.

"Laura," Alex said. "Bingos . . . bingos." Her voice fading in and out.

"Say again?"

"We found another . . . in the name of Leon Begay . . . Tucson . . . Houston area, near . . . university."

"Alex, you're fading out." And gone, the signal bars on my cell dropping off one at a time. I was out of range.

I barely noticed Arivaca, slowing by the old army post and the adobe ruins of Teresa Celaya's house, stopping only once for a crowd of partygoers near La Gitana, one of two bars in the community. Turning south at the T-junction outside Arivaca, my Cherokee shuddered as the automatic four-wheel-drive started kicking in. My map overestimated the road quality, what I'd hoped was a solid roadbed consisted of packed gravel and caliche over dirt, and I'd not gone more than three miles when the flooded washes started frequently. Driving as fast as I dared, the Cherokee bouncing on washboard surfaces, I finally had to get into crawler gear to pass through a wash covered with six inches of water.

Slithering through the next nine miles, crawling through three more washes with higher and higher water, off-road I saw what had to be the old Oro Blanco stage station and a small cemetery. Four miles to go to the Ruby gate, rain spitting here and there but no steady downpour. Ahead of me the lightning veined the entire southwest horizon, occasional thunder loud enough to rumble over the noise of my tires spitting gravel and chunks of dirt. And finally, Ruby.

Locked away behind an iron-barred gate!

I couldn't get inside the ghost town, a sign showing me the phone number I'd have to call to arrange a tour. I drove a mile past, U-turned at a dry shoulder, headed back at crawl speed, looking for any signs of a movie set. Not finding any, I began looking for a way to get completely off-road, pushing the Cherokee across the desert and skirting the gated road into Ruby. Nothing, nothing, nothing.

Past Ruby again.

Nothing. Lightning flashed all around the Cherokee, splitting a huge mesquite tree just off the road, most of the trunk teetering across the road, I stomped on the accelerator, taking a huge risk, leapt ahead on the road as the trunk fell in slow motion just as heavy rain deluged my car and the road, restricting visibility to less than a hundred feet.

I drove steadily back to Arivaca, not daring to try the mountain roads since that would take me directly into the buffeting monsoon winds at their worst. After an hour I passed again through Oro Blanco and almost immediately came to a heavily flooded wash, water gushing across the road, carrying small debris. I didn't stop, just slowed and nudged the Cherokee into the water, reaching the middle of the wash with water almost over my hubcaps, impatient to get out of the stream I goosed the gas and the forward motion set up a bow wave that splashed over and up under the hood so that even though I was going through shallower water I still had ten feet to get to the gravel on the other side and just then the engine stopped, all power off, my brakes not working, the Cherokee slewing half sideways, taking all my strength to wrestle the steering wheel around enough so that my momentum carried me out of the water. I set the hand brake, trembling, shifted into Park, ground the starter motor three times before it caught and the engine purred.

Half a mile later, another flooded wash, this time thirty feet across, water pouring farther out to edges of the road on either side. I realized it was hopeless, backed up to higher ground, turned off the engine, and sat in the steamy closed Cherokee, sweat rolling everywhere on my body, substantial rain striking the roof and hood, the noise almost intolerable, a thousand small jackhammers drilling into the car, inside my head, the noise and humidity finally pushing me near panic and for three years I'd *worked so hard* on surviving panic and anxiety attacks, I wasn't going to give in, so I started the engine, cranked the aircon to full roar and tuned in the single station available on FM radio, somewhere in Mexico and playing a lilting polka and three women longing for their *corazón*.

Her car horn woke me up. I rolled down the window and looked out.

Almost sunset. The rain had stopped, the monsoon had moved on, but clouds blotted out most of the remaining sunlight. At some point I must have turned off the engine, I couldn't remember when. Across the wash, an ancient Land Rover, an older woman in shorts and a Betty Boop–decorated muumuu pulling a cable from the winch on the Land Rover's front bumper.

"I'm coming across," she shouted.

I got out of the Cherokee. "Don't bother," I said. "I'll drive it."

"No you won't. Water's too high, it'll flood your engine."

She turned on the winch motor, pulled the cable across her shoulder, gloved hands clutching the cable hook as she strode into the water. Halfway across, the water splashing up to her belly button, she grinned, bent toward me and kept coming with the cable.

"Drive down to the edge," she said. "We'll hook you up there."

I moved the Cherokee into an inch or two of water, set the gear shift in Neutral, engine still on.

"Hiya," she said, grinning, dropping the cable and extending both hands. "Whatcha doing stuck out here, girl?"

"Looking for, trying to find the location."

The smile faded from her leathered, crinkled face. "The location."

"Yes. It's supposed to be near Ruby."

"Did you find it?"

"No."

"You go hiking up there?"

"No, I didn't."

"Take any geodes?"

"Geodes?"

"Rocks, you know, those funky things people get for their coffee tables."

"I'm not a geologist. I'm not looking for rocks."

"You trying to find the location of the gateway?"

"The gate was locked."

"Girl," she said finally, "you aren't making a whole lot of sense. The gateway is *never* locked."

"I saw it, I was right in front of it."

"You go through?"

"No," glad she'd offered to help me, irritated at her senseless questions, "it was locked, I told you, it was locked shut."

"Ha," she cackled. "You talking about that gate into Ruby."

"Yes. That's what I wanted to do, get into Ruby. A man I know has a movie location somewhere in there. I wanted to see it."

"A movie location."

"Yes."

"So you weren't trying to find the gateway?"

"Can we just get me across this water?"

"Nope. Gotta wait at least an hour. I just wanted to get you hooked up, but when I waded in there, I could see it was no go for a while. You might as well turn off your engine, we'll sit awhile. A movie, you say."

"A Western."

"Lots of movies been made around here. Nothing going on now, though. I'd know about it. George would know about it."

"George?"

"A movie stuntman, lives in Arivaca. Worked in Hollywood, worked at that Wild West dude place in Tucson. Any Western movies being made around here, George would know about it, most likely, he'd be part of it."

"No movie?"

"Nah. I know the caretakers for Ruby, I'd know if they leased some of the town to a movie deal. Unlikely they'd do that. Look."

"Look at what?"

"Over there," she whispered. "Other side of the wash, twenty feet upstream. See her?" She pointed, I sighted along her arm.

"Is that a cat?"

"Cat all right. Name of Bob."

Short tail, tufted ears, with a summer coat of yellowish tan highlighted with randomly placed dark spots and a few black stripes.

"Bobcat. Look, her babies."

Three tiny kittens stumbled out of the brush, round-faced with thick legs and enormous paws, two of them tumbling in play while the mother scanned their side of the wash and then over to us. She froze instinctively, knowing us for humans, uncertain whether we wanted her pelt or just happened to be nearby. I stepped backward, ready to jump into my Cherokee if she came across to us, but the movement scared her enough that she snarled at her kittens, their play ceasing as all four took off in an awkward stumbling run, disappearing into the shrubs and creosote bushes across the wash.

"Cute lil suckers, aren't they. My name's Delilah."

"Laura," I said.

"Guess you're not looking for the gateway."

"I don't even know what you're talking about."

"People say there's a powerful vortex gateway up in the hills."

"A vortex?"

"Yeah. I've got a few on my ten acres."

"Good and bad?"

"You know about that, yeah, one bad and the rest wonderful."

"And the gateway?"

"Who knows? Lots of stories." Picking up the cable

hook, suddenly less talkative. "Let's give this a shot, what the hell. We're late for the birthday party anyway, might's get moving."

"I can't go to a party, I've got to be in Tucson."

"Girl, there's two heavy-duty flooded washes between Arivaca and I-19. You won't be able to get past for at least two hours. This wash here is nothing compared to the others, folks sometimes hole up at the Longhorn bar until midnight, cars lined up for three miles or more waiting to get through the water."

"I've *got* to be in Tucson."

She grabbed my hands, leaned her head back. "You're kinda worked up."

"Can we please get across? Now?"

"You're not listening to me, Laura. No matter how much you might want to be in Tucson, you won't get there until really late. Just chill out a bit, things'll go all right, we can party up for a while."

"Is there another road out of this place?"

"What are you angry about, Laura? You can't be angry about water, you've gotta see past that."

"I don't need a therapist right now. Just give me a tow."

She let go of my hands, leaned against the hood of my Cherokee.

"Girl, you've gotta do some work."

"I'll hook it up, just show me how."

"No. I mean, you should do some work on that anger." She watched as I lifted the cable hook, lay down in the muddy dirt, and fastened the hook to the towing bolt. I stood up, half wet and mostly dirty, brushing dirt off the back of my head. "Look into the water, Laura. Look at the last light, reflected in the water."

Clouds drifting off to the north, opening a tunnel so the moon was imaged in the water, which no longer flowed quickly, almost at a standstill as the desert soaked it up.

"You can get messages from water," she said. "The molecular structure changes if you focus on it, concentrate on the water until it mirrors your anger."

"I don't want New Age stuff right now."

"That bobcat, she's over across there somewhere, probably at home in a hollow log. She's watching you, watching your mirror image in the water. She's feeling your anger."

"Anger," I sighed. "I *am* angry."

"At what?"

"Trying to solve so many things, and here I'm stuck in the desert."

"Just a monsoon, Laura. Nothing you do can stop a monsoon. You feeling irresponsible, that you can't solve things, you don't have control?"

"I don't want to talk about what's making me angry."

"I don't, either. You've got to do the work yourself, girl. You've got to see the mirror image of yourself, you've got to mirror yourself and illuminate the anger you see in yourself instead of just figuring what you want from other people."

"Illuminate," I said shortly.

"Yeah. It's simple. Do the work. See in yourself what you think you have a right to see in other people."

"You mean, see myself in terms of . . . what?"

"Your emotions toward other people. Flip those emotions so you see them in yourself, then you work on what that's doing to you." I shook my head, unwilling to listen anymore. She smiled, touched my hands again, and started wading back over the wash. "Let's get your Jeep across. We can talk about things more at the party."

35

My cell rang just after midnight. I'd crossed the last flooded wash and was on I-19 before the cell signal strength bars lit up. Anxious to call Alex, but she called me.

"Where have you been?" she said. "God, Laura, I've left a dozen messages on your voice mail."

"Did you find anything we can use?"

"Yes. Leon Begay is the registered owner of a house at one nine one two Avocado Place. Between Campbell and Mountain, just north of Grand."

"I know that neighborhood."

"Fries me off," Alex said. "Should've been onto it hours ago. I'm getting old, I'm slipping here. Where are you?"

"Near Green Valley, about half an hour from that address."

"We'll meet you there."

"No. I'll go myself. Anything else?"

"On hold. Can't crunch data if we don't have it."

"My cell battery is almost shot. I'll call when I get to that house."

* * *

Most of older Tucson had no streetlights, the subdivisions planned decades earlier. This wasn't the result of zoning laws, however. Tucson was surrounded by many observatories, and in an attempt to keep reflected city light down, streets were planned without lighting. Some of the newer developments east of town, like the car lots on Speedway, had yellowish lights. But in the area north of the university and west of Campbell Avenue, the older neighborhoods were very dark at nights.

I'd lived here several years ago, when I'd first met Rey Villaneuva and wound up with Audrey dead by a shotgun blast in my kitchen. The house was now gone, bulldozed along with two neighboring houses so the new owner could build a walled new-style hacienda. Most of the houses on Silver were still there, however, and I found myself remembering the neighborhood street names, some of the houses, Jerry's eclectic and amazing collection of welded objects—a camel, several dinosaurs.

I drove slowly past Leon's other house, distinguished in style from its neighbors only by the bamboo fencing along the front yard. Like the kind of bamboo you buy to hang as window shades, except this was stacked vertically and braced every few feet with what looked like ocotillo ribs. A forty-foot mesquite leaned over the bamboo, and several palm trees ringed the left side of the house.

Parking down the street, I walked back, not wanting to use my flashlight but wary of my footing once I stepped off the paved street onto a sand-and-loose-gravel sidewalk area. A mailbox lay atop a stack of three concrete building blocks, the bottom two painted purple. Two feet from the entrance, I stopped, alarmed, as a light flickered suddenly in the draped front windows, and I heard sounds from a TV. It took me a minute to realize that somebody'd set up a timer inside, the cheap-person's burglar alarm, controlling a lamp or CD player or TV so people would think somebody was home. Without hesitating I opened the front gate, moved inside the yard, and refastened the gate hasp. Bushes grew irregularly on both sides of the house, shielding me from the lighted living- and bedroom windows of the houses on each side. Even with their blinds down, I didn't want to make any noise that might cause somebody to take a look. Three steps up to a concrete porch, some wicker chairs positioned around two tables. No screen door, just solid wood with three small windows at eye level.

Every door and window locked tight and covered. I waited ten or fifteen minutes, couldn't detect any changes in the pattern of sounds from the house. TV played, one lamp switched off and another on in a back bedroom, but nobody seemed to be moving around. At the back of the house, a narrow window that wouldn't budge until I wrapped a large, flat rock inside my blouse and smacked the window just enough to break the glass, only one shard falling inside to crinkle on a wooden floor. I removed the rest of the glass and boosted myself over the sill.

A laundry room, an ancient washer and dryer, hoses and power plugs unconnected. Opening the door, I crept into a hallway, saw a crack of light under a closed door. I tapped on the door, heard nothing, opened it to see a totally empty room with dingy white sheets hanging over the windows. Down the hall, the living room, bathroom, and kitchen were also completely empty. One bedroom left.

Entirely by itself, an old Mac G3 computer sat in the middle of the floor, a long extension cord running to a power outlet, the computer unplugged. An old monitor sat next to the box, unplugged. I attached the monitor cable to the back of the computer, plugged the power cords into the wall socket. The monitor jumped on with a sizzle and the screen opened in the middle and slowly expanded to the outer edges, the monitor so old that everything was in green.

The computer ground through the boot-up process until a box appeared asking me for a log-in password. Without hesitating I pulled both power cords out of the wall socket, removing the monitor attachment. Hoisting the computer, I went to the front door, unlocked two dead bolts, and closed the door behind me to stand on the front porch. Two mourning doves hooted their baleful cries, but no traffic moved on the street, none of the neighbors seemed awake.

I went quickly to the Cherokee, set the computer on the floor behind the driver's seat, and called Alex to say I'd be at her place in twenty minutes.

36

The gateway, I kept thinking of the gateway all during my two hours at the birthday party, over fifty people crowding inside La Gitana, packed against the walls, several people dancing outside on the terrace.

A vortex, Delilah told me. An archway into another time. Up there in the hills near Ruby. All kinds of stories about it. People run through and disappear. Somebody throws a jackrabbit through, the rabbit disappears but three lambs run out. You just disappear or reappear around the gateway, you reverse in time or forward in time or who knows, into another world. A few people claim to know where the gateway is, they say the arch has crumbled, it's just two curved columns now, me, I don't go up there, I don't need to know, I'm happy in this time, in this world.

Finally driving up to my own house. Almost two in the morning.

Alex and Steffi couldn't easily crack the computer's log-in requests and after fifteen minutes, I left them running their own cracking software, knowing she'd call me if and when they got something useful.

Driving through empty streets, even the birds quiet,

I expected to find an empty house. Lights shone from the living room and kitchen. I parked in the drive, stretched, did some breathing to get myself calm, I knew my daughter had come home, I knew what I wanted to say to her. Nothing else much mattered.

"Laura," she said with a huge grin. "This is *so* cool."

She'd unboxed the small Zen garden that Alex had given me, she'd poured the almost white sand into the eight-by-twelve-inch framed box, five small rocks placed at different spots and she'd been pulling the small rake through the sand, creating wavy lines in a random pattern.

"Where've you been?" she said.

"At a birthday party. And you?"

"Got back earlier. Whose birthday?"

"Some woman in Arivica, her forty-fifth birthday party and the day she got her divorce papers after years of waiting. Got back from where?"

"Mexico. Didn't you get my phone message?"

"Yes."

"Well, then. I got back about nine tonight. A bad monsoon north of Nogales, Carlos loves his low-rider convertible but the ragtop leaks like crazy. What was her name, the birthday girl?"

"Monica."

She turned to the Zen garden, shifted two rocks, raked out the sand in a different pattern. "Where'd you get this?"

"From Alex." I stretched, felt the Beretta shift and dig into my butt. I took it out and set it on an end table.

"I'd never figure you Zenning out, Laura."

"Yesterday, I wouldn't have figured it, either."

"You seem . . . I don't know, like, you're so calm."

"I am. Tired, but yeah, I feel good. Really good."

"Carlos said you'd jump all over me for taking off. I said you'd understand, once I told you what I'd been doing." I waited for her to continue and my silence confused her. "Laura, what's been going on, you're so different. Look at this." She stood up, turned sideways so I could see her profile, stretched her spaghetti strap tanktop tight over her belly. "I think I'm starting to show."

"I can't see anything," I said, thrilled anyway.

"Well, maybe it just feels that way. From inside, I think I'm showing."

"So you're going to have the baby?"

"Yes, I'm going to have the baby."

"And Carlos, what's he going to do?"

"Mom," she said with exasperation, "Carlos is so *not* the father."

"He's not?"

"Carlos is my best friend." I opened my mouth to ask about the father, realizing that it really didn't matter to me, and she saw that it didn't matter and ran to hug me. "You thought Carlos and I . . . no way. He offered to loan me his car, to go to Mexico, but I wanted him there for me as a friend."

"What were you doing down there?"

"You probably thought, you heard my message, you thought I was down there getting married?"

"Worse."

"Having an abortion? Mom, please." The second time in a single minute she'd called me Mom. "I want this baby. Oh. Alex tried to get you. And somebody else has been calling. After three times I answered, I just let the answering machine take it."

"Okay, I'll listen in a minute. What were you doing in Mexico?"

"I was looking for Dad."

That astonished me, my jaw dropping until I could finally say something. "Spider, he's . . . your father is dead."

"No. He's not. Are you all right?" I'd stumbled to sit on the floor with a thud. "He's still with that peace activist group. They changed their name, but the *policía* and the army still want him for some old charges, so he changed *his* name and went into hiding down with the Zapatistas."

"You're sure?"

"Yes. He called me. Four months ago. He called from Mexico, he needed to talk to me, to hear that I was all right and doing okay. He sounded lonely, but he cheered up as we talked."

"Where is he now?"

"I couldn't find him. Everywhere I went, even with meeting the contacts he told me about, a woman in Caborca who sent me to a man in Guaymas, nobody knew where he lived. Or they didn't trust me. Anyway, after two days in Guaymas he called me. I know it's him, I know his voice. I didn't think you wanted to ever see him again, that's why I didn't tell you."

"I'm glad," I said. "I'm really glad to know that."

"Yeah. Me, too. So, what's up with you? What's happening?"

For half an hour I ran through everything from the past few days. The killings, the houses, the people, the casino and Vincent Basaraba and Wes McCartney and

Bob Good Fellow and then I began sobbing, Spider sat beside me, pulled my head into her lap, and kept stroking my head, smoothing out my hair and the lines and tears on my face. When I finally smiled up at her, she smiled back and gave me a thumbs-up.

"That's my mom," she said. "Every year or so, you get into deeper piles of shit, I can't even imagine this thing, it sounds so operatic. Oh, don't forget the messages on the answering machine."

All from the same person. "Hi. It's Vincent. I've been worried about you. Wes told me he was at your other house last night. I'm really saddened and angered at what he did, I can't apologize enough. He won't ever bother you again. He's going to . . . he's going away . . . he'll disappear, I promise you. Please call me when you get in. The casino will know where I am. Please call? 'Bye."

37

"We've got a database," Alex shouted. "We're reformatting it."

Waiting. Ten the next morning, after not sleeping at all, staying up until four talking with Spider, our first *real* mother-daughter talk, incredible, just when you think your kids have drifted out of your orbit, *pow*, you both realize you're not only on the same planet, but still very much in each other's lives.

I'd finally driven to our main Tucson office where Alex and a crew of four people slid their expensive ergonomic chairs between half a dozen computers.

Data mining. A growing business. And much of it legal.

When I started hacking, only eight years ago, information wasn't readily available. Working with dial-up modems, connection speeds, and bandwidth meant that you had to write password-cracking scripts that ran for hours and hours until you found the right combination of log-in names and passwords. Almost all of what I got, I got illegally. Now, with online databases everywhere, anybody could look up information. Googling for private investigators, you could pay as little as sixty bucks to find out if people you just met at a singles bar told you the truth, if they really were stockbrokers or models or rich or whatever. Pay more money, you could find out what kind of potato chips they bought using their grocery-store discount cards. Take out your wallet, I'm telling you, look at the cards in there with that magnetic strip, you swipe the card at the supermarket, the ATM, a gas station, the transactions were all recorded in databases. Turn those cards over, like, say, look at the back of your driver's license. Does it have a bar code? You know, those weird numbers on things you buy, the supermarket scans them? Almost everything you supply to the state about yourself, just to get that driver's license, *all* of that could be in the bar code. So you're on a long drive, gas running low, you're thirsty, need to find a bathroom, you give the card to the kid at the cash register, when you're not looking, he not only copies your credit card number, he zaps the bar code with a scanner. Then he sells off your information to a data miner.

"We got it, we goddam freaking got it!" Alex shouted.

The monitor listed several thousand names.

"What does it mean?" I said.

"Too early. Too many fields. Whatever else Leon Begay did, he knew how to construct a clear database. Right now, all we've got is columns of data. At a glance, two important columns. Names. Dollar amounts. No way are we going to have time to back-check everything. So how do you want to work this list?"

"Outsource the list," I said.

"That's a lot of money we're talking if we don't crunch the list ourselves."

"Not enough time," I said. "Besides, we've got to work out the most likely names on this list, work them ourselves."

"We're on it. This could take time, just be patient."

Alex used three people to do most of the serious analysis.

Anything corporate, banking, follow the money, Alex gave those jobs to the Two Sarahs. Dee and Vee, they never used a last name, just an initial. When we first interviewed them, they showed us ID with the last names as Dee and Vee. Two women who shared an old home in South Tucson.

They drove to the office only if they needed to get paper data, otherwise they worked exclusively from their home next to a one-acre greenery and community garden. I rarely saw them, but when I did they were always together. Sarah Dee was somewhere in her fifties, long, lanky, hair part blond, part graying, usually in a braid lying two feet down her back. She always wore sleeveless sundresses that hung to the floor. Sarah Vee was at least fifteen years younger, skin naturally dark, almost an olive brown-green, with short red hair curled tight as a Brillo pad.

One day at the office, Nathan, thinking they couldn't hear him, asked me what the Data Dykes were doing. Sarah Vee poked her Brillo-hair head around the doorway, got his attention and held it for a minute until she just shook her head and smiled. *You just don't know how good it is, being a woman*, she said to Nathan.

The Two Sarahs got all the money-trail stuff. When it came to finding data on real people, Alex worked with Lola Darlin, a women of completely indefinite age and sexuality. Probably in her sixties, skinny as a bean pole, nearly six feet tall. Hair dyed in various colors, according to the weather or time of year or some secret mood. She mainly lived out of her 1982 Coupe de Ville, the backseat always loaded with cardboard boxes of indeterminate age. No passenger bucket in the front, a doggie bed for Billie and Babe, her two Yorkies, plus discarded chew toys and scraps of dog bones. At one time, Lola had also lived in Arrivaca, the Two Sarahs brought her to Alex one day, asking Alex if she needed more help.

Still waiting.   •

At seventeen, Alex knew her place in life, existed somewhere between teenage and adult years. Although I hadn't seen or heard from her directly for two years, when Don Ralph died in the plane crash, she reappeared in my life as though she'd been there all the time. Never said where she'd been, what she'd been doing. Extraordinarily beautiful, in two years she'd grown from spunky brat to woman. An adult's body in the neck and legs, slim but not thin, small breasts usually bouncing beneath a tee or tanktop. She'd work a laptop, usually a Mac of some kind, a heat pad underneath to avoid scorching her bare thighs. No makeup, lots of silver rings, at least one on every finger, the only other person I'd ever met with so many rings was Shane Caraveo, the computer guru at Florence Prison. How they both could work a keyboard, I never knew.

Alex never talked about her private life, I had no idea if she had a lover, a boyfriend, a roommate. Once, she saw me looking back and forth between her and the Two Sarahs, wondering, and she read my look instantly. *Nah,* she said, *tried it once, realized it just wasn't me.*

Tried it once. I couldn't imagine myself ever being so casual about lovers.

Half my age, she understood people much better than I did, she could read anybody, take them on by dissembling. Customer pushed against her, Alex immediately sized up the strength of the push, if it was serious, in her face, she got right back into *his* face. But the bluffers, scammers, macho men, weepy ladies, whoever, she could play their weaknesses like a pianist. She always looked people right in the eye when talking to them, yet she projected an artlessness, an honesty of relationship. At seventeen, people trusted her.

I doubted I'd ever get that ease of social relationships.

"Waiting," Nathan said. Fidgeting one moment, absolutely calm the next.

"Done a lot of it. Waiting in Nam was hard, unless you were so far in the rear that no Charley was gonna pop out in front of you. Men wait around, they either drink or dope or they talk, on and on, macho stuff, women they've screwed or, mostly, they've imagined. Lots of war scenes from movies, so men can go over the action, keep themselves pumped to survive like the Terminator. The sounds of waiting, the smells, different all over the world. Daytime, daylight, any light, waiting is not so bad. Night, that's the same everywhere."

"We've got it!" Alex shouted an hour later.

"Tell me." Hands up, palms facing me I waggled

my fingers at her, the universal symbol for *Give it up to me*.

"Credit cards," she said.

"Stolen credit cards?" I shook my head.

"Knew it was credit cards over an hour ago. But didn't want to give you just a piece of the story. Single people come to gamble. They live mostly out of state, they've got so-so jobs, no husband or wife or significant other, mostly not even pets, very few relatives, they come to gamble and soak up the sun for a week. Like Vegas, only a smaller scale, not so expensive. They lose or win a few hundred, they pay their hotel bill with a credit card, they go back home."

"Identity theft," I said.

"Exactly. We selected six at random from Leon's database. The six with the highest figures next to their names. We ran credit checks. All of them have never reported loss or theft of credit cards, but all of them, in different states and even in two different countries, all six have taken out multiple mortgages that were almost immediately cashed in. The number of scams is breathtaking.

"How does it tie to the casino?"

"They all used their credit cards the first night."

"Is there a direct link? Why are you all lit up, what else did you find?"

"That list of seven names, that you called in to me."

"The suicides?"

"The suicides. All seven."

"On the list?"

"On the list."

"Anything tying the names to Vincent Basaraba?" Nathan said.

"Nope," Alex said. "All circumstantial. But why would Leon Begay, brother of casino owner Vincent Begay, keep this detailed record?"

"Exposure," Nathan said. "Leon knew his brother was stealing money." He took my cell phone and walked away to make a call, ran back. "Let's go," he said to me. "Casino. Police have been there for an hour. Vincent claimed two of his employees tried to embezzle money, they attacked him, he shot them both."

"Chavez Sliding," I said. "And Wes McCartney. Wait, wait . . ."

I *flipped* everything I knew on its head, starting with the very first of all the suicides. "Leon's father didn't commit suicide. Vincent killed him."

"Why?"

"I don't know. I just believe it's logical. Vincent shot those two men?"

"Both dead. Let's go."

And on the way to the casino, I remembered Vincent's mesage on my answering machine. The message about Wes McCartney.

He'll disappear, Vincent said.

38

Outside the casino, we sat in my Cherokee, waiting for all the police cars to leave.

Heavy gusts of wind rocked the car, rain fell heavily for a short time.

"I've done too much waiting in my life," Nathan said. "Night, mostly. You're up, it's raining. Everything's dark, everything's got its own time. You're waiting. You're somewhere between the beginning and the end of your watch, somewhere between the real world and the jungle. Sergeant, or maybe the lieutenant, he controls what you're doing, he controls the time zone."

"Sweetie," I said. "Waiting is hard enough for me. No war stories, okay?"

"Yeah, well. Here, we see what we're waiting for. Police leave, we go in. Everything's in bright lights. In the bush, you're nothing but two eyes, a finger on a trigger, maybe another finger on the button for some claymore mines, or flares, in case you think Charley's out there. When you're new in-country, that night goes on for a century. But when you've been there a few months, you get this feeling for the time zone, there's a rhythm to those nights. Ears, eyes, sometimes your nose, they talk to you. Teach you what to trust. Am I right?" I kept silent, waiting for him to stop talking. "Yeah. I'm right.

One police car left in the parking lot, its turquoise and amber lights still flashing. The monsoon rains stopped gradually, the winds still buffeting the car.

Alex called again.

"This guy is a vapor trail," she said. "Absolutely no traces of him being involved in anything."

"Stand by," I said. Still waiting for that last police car. I told Nathan what Alex had just said.

"He's just a few strings short of being our puppet," Nathan said. "That's all. You remember what I want you to do?"

"I'm ready."

"Just checking." The last police car drove away, lights off. After ten minutes the front of the casino looked no different than any other night, a single uniformed cop near the sliding doors, gamblers arriving and leaving. "All right. Here we go."

Braced against the wind, we hurried to the front door where the cop tried to stop us, recognizing my face. Nathan held up his badge. "I've got a coupon."

And the rest went down so fast I hardly marked time, it seemed just a minute or so after we got into an elevator, rode to Vincent's floor, went into Vincent's office. Surprised to see me, he started to protest but Nathan gave him no time to talk, throwing him to the floor. Nathan took one of the wooden-framed office chairs and held it on top of Vincent's body, the frame across his neck. Nathan pulled out a Glock, I didn't even know he had the gun.

"We're leaving," Nathan said to Vincent. "Now."

Vincent didn't move.

"Am I rushing you?" Nathan said, the Glock against Vincent's head. "You don't seem to understand what we want, you don't seem to understand we don't care what you have to say, we'd prefer you didn't say anything. We know all about the bogus movie, the credit card scams, we know everything."

"Not a bogus movie," Vincent said.

"I don't care," Nathan said. "Now, get up. Let's go downstairs, let's go outside. I'm an officer of the law."

"No you're not."

"We're taking you into custody."

"I want to talk to the regular police," Vincent said, the last thing he said as Nathan mashed his lips with the Glock, not breaking skin but so hard against Vincent's teeth his eyes glazed with pain.

"We don't really care who you want," Nathan said. "Now. Let's go outside. You won't say a word to anyone, you won't give a code phrase to any employee, you'll nod and smile and wave off anybody that tries to talk to you." He released pressure from the gun barrel, Vincent licked his lips, sucked the lower lip as he slowly got up. "I know what you're thinking," Nathan said. "It's a long way out to the parking lot, you'll find an edge. If you try for that edge, I want you to know this. You've caused the death of two of my oldest friends."

"I killed nobody."

"And other people, I don't know how many other people. If you don't come with us, come and get in our car, if you do *any*thing to get away from me, I'll kill you on the spot."

"You're bluffing," Vincent said. Nathan stuck the Glock in his belt, pulled his light sweatshirt over the gun. "I get my chance. I'll take you down."

"He thinks this is a movie," Nathan said to me. Vincent actually smiled. "Okay," Nathan said. "Let's start."

"I'm not leaving this room."

"The hard part of playing chicken," Nathan said, "is knowing when to flinch. Except when you're heading into a guy who's *never* going to flinch."

Nathan slowly raised an index finger, cocked his thumb, and aimed his hand at Vincent's head, Nathan stepping off the distance between them, one stride at a time, the hand extending as he moved, arm fully horizontal until the finger rested exactly between Vincent's eyes and he backed up a step, the smile fading as Nathan stepped with him, a slow dance until Vincent bumped into window glass.

"Here's your choice," Nathan said finally. "Come with us, or stay. If you won't leave the room with us, I'll throw you out the window." Vincent's face blanched whiter than his capped Hollywood teeth. "Like the suicide here the other day. Either way, it makes no difference to me."

The brightest people, not so much the most intelligent, but people with street smarts, they figure things quickly. A scent on the breeze, a slight sound, like a dog licking its paws and suddenly stopping, the slightest changes in stimulation sets these people in action. You don't need to feed them much, the less you feed them the more alert they become as they look for an edge.

All the way downstairs and through the casino floors, Vincent looked left and right, trying to find his moment, needing to find an edge.

As the glass front doors slid open, Vincent half turned to the Tucson policeman standing just outside, but a deluge of rain squalled across the parking lot just then and the policeman ducked inside the door to keep dry and Nathan pushed Vincent to keep walking.

He never found another chance.

Nathan forced Vincent into the backseat of the Cherokee and wrapped plastic quick-tie handcuff strips around his wrists and ankles.

"Where are we going?" Vincent said. Still a measured, cool voice. "Where are you taking me?"

"North."

"Phoenix?"

I stretched around, my Beretta out for anything, I didn't know what, but the movement caught Vincent's eyes. "To Monument Valley," Nathan said. Vincent's eyes and mouth opened in the first sign of real panic.

"Why?"

"Somebody up there killed my two good friends, killed off a whole clan family, killed all the Begays left who might know something about you."

"McCartney did it. He told me, he wanted me to sign a document that said I'd embezzled money from the casino. He was going to shoot me with my own gun, with the Colt .45 I got from my dad."

"Henry Fonda's gun?" I said. "From when you were a kid, working on *Fort Apache* with your brother Leon and your father?"

"Yes, that gun, yes."

"That's it," I said to myself.

"What?" Nathan said.

"That's it. The same gun that killed your father."

"He shot himself, yes," Vincent said. "With that gun. Yes."

"You mean," I said, "the gun you used to kill your father. It's not even about money for your movie. Your brother Leon found out that you'd killed your own father. You didn't know who he'd told, you couldn't even ask. You just killed them all. It wasn't about money at all."

"Money," Vincent said. "Name it. I'll pay whatever you ask."

"He thinks that you want his money," Nathan said to me.

"Name it. Then just drop me anywhere."

"After you get us the money?"

"Yes, yes. After."

"You killed your own father, you made it look like suicide."

"No," Vincent said. "No, now listen, no."

"And the other suicides, of those gamblers with big losses, were they all suicides or did you kill them, too?"

"You have *no* proof!" Vincent shouted.

Nathan stood on the brake pedal, the Cherokee wobbling across both lanes of I-10 as he swirled onto the shoulder and then caught the Casa Grande off-ramp. He drove past darkened houses until he found a large, empty desert lot and moved the Cherokee out into the middle of the lot. Nathan stopped the car, unfastened his seat belt, motioned for me to do the same as he opened his door and took out a clasp knife, unfolding the large blade before he opened the back door to reach in with the knife and cut the plastic quick-tie around Vincent's ankles.

"Out," Nathan said. Uncertain what was happening, Vincent hesitated, but Nathan did nothing, just waited until Vincent slid awkwardly across the seat and dropped his legs outside, shoulder against the door frame to balance himself as he stood on the hardpan desert floor. Nathan cut the quick-tie around Vincent's wrists, waited patiently as Vincent rubbed his wrists, slapping them to get more circulation, all this time Nathan standing with the open clasp knife, waiting.

Off to the south, lightning flickered behind the mountain ranges as the monsoon moved steadily away from Tucson, but occasional fingers of the winds swept across the desert and things rustled and moved in the dark and birds flew everywhere, disturbed by the wind, I heard cactus wrens scolding off in the brush and a large bird swooped down and up without a sound. With the Cherokee headlights out, my eyes adjusted to the dark, swarms of stars appearing as the monsoon pushed all remaining clouds away.

"Give me your Beretta," Nathan said to me.

"My, give you what?"

"Your Beretta." I slowly handed it to him. He tossed it in the air, grasping the barrel as the gun settled into his hand, the checkered rubberized grip facing toward Vincent and the muzzle at Nathan's stomach. Nathan lifted the front of his sweatshirt, pulled at the Glock to free it up, and then extended the Beretta to Vincent. "Okay," Nathan said. "You've been looking for an edge, here it is."

"Nathan!" I said. The large bird swooped again, a great horned owl, flying silently despite its size, we'd probably disturbed its stalking prey and the owl buzzed us angrily one more time before flying off.

"Just take her gun. See if you can shoot before I can." Vincent stopped rubbing his wrists, flexed his fingers. Nathan moved closer, extending my gun. "Isn't this how they do it in the movies?"

"You'll kill me," Vincent said.

"We've all got to die. Just a matter of when."

He pushed the Beretta right up against Vincent's right hand and Vincent hesitated and then stepped back, arms to his side, shaking his head.

"No," he said. "No."

"Then you can go," Nathan said shortly.

"Go?"

"Nathan?" I said. "Why?"

"Why?" Vincent said.

"You're right," Nathan said. "We've got no proof."

"No proof. Yes, that's right."

"But just to answer the question, just for me, just to satisfy me, just to give me some closure about my friends who died, I'd like to hear you say that you were part of it."

"No, no," Vincent said. Confidence returning, he smiled, his capped teeth shining in the starlight.

"We're intelligent people," Nathan said. "We're forgiving people. I just want to know, that's all."

"I don't think so."

"Just one thing," I said. "Did you kill your father?"

"That was a long time ago."

"A long time," I said, taking my Beretta from Nathan, sticking it under my belt in the small of my back. "We could never prove anything, Nathan is right, there's no proof. I'd just like to know."

"He didn't want me to be in the movies," Vincent said at last, nodding to himself. "Leon, he agreed, he hated it, anyway."

"And what did your father ask of you?"

"We had twenty-nine sheep," Vincent said. "He wanted to buy more, he wanted me and Leon to raise the sheep."

"And that's why you killed him?"

"It was almost an accident."

"Almost?" Nathan said.

"He didn't want me to have that pistol. Henry Fonda gave the pistol to my father, but John Ford, the director, he said I was good-looking and well built, Ford got a leather holster and gun belt and hung it on me, stuck the pistol in the belt, and offered me a part in two more movies he was going to make. That night, my father tried to take the pistol from me."

"And the accident?"

"I wouldn't let him."

We stood there, the three of us, nobody saying a word for nearly five minutes, the monsoon breezes tapering off and the night creatures settling down. One last flare of lightning crinkled far off to the southwest.

"Well," Vincent said. "I'll be going."

"What about the law?" Nathan asked.

"There's no proof."

"What about tribal law?" Nathan said.

"Tribal . . . what are you saying?"

"You're so far beyond any laws," Nathan said, "that we'll make our *own* law. This is what's going to happen. When we drive up to Monument Valley, there are people waiting for us. They're bringing a coyote skin. We'll leave you with them."

Vincent backpedaled trying to run and Nathan strode to him in a blur, sacking Vincent over his shoulder, Vincent struggling as Nathan bulled toward the Cherokee and dumped Vincent into the backseat, Nathan taking a large roll of duct tape from under the seat and winding it around and around Vincent's ankles and legs and arms until Vincent lay cocooned in tape, screaming for Nathan to let him go until Nathan wound a last ribbon of tape over Vincent's mouth and nobody said another word for the next six hours as we pushed steadily through Flagstaff and Tuba City and past Black Mesa then north at Kayenta and finally a dirt track off into Monument Valley where seven people huddled around a small breakfast fire, waiting for us, waiting for the skinwalker to finally come home for the last time.

epilogue

Weeks later, on our way again to the Navajo reservation, but this time for pleasure, we stopped in Winslow.

"You lived here once?" Nathan said. Looking down the shotgun-straight avenue, old buildings, post office, Elks lodge. A forgotten small city.

"Over there." I pointed at a seedy building, once a motel, now probably cheap rooms for rent. "Came over here from the mesas, spent two nights with Jonathan, our honeymoon." Nathan stared at a silver and black Harley laid against the wall. "Afterward we ran away, but not enough money to drive any farther than Winslow. I worked three days in the grocery store, earned enough so on the third day we gassed the pickup, I hustled a box of stolen groceries out the back door. We went off to Pine Ridge from here.

In Monument Valley, we followed the hand-drawn map to Antoinette Claw's hogan. She told us, in her own way, the last of the skinwalker stories.

"One of my aunts told me this story," she said. "A *yenaldlooshi* story. My aunt, she was home with her husband, their children all gone to other lives and other hogans. So one night, my aunt and her husband are singing songs, getting ready to lie down, and this *yenaldlooshi* comes into their hogan and demands they give him all their valuables, or that's what my aunt said, I think she was terrified, who knows what was said in there. The husband, he turned up the kerosene lantern and the *yenaldlooshi* runs out of the hogan and the husband says, that's the last *yenaldlooshi* I ever want to see in this valley, I'm going to kill him. So the husband, he's got this really old shotgun, it's more like some hunting musket, just a single shot, he loads and primes it all up and he goes outside, meaning to track the *yenaldlooshi,* but it's just standing there, like it's confused and trying to peel off its coyote skin, but the husband ain't taking no chances, he fires the musket and blows a hole in the *yenaldlooshi*'s chest. They know the *yenaldlooshi* is dead, so they drive over to the tribal police station, bring a policeman back. The *yenaldlooshi* tried, before he breathed his last, he tried to get out of the coyote skin, but it was tied all around his body, tied behind his back and onto his leg and hands and head, he couldn't get out of it. Later, when they took his body down to Window Rock, they got the coyote skin off and it was somebody really familiar, they couldn't place him right away until somebody said, Hey, that's Franklin Begay's son, isn't it? And another policeman, or maybe the doctor cutting him open he says, Yeah. He used to be a movie actor. I guess he was trying out for his last part."

And that's the true end of this story.

Enter the World of Laura Winslow

Butterfly Lost

This first Laura Winslow mystery introduces us to the smart and resourceful computer whiz whose business is hacking onto the electronic trail of people who want to stay lost. But this time, when an old Hopi commissions Laura to find his granddaughter, she doesn't want any part of his vision of Powakas or Navajo skinwalkers—or anything else that will remind her of her old life back on the "rez" in Arizona. The Hopi's granddaughter, however, is one of too many girls recently gone missing, and only Laura can bring them home. . . .

"Are you the one who finds them?" he said.

His face was creased, lined, leathered, neutral, and expressionless. He could have been fifty or eighty years old, his breath asthmatic but steady, his body stocky and muscled. A traditional Hopi headband of faded red cloth wound around jet black hair cut at mid-ear length except in front, where short bangs hung over his forehead. He wore an old but clean long-sleeve blue cotton shirt, faded denims, and old black Nike sneakers, and he carried a plastic Bashas' Supermarket bag.

He took his hand off the girl's shoulder, and she immediately began stretching her neck and arms and legs in vague dancer's movements. Without asking, she picked up my binoculars, held them vertical with one lens to her right eye, and scanned round and round the driveway, lighting finally on a small pile of pebbles. She set the binoculars on the table and sat down to begin sorting the pebbles by size and color.

"You *are* Miss Laura Winslow?" the Hopi said politely.

"Yes," I said.

"You're the one who finds the girls?"

His wide-open eyes were as black as navy peacoat buttons.

"I only do that for the high school," I said. "And they're closed for the summer."

"Yesterday, I went over there. I talked with a Missus Tso."

"Billie Tso? The guidance counselor?"

"She said *you* would help."

I had a contract with Tuba City High School to run computer searches in an attempt to locate teenage runaway girls who fled the rez for brighter lights and bigger cities. Girls who hated reservation life, girls who were bored or curious or in trouble or just plain bad. These girls were my soft spot, my social weakness, my one public flaw in an otherwise mostly private life. My own daughter disappeared when she was only two, taken by my ex-husband to some place where despite repeated searches I couldn't find digital tracks of their existence. She'd now be in her early twenties, but I'm still unable to grant her adulthood, having progressed only to admitting that she could be twelve or fourteen years old. By looking for other missing girls, I kept alive my hopes of finding Spider.

"Who are you trying to find?"

He frowned, not yet ready for such a direct question. Hopis' conversations are incredibly circular with people outside their families or clans, responses withheld while they explore the entrails of the stranger's words for signs and possibilities.

"What's your name?" I asked, trying to get him talking.

He pulled off his headband and wiped his neck and forehead with the left cuff of his workshirt, trying to decide how much he could reveal. After putting the headband back on, he settled the knot over his right ear and nodded.

"I am Abbott Pavatea. From Lower Moencopi. My granddaughter, she was supposed to graduate from the high school. But she left a couple of nights before graduation and hasn't been home since."

"Graduation was two weeks ago."

"I thought she'd come back," he said shortly. "She didn't."

"Okay," I said. "What's her name?"

He opened his mouth to speak, his lips moving with no sound as the unspoken name hung in the air, crackling and invisible like static electricity. I realized Abbott couldn't say the name because he believed she was dead. I stretched my arms tighter across my breasts as tears streamed down his face. For a long beat I couldn't hear the barking dogs or even the whistle of his breath, his fathomless black button eyes locked on me like those of a coyote with a lamb in sight and nothing in between them but hunger.

The Killing Maze

Laura Winslow left her Hopi self behind and came to Tucson hoping to start over. Armed with a new name and praying that her past would never find her, Laura now works as a cyber-sleuth for Miguel Zepeda—an aging private detective who lives on the Tohono O'odham reservation. Laura is hiding within the Internet, safe and untouchable . . . for now. But when Miguel suddenly disappears, and an uninvited stranger shows up at Laura's door, she is soon swept into a twisted maze of gangs, Internet scams, and cold-blooded murder. . . .

"Hello in there."

A man's voice.

"It's Rey Villaneuva."

I went to the front door and stood silently behind it, looking through the peephole. But it was too dark to see anything except that a man was standing there. He rang the doorbell again.

I reached for the twelve gauge pump shotgun beside the door.

"I work for Miguel Zepeda."

Hesitating for a moment, I flipped on the outside porch light and opened the door. He blinked at the naked lightbulb, shook his head wearily, and moved back a few steps, allowing me to look him over. His tanned and unmistakably Mexican face was topped by a shock of unruly black hair that glistened with water as though he'd stuck his head under a faucet and run his fingers through it instead of a comb. He wore brown khaki pants, creased sharply, a sky-blue shirt with some kind of dog pattern, and a light, loose-fitting blue blazer.

"Who's Miguel?" I said.

"Let me get out my ID," he said wearily, reading my distrust.

He pulled aside his blazer, revealing a dull black Glock 17 stuck in a nylon shoulder rig. He took out a wallet and flipped it opened to show me a Private Investigation Business License issued by the Arizona Department of Public Safety.

"You are Laura, right?"

"What do you want?"

"Right now, I want to come inside. I feel a little stupid, standing out here in the middle of the night."

"Okay," I said finally.

He stopped just inside the living room and carefully closed the door. Hearing the solid chunk of the door settling into the steel frame, his eyes ran up and around the door and the three dead bolts. I leaned the shotgun against the wall. It fell over and I jumped at the noise.

"Mossberg 590," he said, picking it up. "Nine slugs in the tube, four stored in the handle. Parkerized dull finish, ghostring front sight. This is a serious piece. Are *you* a serious piece?"

His intensely focused eyes were offset by a slight smile. He was either amazed or bemused by the shotgun. He ran a finger down the dull black, matte-finished barrel and laid it against the wall.

Stalking Moon

Hiding out in the Arizona desert, Laura Winslow hopes to escape the past through false names and untraceable Internet phone technology. But when Bobby, her current and elusive partner, rings Laura's cell to brief her on their latest assignment, she soon realizes that the case may risk exposure and arrest unless she can uncover a nightmarish smuggling operation trafficking in the most precious of commodities: human lives . . .

"Here's the wiggle. Funky. I've got two people wanting to pay for the same job."

"Bobby, I don't understand."

"Two different clients. Each approached me separately. I know they've got no idea somebody else is asking for the same information."

"That *is* funky. So?"

"The first client, a package is coming your way."

"At my mail drop?"

"The second client," he continued, ignoring my question, "you're going to have to meet her."

"No. I don't personally meet clients."

"Not even for two hundred thousand?" He sucked in his breath, the sound rasping in my earpiece. "That's a minimum."

Well. Incredible. My biggest score ever. I could take months off work, I could retire for a year, I could bliss

out in northern Thailand with that kind of money. The
phone connection buzzed the way it does when somebody on a portable or wireless phone shifts body posi-
tion and the uplink can't quite maintain the connection.

"Okay. I'll meet. Where do I go? What state?"

"No airplanes necessary. Your own neighborhood.
Client's nearby. Meet her tomorrow night 4:22. She
prefers Nogales. I told her you'd pick Tucson."

"Yes. Arizona Desert Museum."

He hesitated so long I thought there was a problem.

"Just checking her cell phone, had to leave a message
on her voice mail about the meet. Okay. Gotta go."

"Wait! What's the job?"

"Something connected to that videotape on CNN.
Today, when you get the package, you'll understand a
lot more. Um, I've *got* to go."

"Um," I said. "There you go again."

"Don't have time to talk."

"Whoa, Bobby. Whoa. What's the hurry here? I
know you by now. I know when you've got something
unpleasant to tell me about a score."

"What's the tell?" he asked after a while.

"I'm not telling you anything. I'm *ask*ing."

"No. You know, um, like gamblers. Poker players.
Get a good card, they lick their lips, sniff, hunch their
shoulders, whatever. It gives away information to the
other players so they can fold."

"That's called a tell?"

"Yes. Look, I'm really curious. I need to know if I've
got a tell, a giveaway on the phone. Nobody's ever said
that to me before."

"When you're holding back something, you say
'um.'"

"Um," Bobby Guinness said faintly.

"See?"

A long, long silence. But I waited, knowing he was

trying to figure out just how much more data to give me.

"Okay," he said finally. "Things here are getting complicated."

"*Bad* complicated? Or just . . . more difficult?"

"Both. First off. There's a Mexican factor."

"Is there data about that in the package I'm getting?"

"Second off. The package is being hand-delivered."

I was stunned.

"How do you know where I live?"

"That's my business. To know all about people. But . . . um . . ."

Uncharacteristically, he was at a loss for words. I heard a swoosh of static as he shifted his head, a momentary buzzing, like a large moth at the screen door.

"I'm going to freak you out here, I think. Tell you the truth, *I'm* freaked."

"What?"

"You're going to find out anyway," he said, "once the package arrives."

"Find out what?"

"I'm not Bobby Guinness."

Where is this going? I thought, unable to think clearly at all.

"Well. I am Bobby to you. But I'm just a voice, just a person who calls himself Bobby Guinness. Actually, I'm a cutout. I work for . . . for the real Bobby. Who's coming to see you in the next day or so. Bringing the package."

"A cutout? I don't think I like this contract at all."

"You will, once you hear the money that's involved. It's going to be a percentage, not a straight fee. Twenty percent of at least thirty million dollars."

"Jesus!"

"So. You cool? You freaked? What?"

Scorpion Rain

Laura Winslow will do almost anything to conceal her true past—a past too painful and too dangerous to acknowledge. But now a friend has been kidnapped following a bloody shootout, and Laura must risk exposing everything she's tried so hard to keep secret. In Scorpion Rain, Laura must cross the line where civilization ends—entering a majestic wasteland where corruption, lies, and violence are bred and nurtured.

"Laura?"

Kamesh tugged the hem of my flannel nightshirt.

"Laura, wake up. There's somebody outside."

I thumbed at my eyes to clear the sleep film, sat halfway up. My bedroom faced the driveway, and I could see bubblegum police lights flickering. Two men stood in the high-beam headlight shafts, one of them with what looked like a shotgun. Fumbling open my nightstand drawer, I took out my Glock. Kamesh winced as I racked a shell into the chamber.

My front doorbell chimed, again and again. Passing through the kitchen, I flattened against the refrigerator as a shadow flickered across the window. I moved through the darkened house to the front door just as somebody rapped loudly on the door, three times, then three times again.

"Miss Winslow?"

Behind me, I saw Kamesh in the hallway, already

getting dressed. He hated guns, hated whenever I left one lying around the house.

"Miss Winslow! I'm Captain Cruz. INS."

Yeah, well, I'm Donald Duck, I thought.

Anybody can pretend to be anybody.

"Miss Winslow? Please come to the door. I have a phone call for you from Michelle Gilbert."

I punched in my alarm system code and opened the door.

"Cruz," he said. "Border Patrol. Take this."

He held out a cell phone to me, his right arm fully extended, his body slightly leaning away from me when he saw the Glock with the hammer back.

"Ma'am, please don't point that weapon at me."

I took the cell phone, shut the door with Cruz still outside.

"Hello?"

"This is Gilbert. About those other names you gave me. All four of the people are missing. I don't have much time to talk with you, but Captain Cruz will leave one of his men with you. In the morning, when I'm back in Tucson, I'll be at your house to look at whatever you've got on your computer."

"I won't be here."

"You don't have a choice."

"I have a contract job tomorrow," I said. "I can't cancel out."

"That's why Cruz and Gonzalez are there. Protection.

"I've *got* protection. I've also got a job in the morning."

"Something you can do from your house?"

"I have to be in Phoenix at four A.M. At the Perryville prison."

"When will you return home?"

"Early afternoon. Four, at the latest."

"All right." She sighed. "I'm so busy, I probably could use the time down here. Will you be at Perryville all day, in case I need to reach you?"

"No. Going from Perryville to Nogales, then back here. All four are gone?"

"No trace. But none of the families are talking. I think they've paid ransoms and are just waiting to get the person back. But these money people have rules of their own."

"It was Margaret Admiral? The body?"

"Yes. It was her. But it wasn't a body."

"The TV story about mutilation . . . was it bad?"

"I really don't know. All we found was a hand."

She paused, uncertain how much to tell me.

"What?" I said. "What else did you find with the hand?"

"A note," she said finally. "The hand was left so we could take fingerprints. But we'd never find anything else, any other . . . body parts, never find Margaret Admiral. She was dead, the note said. We have no way of knowing if that's true or not, no way of knowing if it's just a ploy for a bigger ransome. Gotta go."

Gilbert told Cruz that I'd be leaving the house at three, which was only an hour away. Kamesh tried to drive off in his '63 Corvette, but Cruz held him until Gilbert said it was okay to let him go.

A hand. All they found of Margaret Admiral was a hand.

I made up my mind right then. Do this last job with Meg, close up my house, move somewhere else. A long, long way from Tucson, far enough away so I'd never again have Hannibal Lecter leaving me messages.

Dragonfly Bones

Of all the dark secrets in her past, Laura Winslow is haunted most by Spider, the daughter she lost years ago. Now Spider is an angry young woman serving prison time, but she's agreed to help the authorities uncover an identity theft ring in exchange for leniency. In Dragonfly Bones, *mother and daughter are reunited and soon face danger together at a secret burial ground near Casa Grande Monument. The discarded bones may be all that remain of dozens of inexplicably missing women, and Laura fears that unless she can uncover a terrible conspiracy, her daughter may be the next body added to the shallow grave.*

"Spider," I said, lips dry, tongue in knots, my whole *head* in knots.

"Dominguez."

She cut me off, her lips barely a pencil line, they were clenched so tight, the word emerging like a hiss, lingering on the last *ahhh* syllable, teeth apart, for a moment I thought her tongue would dart out. Like a stinger. Like a snake.

"Help me here, Spider," I said.

She fingered the ID badge clipped to her orange tee. Waited for me to read it.

DOMINGUEZ, ABBE CONSUELO
ADC 49-353424-F

Finally, not knowing what else to do, I took out the photo that Jonathan gave me two years before. I traced my finger over the smiling woman, trying to discover some link, some blood, some connection between my memories of her at two years old, when Jonathan took her from me and disappeared.

Trying to make a connection between the smiling photo and the enraged face in front of me. I just kept staring at her, a tiny smile flickering on my lips, fading, more a twitch than a smile. I had so much invested in discovering this moment, meeting her for the first time in twenty years, I'd built this mythic meeting scene, I don't know what I'd built, but the daughter I'd imagined was nothing like the woman across the table.

Her concentration broke. Blinking, suddenly looking down, nothing else changing in her body, still sitting like she had a pole up her ass, years of anger at me, at somebody, and here I was as a release for the anger. And then she took a deep breath, hunched her shoulders, let the breath out with a slow sigh, and rolled her head side to side, muscle tension probably cramping her neck.

It was something to build on.

"Dominguez. Where did you get that name?"

"Run one of your hacker searchers. You'd find out." Rude.

A whole different attitude. For the first time, I wondered if she really knew what to do with me, with her mother, facing her mother, two adults, two strangers.

"I've searched for your real name for years."

"I have no *real* name," she snorted. "Like you, I have lots of identities."

"Spider Begay." She shrugged. "I filed the birth certificate. In Flagstaff."

She shrugged again.

"So Spider Begay disappeared two years after that birth certificate?"

"*You* disappeared. That's what he said. What Daddy said. When I met him in Mexico. Do you know where he is now?"

"No."

She nodded toward the steel door at the far end of the room.

"Where is he?" she asked.

"Who?"

"Mister Law."

"Nathan Brittles?"

"Oh, c'mon, mom. You don't believe that's his real name, do you?"

"He has a lot of ID. But I really don't care about him right now."

She saw I was curious.

"Check out John Wayne," she said cryptically.

"I saw the movie. What do we do here? *Why* are we here?"

"He coming in? Or what?

"Tell me, Spider."

"Dominguez!"

"Abbie, then."

"It's not *aaaaa-beeee*." Flat A sound, long E sound, said derisively. "*Ah. Bay.* Ahbay. Don't you, like, know any Mexican?"

I swore. A border phrase, a slang phrase, the rudest I could think of. That shocked her. No telling if it was because of the insult, or because it was said by her mother. Another attitude. Negotiation with anger.

"Let's get to it," she said flatly. "Call him in."

"This is between us," I said, standing up. "You want him in here, you deal with him and I'll just go home."

After a minute of standoff defiance, I headed toward the door. I'd only gone a few steps when she surged out of her chair, slamming it against chairs behind her, grabbed a plastic ashtray from another table, and hurled it like a Frisbee, like a discus, like a deer slug out of a twelve-gauge, sailing it three inches from my head. I ducked, but she wasn't aiming it at me. Flew all the way down the room in a flat trajectory, cracking against the door and dissolving in shards. The bolt shot back with a loud click, a CO appeared with her hand on a baton.

"Get John Wayne," Spider yelled.

The CO cocked her head at me.

"Brittles," I said.

"Wait one."

She closed the door, the bolt shot home. Neither Spider nor I moved. Two minutes later the CO came in again.

"On the phone."

"Get him *off* the fucking phone, get him in here!" Spider screamed.

"Your call," the CO said to me, arms out wide, palms up, a shrug.

"We'll wait."

Spider immediately went to the other door and pounded on it with her hands. The CO quickly shut and locked her door, the second door opened, a second CO appeared. Spider held out her wrists to be hooked up. Once the handcuffs were on, she left without a word.

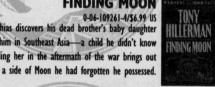